The Villain Edit

OVER THE TOP LOVE BOOK THREE

SARAH BRENTON

Contents

Content Notes

While I don't write grief or trauma-heavy books, The Villain Edit sits more in the contemporary romance category than in the rom com category, and does contain a few things worth mentioning. Below the *** you'll find a list of things you'll find in this book. While I've tried to keep it vague but informative, there may be light spoilers. Please take care of yourself. xx

***

On page explicit sex, course language, near drowning (on page), a main character raised by a drug-dealing father, (off page) death of a parent via drug overdose, a main character briefly in the foster care system (off page), a main character raised by manipulative narcissistic parents and often neglected (a little on page), infidelities (NOT between the main characters though in the first chapter Ashley does attempt to break up her cousin's marriage), drug use (off page), light drinking (on page), abortion (side character, off page), sex tape, light spanking not talked about before delivered but very much appreciated.

For everyone whose moral compass is a little off.

Chapter One

Ashley

I'm the villain of several stories, but mostly my own.

Maybe other people tell themselves they're the heroes of theirs, but there's power in embracing the truth. I'm at my best, truest self when I'm at my worst.

Take tonight. My cousin invited me to her wedding and I'm here to steal her man.

Any minute Dominic Fontana will walk into this boudoir-styled dressing room and see me draped seductively on a chaise in lingerie that reveals everything. I hope he'll see me, sweep me into his arms, and take me on this chaise, but I don't expect him to. I don't need him to. He only needs to be in this room with me for a few minutes.

He might not be happy, at first, but he'll come to see how much better we are together. I'm doing him a favor, showing him now so he won't discover it down the line.

We've had this connection since childhood, but our timing is off. I can't wait one year, or two or more, for this inevitable divorce. Something in my life has to change, and I'm afraid if I don't take this opportunity, the universe might not give me another chance.

I have nothing to lose. My career is effectively over after my season on the reality TV show *Love on the Line* and my extended family...well, they don't like me anyway.

Footsteps come down the hallway and stop at the door.

This is it.

There's a mirror on the dressing table, and I turn my head for reassurance. My platinum blonde hair is perfectly tousled, my lips are the perfect shade of *fuck me* red, matching the delicate lace of my lingerie. It was a bitch to put on, ribbons crisscrossing my body. Uncomfortable under my black dress.

Yes, I wore black to this sham of a wedding.

I don't look too closely at my reflection. If I don't see the slim shadow of fear in my eyes or the uncertain tremble on my lips, they don't exist. All I see is what Nic will see when he opens the door.

Me.

Hot as hell. Ready to commit a sin or two.

The door opens and I say a quick prayer that the tits I gave myself for my twenty-third birthday will keep him in the room long enough for this to work.

The lighting is dim, but the man moving through the shadows of the short hallway has a natural panther-like grace. Nic, for how incredibly hot he is, doesn't move like this. I frown. I don't think his shoulders are this broad either.

Sitting straighter, I peer into the darkness. Something's wrong.

This isn't Nic.

Oh fuck.

The man steps into the light and sees me, his jaw dropping.

My eyes are burning with tears I don't dare shed. I am going to murder my assistant Lea so dead it will be like she never existed. *How could she mix them up?*

Gabriel Sinclair, Hollywood's golden boy, is staring at me like someone dropped a whole live squid on his plate and he's not sure if it's a prank.

Gabriel and I have never met, but everyone knows him. He rescues kittens from trees (twice) and helps old ladies with their shopping. *Literally.* It was on the damn news. He's an obnoxious do-gooder who manages to pull off the *I'm so much better than you* without opening his damn mouth.

He clears his throat as he tugs at the cuff of his suit, and it sounds like the universe slamming another door shut on my path to Nic.

No. I refuse to accept it. This still could work. They look a little alike—a *very* little. Enough that Gabriel Sinclair was cast as Nic's replacement in the Warwick superhero franchise. They're both white, but Gabriel's skin has a golden hue compared to Nic's porcelain. Gabriel's hair isn't as dark, his eyes are dark brown not gray, and he's a smidge bigger, his features a little stronger.

Gabriel Sinclair is also the kind of guy who needs six months of dating and a diamond ring before he'll take a woman to bed, only to fuck her in missionary. Once. With the lights off.

Nic would fuck a woman against the wall in a club without needing to know her name.

"I'm sorry." Gabriel's voice is deep. Plush. "I must have the wrong room. I'll—"

He starts to say *go* but stops.

He doesn't go. Of course, he doesn't. I'm the fantasy and he's the fly in my web. The wrong fly, but seriously, I think this might work.

"Stay," I say in a breathy whisper, sliding my hand over the soft velvet of the chaise next to me.

He's frowning, his eyes maddeningly stuck on my face when the rest of me is right here on display. Instead of accepting my invitation, he pulls a chair over and sits. He's at ease in his Tom Ford suit, leaning back, crossing his legs so one black leather wingtip shoe rests on a knee, looking for all the world like he's in control of the situation.

He's not and I want to break him. Mess him up. Leave him looking on the outside how I feel on the inside.

"What's this?" he asks, sounding tired. Worn. The perfect place for me to pick and pull until every thread holding him together is in a tangle on the floor.

Instead of answering, I take my time rising to my feet.

His gaze stays on my face. "Some woman claiming to be my assistant told me Gabriel Sinclair wanted a word with me in this room."

The seductive smile I've been holding in place falters and I catch it before it can break into a scowl. Lea is fucking *dead*.

"But the thing is," the insufferable man continues, "*I'm* Gabriel Sinclair, and my PA is a man who went back to his hotel room two hours ago." For the first time, a suggestion of a smile crosses his lips. It's not a happy one. It's vaguely threatening, even. It's surprising on him and I like it. I'll tell him the truth. A version of it, anyway.

"I'm waiting for a man," I say. I still have my heels on and they make my legs look endless. I sway my hips as I move closer, but he still won't glance at my body. It's insulting.

"Me?" He sounds annoyed by the idea.

Same, asshole.

"No." I stop in front of him. He hasn't sat up any straighter, hasn't dropped his gaze down my body. Either this man has superhuman willpower, or he isn't sexually attracted to women. The tabloids have photographed him with women outside the industry, but those women could be paid decoys.

"So the woman who told me I wanted a word with myself—?" One thick eyebrow arcs up.

"Had nothing to do with me," I say with an innocent little shrug that bounces my tits—not that he looks.

His frown deepens as his eyes flicker over my face. "Have we met?"

I bend forward, placing my hands on his thighs and my lips inches from his, putting my tits on full display. The muscles under my hands tense and goddammit I don't need the little flicker of desire that inspires. They're just thighs. Thick and hard but not Nic's.

His eyes though. Now that I'm closer, I can see the lighter shades of brown dancing in the dark like flames around his dilating pupils. He has the kind of eyes I could drown in.

"We haven't met." I focus on his lips and unfortunately, he has a mouth made for all manner of sinful, despicable things. Not that he would ever do sinful, despicable things. "But I wouldn't mind becoming better...*acquainted*."

He laughs.

And then he moves.

His massive hands take mine, pulling them off his legs as he stands.

The man towers over me. I'm not frightened—Gabriel Sinclair wouldn't hurt a bug—but I am intimidated. This is going to be hard if he isn't going to play along.

"Lady," he says in that deep, serious voice, releasing my hands, "you need to examine your life choices."

He turns away, but I snatch his sleeve and pull him back. He tries to shake me off, but I hold tight.

"I'm not interested in whatever scam you're—"

I grab his tie, yank him down, and shut him up with my lips.

He's not Nic.

But he looks enough like Nic, and in this dim light, through the open window to the balcony across the courtyard where the photographer is hiding, the whole world will think I'm kissing Nic. My cousin Jessie will think I'm kissing Nic.

I'm getting my chance if I have to burn down the world for it. Gabriel Sinclair is collateral damage.

He grabs my arms, but he doesn't push me away. He doesn't pull me in or kiss me back. He makes a surprised noise and freezes, hopefully giving the photographer a few extra shots.

Ideally, Gabriel would take me over the chaise. I could close my eyes and pretend he was Nic for the two minutes it would take. Photos and grainy videos of that would have Jessie running for a divorce. But this is Gabriel Sinclair, so *of course* he won't even kiss me back.

When I pull away, he's looking at me like I've lost my mind. He's wearing more of my lipstick than I am. I've managed to muss his hair up, not to mention nearly strangle him with his tie.

I hum, satisfied.

It's done. We'll be trending on social media before we step out of this room, although I guess technically Gabriel Sinclair won't be. Not that he'll want to correct them.

He stays perfectly still as I walk around the chaise to retrieve my dress off the hook on the door. Maybe I've broken him.

That was too easy, no fun at all, really.

"What's your name?" he asks gruffly.

"Ashley Foley."

He blinks. Swears. A mild *dammit*.

I feign offense at the obscenity, clutching at my chest with a gasp. His eyes narrow. But yay! He knows who I am. It finally clicked in his empty head.

"Zip me." I turn my back to him and pull my blonde hair aside.

He ignores me, looking upset as he paces his side of the room in short bursts. "How close are you to the bride?"

Ugh. "We're cousins. Why?"

His hands are in his thick hair, making more of a mess than I did. He's talking more to himself than to me, so I let him ramble on as I do my zip as high as I can. Maybe it would be better if I came out half-zipped, looking freshly fucked anyway. I turn to the mirror to transform the mess I've made of my carefully chosen lipstick into something artful.

I only look at my lips.

"I shouldn't have come to this wedding." Gabriel is still having his boring existential crisis, muttering to himself. "How am I going to explain to Nic I'm taking a restraining order out on his cousin-in-law?"

I stop. "Restraining order?" That would ruin everything. "That's not necessary—"

He shoots me a filthy look. Not the fun kind. This kind says I am worse than a shoe-ruining pile of dog shit. "I appreciate my fans, but you just crossed all sorts of lines."

A wild laugh rips out of me, pushed by the surge of anger because I never wanted him in this room. I stomp up to him, but already his hands are up in the air. "I am not a fan of yours."

His look suggests he doesn't believe me but might play along in case I turn dangerous and honestly, I am *this* close.

I lean in and to his credit, he doesn't back away. "I despise you."

His glare intensifies. "Two minutes ago you were trying to suck my face off."

"I didn't enjoy it." I push past him for the door. My half-zipped dress is already slipping down, exposing the top of my lingerie. "If you'll excuse me, I have a party to—"

I open the door to a camera flash. A dozen camera flashes.

And I freeze. My heart pounds in my ears and I'm going to be sick. This wasn't the plan. Where did they come from?

The first volley of flashes stops and a second of shocked silence falls.

"Gabriel Sinclair?"

Stunned voices. Stunned voices saying his name, turning hungry. Rushing toward me, cameras flashing.

I'm yanked back into the room, the door is slammed shut and locked.

I stumble to the chaise and drop onto it.

Fuck.

Gabriel Sinclair, golden boy, says it out loud.

Chapter Two

Gabe

Celia Foley is terrifying.

America's Tipsy Kitchen Aunt cleared the venue of anyone who could be paparazzi with the efficiency of a general. For the last ten minutes, the TV chef has been pacing the empty Wisteria Bar and talking in a tense, shushed voice into her phone.

Her smoky blue pantsuit is the softest thing about her. The expression on her face is stormy as she pushes aside a stray lock of gray-streaked auburn hair.

She hasn't glanced at me since she pointed at the chair I'm sitting in, though she's cast more than a few Angry Parent looks at her niece.

I feel like I've been put in time-out.

My publicist and agent aren't answering my calls, which is terrifying. I've never been touched by anything even a little scandalous, so this is a great time for my team to ignore me.

My phone sits on the table in front of me, but I don't need to look to know those pictures are everywhere.

Little Miss Look-At-My-Tits is upset as she scrolls through her phone, though she's trying to appear unaffected and bored. The subtle lift of her eyebrows and tightening of her lips give away her true feelings. As does her throat working to swallow before she remembers her cocktail.

Her cocktail is the same bright red as her lips. And her lingerie. The contrast against her creamy skin is seared into the lizard-part of my brain. I'm going to be seeing her curvy body in that damn lingerie in my dreams for weeks. She's dressed to seduce in a little black number, not attend a family wedding. I don't know that I've ever seen someone embody the blonde bombshell/femme fatale look the way she does.

Unfortunately for me, she's exactly my type—hence my inability to run from the room as soon as I sensed danger.

The woman who sent me to Ashley's trap is sitting next to her, teary-eyed. They haven't spoken, so I doubt they're friends. They don't look enough alike to be family—this woman has a cloud of curly brown hair and a more angular face—but who knows? Family takes all forms.

My attention returns to Ashley, and I rub my jaw. There was a moment on the way to this room. A door opened and Nic and Jessie stumbled out, mussed and laughing, color on their cheeks. Far enough ahead of us that they didn't notice our solemn march to the Wisteria Bar.

Ashley faltered. Her shoulders slumped. In an instant, she went from cool indifference to a palpable sadness.

I felt bad for her. Until I saw my face in a hallway mirror, lipstick smeared all over it.

The door opens and Celia spins around as my real personal assistant slides into the room. Thank god. If anyone can help me sort this mess—outside of my agent and publicist—it's David.

"I'm Mr. Sinclair's assistant," he informs her. She motions for him to come in as she continues her hushed conversation.

David quickly makes his way to my side, shooting Ashley a glare that goes unnoticed as he drops into the chair next to me. He turns his back to her and leans closer to me, speaking in a hushed voice. "What happened?"

"I have no idea."

It was a con. Obviously. But I can't understand what she hoped to gain. She'd kissed me, hadn't cared when I didn't return her kiss, and told me she despised me on her way out the door. She panicked at the cameras like she didn't want to be photographed with me. None of it makes sense.

"Well, she's bad news," David continues, dropping his voice lower. "She was on the last season of *Love on the Line* and she does *not* have a lot of fans. Check this out," he pulls his phone out of his pocket, opening some gossip site calling her Reality TV's Bad Girl. "No current boyfriend or girlfriend—she's bisexual. Often photographed with the lower rung of professional athletes and musicians, the odd model or influencer, but nothing lasting more than a few weeks. She's—"

"Still in the room, boys," Ashley calls out in a dry voice, not looking up from her phone.

David tenses, then stands and motions for me to follow him over to the windows, about as far as we can get from Ashley's table. The heavy curtains are drawn given...well.

"I'm sorry I interrupted your night," I tell him in a hushed tone.

"Not your fault."

I knew he'd be on my side, but I'm still relieved David doesn't believe I was responsible for what happened tonight. He was my uncle's personal assistant for years, and Michael Sinclair was his idol. When my uncle died, I kept David on as my PA.

"What are they saying?" I ask David, jerking my chin at his phone.

He hands it over like a hand grenade with the pin pulled.

Not a Saint After All! Gabe Sinclair Hooks Up With TV's Bad Girl

Gabriel Sinclair Gets into Character for Upcoming Warwick Role with Steamy Hotel Hookup!

A Little Bad Boy in America's New Hero?

Gabe's Naughty Side.

"*Naughty side*?" I hiss at David.

He wrinkles his nose. "Look at the picture."

I do and it's a punch to the gut.

I wish I'd never come to this wedding.

My invite was an afterthought, a courtesy extended thanks to fate and filming schedules. I'm taking over the role of the superhero Warwick and it was strongly suggested that in preparation for the role, I get to know the man stepping down from it since we've never worked together. We might travel in some of the same circles, but I don't really know Nic.

Two weeks hanging out with him and I still don't think I know him. I'm not sure what it is about him that the Warwick fandom has latched onto—Nic didn't know, either—which is not promising for my career goals.

Beyond a slight resemblance to Nic, I'm not the obvious choice for a gritty superhero, but it's the opportunity of a lifetime and I'm going to work for it. Hell, if I want meatier roles beyond the lighthearted good guy ones I've always played, I need this. By the time this movie is over, I'm going to have all of fandom wondering how they ever doubted my suitability. I'm going to get cast in something that will win me a goddamn Oscar.

A little voice in my head tells me my future Oscar win won't matter if I'm not respected by my peers, the industry, or the audience.

The photo...

I look lecherous, my eyes caught on Ashley's backside, my mouth twisted into an expression I don't recognize. It's primal. But the look on my face, the mussed hair, crooked tie, and her smeared lipstick, is PG-13.

Ashley's appearance is straight-up Rated R.

Her dress had slipped below one breast and her hand, clutching the fabric, hadn't pulled it up yet. Her see-through lingerie earned her a censored bar. The smile on her lips—taken the moment before she glanced up—is one of satisfaction. She looks like she got *exactly* what she'd come to the room for.

From me. And I look hungry for more.

I push the phone back into David's hand. I can hear the disapproval in my uncle's voice. *Sinclairs do not get caught in embarrassing situations.*

My mouth goes sour. Up until a few weeks ago, I thought it was about integrity and doing the right thing. Turned out it was about not getting caught.

"Emma and Rose aren't returning my calls," I say softly. "Have you heard from either of them?" We're twenty minutes into this disaster and it's all over the internet. They should be blowing up my phone.

"No. Went to voice mail. Shit," David exhales, his face lit up from the light of his phone. "You should see what they're saying about her."

That sour taste intensifies. I know the kinds of things they say about the Hollywood darlings, so I can imagine how much worse it is for someone people love to hate. I don't know Ashley, and I'm not happy about what she did, but she doesn't deserve the vitriol.

I can't stand here anymore, with David scrolling through the trash. I go back to my table and take a drink of my sparkling water. It dilutes the taste in my mouth, but I wish I had asked for something alcoholic.

The door slams open and retired stuntman Timothy Foley walks in, waves at me, and drops into a seat next to his cousin.

Ashley sniffs discreetly, leaning away from him.

Timothy leans closer to her.

He's had a few drinks, by the bright look in his eyes. He's lost his vest and suit coat and a few buttons of his dress shirt are askew, his hair standing up. I assume it has to do with the goats he unleashed at the reception an hour ago. I don't know what the hell that was about, but I do know the man. He was professional on set the couple of times we've worked together, but off set, he's walking chaos.

He pokes Ashley in the arm and she hisses at him.

"I know what you're up to," he hisses right back. "The moment you sent your assistant asking—"

"*You* pointed her at *him*?" she asks, slamming her phone onto the table.

I'm not trying to listen in, but Timothy's voice carries and it's obvious I'm the "him" in this conversation.

Timothy glances at me, mouthing a "sorry" before turning back to Ashley. "If you ever, ever try this shit again—"

"It's over," she snaps back. "I'm done."

"You don't know how to be done or you would've been done years ago." His voice drops until I can't hear what he's saying, but her eyes almost tear up before she snaps her spine straight and pushes him away.

"Get off me, you drunken dickwad."

"You," he says pointedly, getting to his feet, "need to grow up."

"Real inspiring from the man who unleashed a herd of goats at his sister's wedding reception," Ashley says, eyes on her phone, without missing a beat.

"Out of love," he says, winking at me when he catches me watching them.

"Same," she mumbles, but Timothy's lost interest in her. He gets up and dumps himself into a chair across the table from me.

"I'm sorry my cousin is…well." He blows a strand of hair off his forehead. "An Ashhole."

Under the table, I clench my hands into fists and release them, trying to work off some tension. "She made a mistake." I'd threatened her with a restraining order, but whatever role I played tonight in Ashley's scheme, I don't think it's something I have to worry about repeating.

I despise you.

I'm not exactly her biggest fan either.

"You're leaving in the morning?" Timothy asks, a wide grin spreading across his face. "You sure you don't want to stay another day and let me drive that sweet car of yours?"

I've been following Nic around, and everywhere Nic goes, Timothy goes. He's been after me the whole time about driving my car.

No way am I letting the ex-stunt performer drive my 1969 Camaro.

"All right." Celia's off her phone now, glancing between me and Ashley, a furrow in her brow as David hurries over and takes a seat beside me. "I talked to your agents—"

Our agents?

That's why I went to voice mail?

Ashley's jaw drops. "You can't—"

Celia whirls on her. "Oh, I can. I'm not any happier than you to have to clean up your mess at my daughter's wedding, so don't start with me." They stare at each other for a long minute before Ashley looks at her drink and Celia's eyes swing my way.

She notices Timothy and rests her hands on her hips. "What are you doing here?"

He shrugs. "Following the chaos."

She jerks a thumb over her shoulder in the direction of the door. "Out."

He stands up, mimes driving at me, and mouths *call me.*

When the door closes, Celia sighs. "I've spoken with your people and we've all agreed the best course of action, for everyone, is to let slip that you two are dating."

"Absolutely not," I say over Ashley's *no fucking way.*

Ashley glares at me. I meet her thickly lashed, tawny brown eyes with a glare of my own.

Celia turns to her niece. "You are the least popular contestant to come off *Love on the Line,* and on a show known for churning out constant trash, that's saying something."

Ashley crosses her arms. "Is this your idea of revenge? Publicly chaining me to *him*?"

"Oh, sweetie," Celia says with a shake of her head. "If I wanted revenge, I'd destroy your parents. Not you."

My jaw drops, and I hastily shut it. What the hell is happening? Christ, I get that families have drama—mine has plenty—but this is next-level and I do not want a part of it.

Ashley gives a bored shrug but keeps her mouth shut.

"This is for your benefit," Celia continues saying to her. "If you want something better from this industry, you need to launder that reputation of yours. I'm sorry the patriarchy punishes a woman for being, well...a bitch, sweetie, but until we manage to burn it down, if you want work, you need to be less...unlikable." She winces at that word, but Ashley just rolls her eyes.

"And you," she turns to me and softens. "Sweetie. A little edge before you take on the role of a gritty superhero might not be a bad thing. Your reputation is so pristine that even dating Ashley can't tarnish you."

"Wanna bet?" Ashley mutters darkly, scrolling through her phone again.

Celia ignores her. "Your team thinks it's a good idea. They like what they're reading online. Your fans are, uh...interested in certain aspects of your life previously assumed to be..."

"Boring?" Ashley pipes up.

Celia nods. "Predictable. And sex sells."

Great. My sex life is predictable. In reality, it's nonexistent, and right now, I don't know which is worse. But Celia's right about the fandom. They are frothing mad the studio cast me as Warwick, saying I'll ruin the movies because I'm too clean-cut. My agent has been getting nervous about it, fearing they might recast the role if the fandom gets any louder.

I need this.

My phone rings.

Ashley's phone rings.

"That'll be your people." Celia points Ashley to one end of the room, and me to another, and we take to our corners.

The conversation is short and brutal. Both my agent Emma and publicist Rose agree: being caught with Ashley has enough people finding nuance in me. If fandom warms up to the idea that I'm not a Boy Scout, the producers and director will feel more confident in me, and they'll be less likely to drop me.

I have no choice. It's the safest way to give my reputation an edge and it will hardly be my first fake relationship.

One week, I offer. They can spin it as a passionate vacation fling. One where I quickly come to my senses.

Ashley's agent refuses, my team soon finds out.

"Six *months*?" Ashley shrieks at her agent's suggestion. "I'd rather go to jail for assault." It doesn't take long for her to cave to her agent. They want three months and a financial penalty if either of us breaks the contract early.

Ashley is staring at the ceiling like she's willing it to fall and put her out of her misery. She hates this as much as I do.

"Fine." I can take her out for dinner every Friday for three months without wanting to walk into the Pacific. Probably. "I'll have David set up a date when I'm back in LA in a couple of weeks."

"That won't do." Rose is brisk and I imagine her sitting ramrod straight behind her desk, her golden blonde hair tightly pulled back, the slightest scowl on her face. "You hooked up at a wedding and we need to keep momentum."

Emma agrees. "You're still planning this road trip? Take Ashley. You can post your relationship on social media as you go."

My stomach crashes. This trip is personal. The man who saved me, who put me on this path and gave me standards to live by, turned out to be a fraud and I need the escape from the world to stop this existential crisis head-on before my schedule makes it impossible. I need to be alone. "No way."

"It'll give you a chance to get used to her without cameras constantly on you," Rose points out. "I doubt any paparazzo will follow you into the middle of nowhere. Not with the price of gas—"

Rose is a talented publicist and I trust Emma with my career. If they both agree driving Ashley Foley across America and throwing pictures of us holding hands and sightseeing to the hungry masses will assure fans I'm up to the task of playing an edgy superhero, I guess I'm doing it.

But two weeks in a car with her? No. I drop it to five days—a straight shot of eight-hour days to get to LA. My team ups it to ten days and throws in a few publicity events along the way. Tour a winery in upstate New York. A bourbon distillery in Tennessee. Stop some place wholly American, like the Grand Canyon.

Across the room, Ashley's shoulders sag and she drops her head into her hand. Guess we've reached an agreement. It's a lot, but I've sacrificed plenty to get this far. I'll sacrifice even more to hold on to this role.

We come out of our corners and Celia gives us a smug smile.

Ashley's as happy about this as I am—which is not at all—but there's something about her that makes me think she's barely holding it together.

"I'll pick you up at seven," I meet her eyes for long enough to let her know I mean exactly seven o'clock, not a minute later, and stride out of the room.

Chapter Three

Ashley

Surprising only Gabriel Sinclair, I oversleep.

After the shit with the paparazzi last night, Aunt Celia put me up in a hotel with security, so I know who the pounding on my door is. I'm living a nightmare.

I sit up and rub my temples. My head isn't the only thing hurting this morning. My heart aches. Nic and Jessie, stumbling out of that room last night...

It should have been *me*.

It's always been Nic for me.

I spent a lot of time at my Aunt Celia's as a child, but I didn't look forward to those visits until Nic moved into the house across the street. He was five years older than me, the same age as Timothy and Jessie, but unlike my cousins, he saw me. Included me. Protected me from Timothy's wild ideas and Jessie's cutting words. And when Timothy was in trouble and Jessie was off painting, he'd spend time with me.

He didn't look at me the way I looked at him, but that didn't matter. We had so much in common, both being quiet and unwanted by our parents, with no siblings to play with, at the mercy of Timothy and Jessie. He won me over with a dozen small acts of kindness given with no expectation of a return. He didn't want anything from me, and I loved him for it.

Last night, I told Timothy I was done, but that was a lie and we both knew it. I don't stop until I get what I want, and I always get what I want, whatever the cost.

Timothy's angry voice still echoes in my head from when he cornered me later. *You tried to ruin a marriage. That's low, even for you.*

No. It's so like me he should've seen it coming. Especially since he's the one who has effectively kept Nic away from me for years. Ever since he caught me trying to slip into Nic's bedroom at a house party I hadn't been invited to when I was seventeen.

There's another insistent knock on the door, and I swing my feet over the bed.

My agent Neve was clear on the phone last night—the jobs aren't exactly flooding in. Not even a trickle. I need to become someone people want to work with before my savings account runs dry.

I'll fake date Gabriel Sinclair. I'll rehabilitate my reputation so I can get somewhere in the entertainment industry. I'll find a way to get Nic back to LA and away from my interfering family. Jessie invited me to the wedding—I'll send her a text after the honeymoon. If she responds, I'll know Timothy didn't tell her about my seduction attempt. I'll gain her trust and wait for the right time.

Gabriel's leaning on the frame when I open the door, glaring down at me. My face, only, because he's a saint.

Shit. I didn't wash my makeup off last night. My face has to be a wreck from crying and drinking. He doesn't have the courtesy to look down at the silk camisole barely covering my tits instead.

"I told you to be ready at seven," he says gruffly while I shamelessly take in his white button-up and dark jeans. Christ, we're going to be in a car all day—why is he dressed like casual Friday at the office?

I leave the door open and walk back to my bed. "You could have brought me a coffee," I complain. He says nothing, but closes the door and leans against it, his eyes now shut. Probably so he can't see my ass in my tiny silky shorts.

I'm irritated. It's not fair that I need to pretend to date boring Gabriel Sinclair to make people like me. A man finding me worthy doesn't define my worth and it shouldn't.

Why does he even need me? How hard would it be for him to let loose and live a little? Get drunk in a club? Make out with a porn star? Do a line off some guy's abs? I did all those things during my first week in LA.

"You could have gotten up early and had time to get yourself a coffee," he points out.

"I overslept," I mutter, tossing my suitcase onto the foot of the bed.

Last night was the worst night of my life. I barely held it together until I hit my room and my minibar. I'm hungover and Gabriel Sinclair can turn his nose up at my current state all he wants—fuck him.

"I expect you to be ready at the agreed time," he says, walking over to the desk—about as far from me and the bed as he can get without loitering in the doorway. He doesn't look at me. My DDs are a work of art, but he stares at the generic pastel painting on the wall instead.

I half-heartedly throw some clothes at my suitcase. Most end up on the bed. "I doubt it will be a problem." My soul is leaving my body, that's how much I want to escape from this. "We'll be sharing a room until we get to LA."

"No."

He sounds so stunned that I laugh. "We're supposed to be passionately in lust, fucking our way across the country on your ridiculous road trip. You think separate rooms are going to work?"

He frowns. "The paparazzi aren't going to follow us."

I shrug. "Probably not, but how is it going to sound if some hotel clerk spills that we're in separate rooms? And don't give me some 'waiting for marriage' bullshit—you know what those pictures looked like."

"They don't prove—"

"That we didn't fuck?" I stop, hands on my hips.

Something dark and unexpected flashes in his eyes. His hands curl into fists in his pockets and he's so tense he's in danger of shattering.

Awareness cuts through my hangover, washing over me, pulling something tight deep in my core. Maybe Gabriel Sinclair isn't boring after all. Maybe he's just very good at pretending. Maybe someone needs to cut that bind and release whatever he's trying to keep inside.

I might consider doing it for him. If he begged.

I pull the silk camisole over my head, tossing it onto the bed, and it finally happens. His gaze drops to my tits. His brain is still working, telling his body to turn away, but his eyes are reluctant on the follow-through and linger until his head finally snaps around.

It's the smallest victory, but I'll take it.

"We're going to have to kiss in public," I inform him, finding a bra and slipping it on.

"I realize that." He says it so tightly I suspect he's lying. The Great Gabriel Sinclair. Lying.

It turns me on.

The idea of dragging this man down to my level, to be clear. Not the man himself.

"You're going to have to touch me," I say, adjusting my tits in my bra. "Intimately."

"We can keep it family-friendly." His voice is tight. A little uncertain. He hasn't given this fake relationship much thought.

Lucky for him, I had all last night, when I wasn't crying over Nic, to imagine all the ways I could mess with Gabriel Sinclair's handsome little head.

"That's not what Warwick would do," I say. It brings a pang of sadness at the thought of all the things Nic would do, and not with me.

"I'm not Warwick." He looks over at me again, but not until I've slipped on my sundress. He's regained that tiny bit of control. "We should discuss what we're willing to do for the cameras."

"You can finger me at a truck stop. We can fuck at a dive bar. We can release a sex tape for all I care." I don't mean any of it, but I want to push him back into his caveman version. I saw a flash of it, and it was in his eyes in that photo.

Anger is what I get instead. "A few people are waiting outside. I need to know what you're okay with."

I'm not okay with anything. I stomp off to the bathroom to brush my teeth and pack my toiletries.

"Ashley," he calls. "If you want to call it off, we can say it was a one-night stand and drop the charade."

Tempting, but I'm not going to take the blame—or incur the penalty fee my agent foolishly insisted upon—by backing out first.

I decide to take a shower.

His exasperated complaint makes it worth it.

When I get out, there's a message on my phone.

WHAT THE HELL HOW ARE YOU DATING GABRIEL SINCLAIR? DETAILS NOW, BITCH.

WENDY

shut up.

ME

Oh my god, you are dating him??? HOW?

WENDY

Since I'm feeling salty, I spend a good ten minutes telling my only real friend what happened. Sadly, she is not on my side.

I told you not to mess with Fontana at his wedding.

WENDY

But I want him.

ME

Well you got Gabriel Sinclair and no offense, that's a trade-up.

WENDY

Sure, if I had insomnia and needed a cure.

ME

By the time I finish my hair and makeup, it's nine. I slip into the sundress sans panties—forgot to bring them in with me—and walk out to find Gabriel sitting at the little desk, a cup of coffee in his hand, reading glasses perched on his nose as he reads something on his phone. A tall iced white chocolate mocha waits untouched on the table.

"Aw, Gabe. You know my coffee order."

He glances up, frowning at the nickname. I vow to only call him Gabe from now on. "Lea brought the coffee," he says. "She was kind enough to ask if I wanted one."

Ugh, I want to fire her again. The urge will pass in a minute or two—it always does. Lea knows where the bodies are buried. Unsurprisingly, I don't have many friends, and I'm not sure I can count Lea since I pay her, but whatever. She messed up but was appropriately outraged at the idea of me having to date this boring prick, so I've forgiven her.

I dump the last of my clothes into my suitcase, then hold up two thongs, a white lace and a black silk. "Gabe, baby, which one?"

He glances up again and gives me an *are you kidding me* look. "You'll want something more comfortable." He lifts his coffee to his lips. They're sensual in a way Nic's aren't. Fuller on both the top and bottom. Soft, but a little cruel. For one irrational, confusing moment, I want them wrapped around me the way they're wrapped around his cup.

I'm jealous of a cup. What the hell is wrong with me?

I drop both thongs in the suitcase, slamming it shut. "No underwear. Got it."

His spit-take at my words would make a top-shelf GIF.

"The black pair," he says, wiping his mouth with the back of his hand, "or you sit on a towel."

"What a gentleman." I pull the black thong out of the suitcase and step into it, holding his eyes the entire time I pull it up. "Every time you look at me, you're going to think about this tiny scrap of fabric."

"Every time I look at you," he responds flatly, tucking his glasses and phone into his shirt pocket, "I'm going to question my judgment. Are you ready?"

I point at my stack of luggage as he pops a mint into his mouth without offering me one. "Right there, baby."

He glares at the *baby* but takes the two larger suitcases. I grab my coffee and follow him out with my smaller bags.

He wasn't lying about the paparazzi. There's a small knot of them hanging out across the street under the watchful eye of hotel security. Two cars are waiting for guests—Gabe's must be the black Lexus. The other car is a metallic fog-gray muscle car from another era. Not something boring assholes drive.

Lea and Gabe's assistant are standing a few feet apart, ignoring each other. When Gabe's assistant—a tall Asian man—leaps to help Gabe with my luggage, Lea rushes to my side to help me with the smaller bags. My money's on Lea. She might look like she spends her days lost in libraries, but she goes balls to the wall at times.

I get it. I'm feeling the same with Gabe right now. I want to win, so I slip my arm through his and pull him to a stop. His dark brows reach for the sky when I wrap my arms around his neck, pressing myself against him.

"What. Are. You. Doing?" he grits out, his minty breath puffing against my forehead.

"We are madly fucking each other, remember?" I toy with his thick hair within view of the cameras. "I thought you were an actor."

"Challenging role," he mutters, but, hands at my waist, he grabs a fistful of sundress in each. There's no way he's aware of how high he's hitched my skirt up my legs, but I feel every inch, my skin tingling at the exposure, my breath catching.

"You could pull out," I say coyly, staring up into his eyes with enough admiration and love to win an Oscar. *This* is how it's done.

Instead, he's gone stiff, and not where it counts. Well, maybe there, but I don't press my hips to his to find out because I've had enough disappointment lately.

"No," he says, but he doesn't sound certain.

"Then kiss me."

He turns us a bit for the cameras and kisses me.

Wow.

This is, without a doubt, the worst kiss of my life. It's dutiful, his lips unmoving against mine, and when I snap out of my shock enough to try to show him how it's done, the mismatch between us feels like a bad movie kiss. The kind where the actors have zero chemistry and barely tolerate each other—which, fair. It's us.

I could continue to try to force my tongue into his mouth or draw his into mine, but to what point? If it feels this terrible, it must look worse, so I pull back.

His hands tighten on my waist before he pushes me away. It's a gentle push, but unmistakable.

I can't help it. I laugh.

He shoots a panicked glance at the cameras and grabs my arm.

"Are you a robot?" I ask as he ushers me toward the car. My voice probably doesn't carry to the paps, but honestly, I'm not sure I care if it does. They witnessed that train wreck of a kiss. "That was terrible."

"Maybe if you stop trying to suck my face off." He opens the car door for me and I stop.

Blink.

Step back.

"Wrong car. This"—I gesture at the muscle car. It's vintage and I have no clue how old it is, but it's in perfect condition.—"is the car of a man who knows how to kiss with his tongue and teeth and his whole body. You, with your closed-mouth church-kiss, drive that." I fling my hand toward the Lexus.

Gabe glances at the Lexus and back at me. His back is to the cameras, so they can't catch the resentment in his eyes. I think I struck a nerve. His jaw could crack a walnut. "This is fake," he says to me like I'm a kid who won't listen.

"That kiss wasn't real."

I step closer, jabbing his chest with my perfectly manicured nail. "Say it a little louder, I don't think they all heard you."

He winces. "Are we doing this or not?"

"Do better."

"You too," he shoots back, and I'm surprised at how much that hurts. He doesn't mean do better fake kissing. He means be a better person. And I can't.

I can only be me.

The woman who ruthlessly uses people to get ahead on a TV show. The woman who tried to end a marriage and will keep trying. The woman who nearly destroyed her family. I've had my reasons, but it always comes down to wanting something. Wanting to win, wanting to be loved, wanting a goddamn break.

I rub at my chest with the back of my coffee-clutching hand and suddenly the inside of the car is too small, the freshly re-upholstered black leather smothering. I have to survive ten days of this bullshit, in there, with him.

"Fine," I say when I realize he's waiting for something from me.

He pulls my coffee out of my hand. "No food or drink in my car."

I claw for it, but he's already passing it off to his assistant.

"Do you want to die today?" I growl at him, and this time the paparazzi can hear. An excited hush falls over them as they strain to catch more.

Lea snatches the drink off Gabe's assistant and hands it back to me. "Drink," she says, and I do, pulling the sweet, sweet coffee through the straw.

"You don't have to win him over," Lea says in a hushed voice as I slowly drain my drink. "You don't have to compete with anyone. All you have to do is convince people you're dating. You do this, and the jobs will flood in."

She's right. I'm using him to get work, to keep myself busy until I can get to Nic. Gabe doesn't have to like me, not when he needs me too.

I drain the last of the coffee. I can do this.

"Last chance," Gabe says. He's put his body between me and the paparazzi across the street, thank god. "We can go our separate ways and pretend none of this ever happened."

I hand my cup to Lea and step close to Gabe, running my hand through his thick, dark hair for the cameras. "I'm not backing down. Are you?" I ask.

He has the gall to look exasperated. "Then get in the car."

Because I can, or because there are cameras, or maybe because I want to throw this man off-kilter, I tighten my hand in his hair and bring my other hand up to grip his chin. He stares at me, his dark eyes flashing, but he doesn't move as I slide the pad of my thumb over his thick lower lip, dragging that soft flesh down. Christ, this mouth. Quick, before he can stop me, I rise on my toes and kiss him, sucking lightly on that lip. The surprised, strangled sound he makes is delicious and I eat it up.

I'm smart enough to end the kiss first, slipping away from him and into his car. When I smile coyly up at him, he blinks away the dazed look on his face and slams my door.

Chapter Four

Gabe

David stops me in the front of the car.

"What was that?" he hisses.

I motion weakly to my unwelcome passenger. "She's so…" If I'm being completely honest, she has me wound so tight I'm not sure I'm going to survive one day in the car with her, let alone ten. I like a challenge, but I'm not winning and I don't know how to even the playing field when I'm constantly on defense.

"Awful," David finishes for me. I nod, though that's not what I was thinking.

She's maddening, but what's making me unreasonable right now is how hard it is to get the taste of her out of my mouth and the image of her breasts out of my head. I am better than this.

I thought I was.

"We need this," David says quietly, glancing at the paps. "The publicity she's giving you is good." His eyes fix intently on mine. "It's only going to stay good if you can make this believable, and whatever *that* was? It looked bad."

"You try kissing her," I mutter, not caring how petty I sound. She tastes sweeter than she has any right to. Not kissing her the way I wanted was an act of self-preservation.

"You couldn't pay me enough," he says with a gag. "So I get it. I do."

He clearly doesn't.

"But you need to make this look real," he says, landing the knockout blow.

I scrub my hand over my face and all it seems to do is rub the feel of her lips on mine deep under my skin. I itch, everywhere, all at once. My eyes drift to the car. To her.

Ashley is giving me that bratty little smile of hers. She drags her perfectly manicured fingernails over my dashboard and I feel it on my skin beneath my clothes.

I tamp it down and glare at her.

She blows me a kiss.

"We can't change who she is, so let's approach this strategically," David continues. "This isn't your first rodeo."

My other fake relationships were easy. The women were kind, and we were able to be friends. I don't see that happening with Ashley.

"The Savannah Protocol." David at least has the good grace to wince as he says it.

"She's nothing like Savannah." Savannah was a shy kindergarten teacher who had never been in the same room as a celebrity and had the misfortune of being the sister of my publicist's best friend and single at a time when I needed to not be. David developed a structured way to overcome her shyness and put her at ease, but Ashley isn't uneasy around me. She isn't shy or intimidated.

"Maybe digging a little deeper will help you relate to each other so we can avoid whatever the hell that performance a few minutes ago was." David throws his hands up into the air. "Or not. I wouldn't want to dig into that muck either. She's awful. But you need to make this look real."

There are flashes. Little moments when I think I can glimpse the real Ashley behind the walls she's put up. There and gone so fast I might be imagining them.

"Try the questions," David says. "Open up and see if—"

"No." I snap, my chest going tight. I'm not offering myself up to a woman who will use any information I give her as a weapon against me. "I don't need to know what her favorite color is or what song she puts on repeat after a breakup. I just need to be seen with her."

David jumps back, his eyebrows up to his hairline.

Shame hits me hot and hard. I've never interrupted him before, and never in that tone.

I can't let her get to me like this.

"I'm sorry," I say, rubbing the back of my neck. Ashley's still staring at me. Her gaze burns. "If I need the questions, I'll call you."

David clasps me on the arm like I'm going into battle. I'm pretty sure I am.

"If you need anything, give me a call. I'll handle it," he promises.

I nod. Shore up my determination, straighten my shoulders, and open the driver's side door.

Ashley's hand is wrapped around the gear stick, stroking it slowly, a slight twist on the knob...

Blood is already heading south and I sit, trapping my cock in place. My pants are tight enough to guarantee any erection will be too uncomfortable to maintain, but I'm not taking chances. I wrap my hand around Ashley's and for a few terrifying heartbeats, my hand rides hers as she pumps the shaft.

"Don't," I say when I finally manage to pry her hand off.

"I could play with your other stick," she offers sweetly.

My cock is on board, going fully hard in anticipation. I shift to face her, threatening myself with castration. "You need to tone it down when we're in front of the cameras," I growl at her. "And when we're alone, you need to turn it off. Got it?"

"Fine," she says with a bored sigh. "I don't need to add your dick to the list of things that have disappointed me in the last twenty-four hours."

She wouldn't be disappointed, but I bite my tongue and start up the car. Usually, the rumble of the engine gives me a sense of calm. Not today.

A camera presses against my window and Ashley leans over me to flip it off.

I grab her hand, bringing it to my lips. I want to bite her finger—not hard, just enough to make her gasp—but I kiss the back of her hand instead because that's what Gabriel Sinclair would do. Since the camera is still bumping my tinted window, I place her hand on my thigh.

She slides her hand right up, and I don't think she means to touch my hard cock—she's not even looking at me—but she does. Her hand goes still. I hold my breath. She squeezes, ever so slightly, like she's looking for confirmation.

She fucking gets it.

"Oh," she exhales, her hand sliding right off. She clasps her hands together and stares out the window.

Slowly, so I don't hit the asshole who got that on video, I accelerate.

"Disappointed?" I snarl.

"That dick is wasted on you," she says without hesitation.

My laughter is sharp. "What makes you think it's wasted?"

She shifts in her seat, bending her head down to my lap and I nearly rear-end the car in front of me. What the—

"Baby," she coos to my groin, "Does he ever take you out to play? Do you get sick of his hand?"

"Stop it," I grumble, using my elbow to push her out of my space.

"Oh, god, Gabe," she groans, "Please tell me you're into anal because I want to grab the stick lodged up your ass and pull it out."

My dentist is going to kill me. I already grind my teeth in my sleep and I'm grinding them now.

Meditation playlists. That might help me survive the next ten days. I'll download some tonight.

"*Are* you into anal?" Ashley's shocked voice wrecks my attempt at unclenching my jaw.

"My sex life is none of your business."

"Except it is. Because we're 'fucking.'" She uses air quotes. "What am I supposed to tell people when they ask what you're like in bed?"

"You tell them nothing." We've signed NDAs. I only need to be seen with her. We don't need to do interviews. She won't be telling anyone anything about me.

"Boring." She digs her phone out of her handbag and spends a few minutes scrolling in silence while I drive through traffic. I don't for a minute believe she won't improvise and say something unflattering about me in bed.

"Ashley—"

"Fine." She dismisses me with a flick of her wrist. "I won't say a word. I'll smile like you're the best lover in the world. Because I can act." *Unlike you*, she adds under her breath.

I bite my tongue. Ashley goes silent.

Four long hours pass, and Ashley scrolls on her phone or stares out her window. I don't know what music she listens to, so I stream a top forty playlist. She doesn't sing along, but more importantly, she doesn't complain.

We have a townhouse booked at a palatial inn styled as a Tuscan villa on Lake Seneca. There are no photographers around when we arrive, and Ashley follows me in without a word.

It doesn't last.

She takes one look at the décor inside and laughs. "Wow, I feel like I'm at my grandmother's." She sniffs discreetly. "Disdain and Chanel Number Five."

The décor is stodgy in a moneyed New England way. Ostentatious in a style that hasn't changed in a century. David booked this place off Rose's recommendation, but I don't think the aesthetic was the selling point. Privacy and comfort were. And the two bedrooms.

"You can take the master bedroom." Knowing Ashley, she'll claim it anyway.

She runs her hand across the back of the couch, her pink nails scraping in a way that's both ordinary and obscene. "This sofa is begging to be defiled. Do you think the middle-aged rich guys who stay here ever fuck their wives on it?" She bends over the back of it, gripping the wooden trim along the top like she's being railed from behind.

"Ashley." I can't grit out anything beyond her name because it's too easy to picture myself behind her, gripping her hips and making her scream in pleasure.

"You're right." She straightens. "They fuck their mistresses on this sofa while their wives are at the spa. So. Now what?" Her smile is suggestive, her hand stroking the trim as she walks around and sits down, crossing her legs, looking somehow prim and naughty at the same time.

She's killing me.

I pick up the spa voucher from the table and hand it to her with a smile. "You have an appointment."

She barely glances at it before tossing it on the sofa next to her. "Are you going to fuck your mistress while I'm getting a facial?"

I raise an eyebrow. "Do you think I'd have a mistress?"

Ashley stands with a sigh. "You'd be a lot more interesting if you did."

"Something tells me you're not the sharing type."

Her eyes go hard as she snatches up the spa pass. "I'm not. What time am I meeting you for dinner?"

"Seven thirty."

"That gives you...five hours to work up the courage to hold my hand and maybe kiss me over dessert. Think it'll be enough? Would it be easier to follow if I wrote a script?"

I've had my fill of Ashley Foley, so I walk to the door. "That won't be necessary."

"Where are you going?" she asks.

I don't answer her. She doesn't need to know. "I'll see you at seven thirty."

Some things are impossible to escape. Ashley's perfume clings to the Camaro's interior, following me as I drive two hours to Buffalo. It's spicy and rich, intoxicating. I hate that I like it. I hate that I want her so bad I can taste her.

She might be my type right down to that bratty mouth on her, but she's not Gabriel Sinclair's type, and I've always managed to avoid getting involved with women like her. I'll deal with it. Somehow.

Frustrated and frayed, I park in front of an old house clad in pale, peeling yellow siding. Ever since I found out about Michael, I've felt this powerful need to see my childhood home.

The house is shabby and run-down, with a chain-link fence surrounding it. It looks darker and more dismal than I remember, but maybe I'm used to marble and chandeliers now.

This is the only stop I had planned before I got stuck with Ashley and I don't know what I expected to feel when I arrived, but...I don't feel anything. That part of my past is so disconnected from who I am now that even when the memories flood back, it's like all those years happened to some other boy.

The sound of children playing somewhere in the neighborhood floats through the summer breeze, and it could be any day from my childhood, some twenty years ago. Sometimes I'd roam the neighborhood looking for trouble with other kids, but just as often I'd hang out while my father worked in the garage, because I never knew when he'd disappear—to jail, on the run, on a bender.

The detached garage where Dad spent all his free time held the scent of engine oil, exhaust, and stale cigarettes. The memory is so strong it briefly overpowers Ashley's perfume.

There were other smells in that garage sometimes. Later I would recognize them as cannabis and cheap perfume, depending on who visited Dad. I seldom saw them. I was always sent into the house and told to watch TV.

But Sundays were our day. We ate bacon and eggs and hash browns and changed into our grungiest clothes before going out to the garage. Dad would work on cars, showing me the parts he was working on, and how he fixed them. He would smile proudly when I could recall the instructions he'd muttered with his head under the hood. He'd ruffle my hair when I could identify parts of an engine. Beam with pride when I learned to do simple tasks like changing the oil.

We'd stop for lunch—sandwiches, or sometimes fast food—at the workbench, ignoring grease-stained fingers. After, Dad would light up a smoke and gaze at the pictures on the wall, torn from magazines over decades and tacked to any surface not covered in tools. A few were naked women. I liked those most, with their ample tits and red lips. Not that I had a clue why I was drawn to them. Dad didn't seem to see them. He always stared at the car.

A sleek silver 1969 Chevy Camaro. It was like something born from the storm gathered on the desert horizon behind it. A car fast enough to escape everything—or so my young brain rationalized. To leave behind the school I had to go back to in the fall and the scary-looking guys who visited Dad.

His father had the same Camaro, once. Lost it when he couldn't pay his bills. Dad would tell me of the road trips his father had taken him on when he was a kid. They'd drive for days to visit family. Through sunbaked land full of so much nothingness it made a man's heart hurt, with skies so big he felt small. Until he felt half mad with the need to see something, anything.

It wasn't some family reunion out at the old farm in Oklahoma Dad would daydream about. It was the car and the open road. Escape. He'd look at me, his eyes full of something that made me feel sad but protective and fierce all the same, and say, "We'll get this car one day, son. We'll drive far away from here, just the two of us."

We never did it. Dad never got the car. He went to prison, and I went to live with a series of foster families before my mother's sister found me and gave me a new name and a new home. A new life.

I slide my hand over the dash of my car. *The* car. Dad's car, my grandpa's car. The same model, anyway. Their dream. It drives like freedom and rumbles like thunder. My past has hounded me, nipping at my heels for years, this fear that the world will find out I'm a fraud. I'm not some perfect angel, even if my uncle made me out to be one, in his image.

He was far from perfect, turns out. And all this time, I didn't know.

Michael Sinclair, the man with a solid gold reputation for always doing the right thing in an industry that rewarded the opposite, was a liar and a cheater who couldn't live by his own rules.

I have to be better than him, but if the great Michael Sinclair couldn't help himself, how do I stand a chance when I come from some place like this? From people like my parents? My mother ran off after I was born and my father died in prison.

I need the escape my dad used to dream of so I could figure out what's real and what's a lie about my own life, and now I'm stuck with a woman who would happily ruin me because she dislikes me.

And I need her.

Michael wanted that Oscar for me almost as badly as I want it for myself. The critical reviews, the reputation, being the best. I want it, and Ashley Foley is a means to that end, so this fake relationship has to be a good thing, right? Would Michael approve? Should I still care, now that I know he kept a second family hidden away from the world and from my aunt?

There are no answers. There's only me, alone, trying to be my best while tamping down my worst.

With a deep, shaking breath, I start up the car I bought and restored so I'd have an escape ready. I never expected to need that escape so soon.

My car still smells like Ashley's perfume. It gets under my skin, so I stop at a

public beach on Lake Erie for fresh air. Sitting in the sand, baseball cap pulled
down low, sunglasses on, no one snaps a photo or asks for a selfie. I'm nobody,
staring at the flat expanse of water.

I think we came here once, as a family. Maybe after my grandfather's funeral.
A picnic in the sand. A dip in the icy waters. I was told my dad's ashes were
scattered nearby.

When Michael and Cora Sinclair adopted me, my past died. They snuffed it
out. No one has dug it up. Guess Michael was right—his reputation was enough
for people to accept me. To never look beyond the surface.

I scoop up a handful of sand and let it slip through my fingers. Michael and
Cora gave me a radically different life, saving me from following in my father's
footsteps. I'm grateful, and I'll do my damned best to live up to the legacy my
uncle left me, but when did it start to feel so suffocating?

The last of the sand trickles through my fingers. I scoop another handful and
do it again. It's irritating having to fake date Ashley to appease the fandom. If
they knew a tenth of how I grew up, they'd see I'm more suited to the role than
Nic ever was. He was nothing more than a placeholder, waiting until my star
had risen high enough.

And my star is going up.

Ashley, my Camaro, and an open road are a recipe for disaster, but her disdain
and attitude are my saving grace. So long as she keeps acting like a nightmare, it
will be easy enough to remember she's not my dream.

Sand trickles through my fingers, again and again, my thoughts drifting on
the cool breeze coming off the lake. I don't know what I hoped to accomplish, revisiting these old memories. Maybe to reaffirm that, despite Michael's
hypocrisy and betrayal and my rough upbringing, I'm not destined to fail. That
I can be the man I'm supposed to be, even if my idol couldn't.

The sun goes down and I feel more like a fraud than ever.

I'm halfway to the car when I realize it's nine thirty. I've stood Ashley up for
dinner.

CHAPTER FIVE

Ashley

IT'S NEARLY MIDNIGHT WHEN Gabriel returns to the townhouse.

I desperately wish I didn't care that he stood me up, but the truth is, with pictures of me sitting alone at a table set for two all over social media, all over the gossip sites, I do care. I care enough that, for the last two hours, I've sat on this uncomfortable, ugly-as-hell couch waiting, drinking wine, and stewing.

There were pictures of Nic and Jessie's wedding—the official ones released to the world—and pictures of them getting off the plane on their honeymoon, each one a tiny cut that stings like hell. Burying my feelings in my anger at my fake boyfriend makes it hurt a little less, but I won't be thanking him for it.

Gabriel flips the light on and startles when he sees me.

I wait, refusing to ask what the hell happened.

"I'm sorry," he says, stuffing his hands in his pockets and walking into the room. His face is calm and controlled like he might be hiding that he's as raw as I am.

"You should be." I keep the snarl out of my voice, barely.

He nods like that's it. Like it's over.

It's not. "You fucked the whole thing up."

He scoffs. "David put out that I was feeling unwell and told you to go to dinner without me. Nothing's fucked up."

"You should have told me. I wouldn't have sat around obviously waiting for you," I snap, draining my glass and setting it on the table. I stand, still in my heels, still dressed for dinner, possibly two inches taller after an afternoon of having all the tension massaged out of my body. Could have been three inches and I'm pissed Gabriel Sinclair stole a hypothetical inch off my height. I walk right up to him, not stopping until my breasts touch his chest. "*Where were you?*"

He steps back, turning to the open bottle of Riesling one of the local wineries had delivered to us ahead of the tour we're supposed to do tomorrow. He pours himself a glass. "It's none of your business."

"You made me look like a fool tonight." I wish I could keep the emotion out of my voice, but I'm unspooling fast. "I think you owe me an explanation."

"You're the one who owes me an explanation," he barks back, and I jump. "What happened at the wedding, Ashley? Because whatever that was is the reason we're here, and I think I deserve to know."

I blink at him, stunned that he snapped at me.

God, I'm such a fool. The man I love will probably never love me back and the man I'm stuck with doesn't respect me enough to show up for dinner. It's a miracle I'm not falling in love with Gabriel Sinclair for despising me as much as I despise myself.

"You need me," I manage to get out. I don't care what this man thinks about me, but I can't confess what I tried to do. Not to Mr. Perfect. Not ever.

"You need me more." His dark brown eyes are angry and I hate that he's right.

I leave him to his wine and go to my room, keeping it together long enough to wash my makeup off, slip into a camisole, and brush my teeth.

That summer when I met Nic, my parents were together, which meant I wasn't necessary. I spent a lot of time at Aunt Celia's house because my mother refused to get another nanny after my father slept with the last one.

Plus, Nic was there. I watched him with Timothy, but the best times were when my cousin wasn't around and Nic would hang out in my aunt's kitchen. He'd let me help him when he'd bake a cake and we'd sit together at the island, licking the beaters. We didn't need to talk, but sometimes he'd tell me about his life. His parents. They were too busy for him, like mine were too busy for me.

One hot day, I followed the sound of laughing and shouting down to the lake. Nic and Timothy were swimming, splashing each other.

"Hey, Ash," Nic called out when he spied me. "Want to join us?"

I wanted to. He was so handsome, and it was sweltering.

"You'd better not," Timothy said with a laugh. "There are fish in here that would bite your toes off."

"Stop scaring her," Nic said, and my heart swelled. "There aren't any fish that big in this lake."

If my cousin wasn't there, I'd tell Nic the truth—I didn't know how to swim. Nic would take my hand and wade out with me, I was sure of it.

While I stood on the shore, wishing I was older and daydreaming of Nic kissing me in the lake, Nic and Timothy took off, racing each other.

Glancing down, I spied their hastily discarded clothes. I didn't even think. I scooped up Nic's shirt and took off.

The shirt is worn now. It was too big for Nic's lanky frame back then, but it still fits me. It wouldn't fit Nic anymore.

I pull it out of my suitcase, wrap it into a ball, and hold it close to my chest. I've spritzed it with the cologne he favors according to magazines. The scent is barely there tonight, though, and as I take it to my bed, burying my face in it, I mostly inhale my perfume. Tears fill my eyes and I let them fall onto the soft fabric.

Gabriel knocks gently on my door. When I don't answer, he pushes it open a few inches.

"I'm sorry," he says quietly. The remorse in his voice sounds genuine, but that changes nothing. "I owe you an explanation. I grew up in Buffalo. I wanted to see where I used to live. See if it changed. I lost track of the time."

I stuff Nic's shirt under the bedding. "I don't care."

His face softens and I remember too late that mine is a teary mess. He takes a step into my room. "I really am sorry. It won't happen again. I promise. I want this to work out for us."

Stupid, hateful tears. His pity is wasted on me. I wipe them off my cheeks and dry my eyes. "I'm not crying over you."

He arches an eyebrow and I hate that he doesn't believe me. I hate it even more when he takes another step toward me. "Do you want to talk?"

"No, I do not want to talk, Gabriel Sinclair." I huff.

He cracks a small smile at that, but it's a warm smile. An invitation. "I'm down the hall if you need anything."

Oh my god. He means it. Maybe it's guilt, or maybe it's more golden boy shit, but he wants me to—what? Spill my feelings about Nic? Maybe he's as good as a priest and would take my confession to the grave, but I'm not willing to trust him, despite the NDA. Ever.

"What I need is something you can't give me," I shoot back. I want to claw him to shreds, make sure he understands that I don't like him.

"Try asking nicely," he replies in a smoky voice.

Something shorts out inside me. I stare at the shadows defining his arms, cast by the warm light of my bedside lamp. The thick stubble on his jaw. The dark color of his eyes. My body goes all warm and honeyed.

I am not okay with this.

There's a look in his eyes like he can see right through me. That he knows what he did, and he likes it. "Good night, Ashley," he finally says, closing the door.

I go to sleep mad, but that's better than going to sleep sad.

There's no chance for me to oversleep. Gabriel knocks on my door with the promise of coffee and breakfast. It's enough to get my half-hungover ass in the shower.

The winery tour is awkward as hell. Gabriel is kind and attentive to everyone, including me, but spits his wine like a douche. Since I don't get to drive, I swallow my drink, but the pours are small. Too small for holding his hand and smiling at him. It's excruciating.

Then we're on the road.

From time to time, Gabriel attempts conversation. Since we aren't being photographed anymore and I'm careening between anger at being stood up and confusion over his following attempts at what I guess is kindness, I shoot him down with one-word answers and hide behind my sunglasses as I scroll through various social media platforms.

Nic is everywhere.

Some asshole has snapped photos of Nic and Jessie in the ocean off a private beach, and though it's not obvious at first glance, Nic's hand is down her bikini bottoms.

"This"—I show Gabriel when he stops for gas—"is how someone playing Warwick does a public relationship."

He leans back into the car, glances at the picture, and frowns. "They're standing in the water."

"Look at his arm, the way it's turned. Her face. He's fingering the shit out of her, right in front of the cameras." Nic's face is intense in all the right ways, protective, and full of absolute worship. I want it—him, looking at me like that, touching me like that. I want it so bad my bones ache.

Gabriel's eyes narrow on the picture, and he sees it now. The tips of his ears go red and he abruptly closes the door.

Gabriel Sinclair would never.

Maybe he *should*. I overheard the call between him and his agent this morning. Standing me up isn't exactly the bad boy flavor they are trying to spice him up with. Unfortunately, I was also the recipient of a call from an annoyed agent. Mine assumed I was to blame. Naturally.

Gabriel takes forever inside. I suspect he's autographing postcards or some ridiculous shit. He's pulled a baseball cap low over his head, but he still stands out. That faded dark gray T-shirt and his perfectly distressed designer jeans are doing things for his body that only happen in movies. Hell, his body only happens in the movies.

He doesn't say a word when he gets in. Soon we're back on the road, cruising along Highway 5. I stare out the window, glimpsing Lake Erie between trees. I don't know why we're taking the scenic route except it seems a very Gabriel Sinclair thing to do.

His phone rings and he shoots me a glance before answering on speaker.

David's voice replaces the generic pop music on the radio. "Okay, I have the list of questions. I'll read them out and both of you answer."

This is hell. I am in hell, paying for my bad deeds. That is the only explanation. "I don't want to play twenty questions."

David sighs like the weight of the world is pressing down on his probably generic-cotton button-up-covered shoulders. "That performance you put on yesterday was abysmal, and this has only gone downhill since. *Tolerating* each other would be an improvement."

It's clear from the tone in his voice that he thinks his boss is perfect and I am irredeemable trash. No surprise, the world agrees.

It's possible I hate David more than I hate Gabriel Sinclair right now. "I'm not doing this."

"You're stuck in a car. What else are you going to do?" David asks.

David can't see me reach over and stroke the stick shift, but Gabriel can. He scowls and flicks my hand away.

"Do you want to make this work?" he asks me, his stern brown eyes pinning me to my seat.

Ugh. "Fine. But I don't want David listening to my answers like a pervert."

"I'll put the call on mute. That okay, David?"

He huffs. "I don't want to listen to her vapid answers. Unmute me when you're ready for the next question."

I guess since I'm stuck in this car for untold hours—going the speed limit down the scenic route all but guarantees it—I might as well play along. "Fine."

David clears his throat. "Given the choice of anyone in the world, whom would you want as a dinner guest?"

Goddammit.

I want Nic, obviously. And I want to be the main course. But I can't say that to Gabriel Sinclair, even after he mutes the phone.

He's chewing on his lip, staring out at the road.

Maybe he's in a similar predicament, longing for someone he can't have.

Wow. I don't know anything real about this man I'm supposed to be fake dating. Maybe he has some deep, dark secrets. There's more to him than his Boy Scout image suggests—the muscle car, for one. Maybe he has a lifetime membership to an exclusive sex club. I flick my phone on and send a quick text to Lea. *Find out everything you can about Gabriel Sinclair, please.*

Research is her superpower. I wonder what she'll turn up.

"My dad," he answers, jolting me out of my little daydream where I step onto Gabriel Sinclair's bare ass in my pointiest stiletto as he lies on the secret sex club floor.

His dad? The famous director who died sometime in the last decade? Is he kidding me with this shit? Hollywood's golden boy has the purest answers.

I twist them. "Daddy issues?"

I expect him to snap back. Or glare. Something.

Instead, he shrugs. "I didn't have a perfect childhood. You?"

My laugh sounds brittle, even to my ears. "Do you think someone with a perfect childhood ends up like me?" I try to come off as flippant. It doesn't work. The concerned look he shoots me only makes the old pain burn hotter.

I dip my chin, staring down at my phone, letting a curtain of hair hide my face from him. Lea texts back with a thumbs up.

His hand lands softly just above my legging-covered knee and the heat from his palm seeps slowly up to the juncture between my thighs.

What.

The.

Fuck.

Is happening?

"I'm sorry," he says.

I continue to stare at his hand. It's huge on my leg, his fingers long and thick and his nails short and tidy. Tan skin stretches over ligaments and veins I could trace for several long, lazy minutes.

He squeezes my leg softly. It sets off a pulse between my legs and I'm un-comfortably aware of the vibration of the car now. My brain goes there. Gabe, sliding his hand up my thigh ever so slowly as he drives. David waits on mute, unable to hear my moan when Gabe's fingers, rough through my leggings, find my clit, circling until I'm soaked.

What the hell is wrong with me?

He'd ask me to sit on a towel, lest I leave a snail trail all over his custom leather.

His hand is already gone.

"Who's your guest?" he asks after a moment.

I turn to look out my window and say the first name that comes to mind. "Wendy."

"From *Love on the Line*?"

Shit. Guys like Gabriel Sinclair don't watch trashy reality TV. They watch documentaries or sports or…god, I don't even know, snobby indie films. They certainly don't watch a show where attractive people hook up and play each other for a huge cash prize.

But he knows who Wendy is, and it leaves a bad taste in my mouth. I have to know. "Have you watched it?"

"No."

There's no judgment in his voice, something I didn't expect to be relieved about.

"But you know about Wendy?" I can barely say her name without my stomach dropping. Getting her sent home cemented me as the villain of *Love on the Line* season five. The producers didn't have to give me the villain edit. Not only had she been my friend and confidant, but she was the girl next door, with wide dark eyes, deep golden skin, and a Miss America smile. The audience loved her and I betrayed her for a man I wanted to use as a pawn. It's more complicated than that, but only Wendy and I know the truth.

"David told me."

Of course he did. Every awful moment, I'm sure of it.

Gabriel glances over at me with a sympathetic look. Because he's trying or he's a better actor than I want to give him credit for, I'm not sure which. "I know how these shows work," he says quietly.

"No, you don't." I reach over to his phone, mounted on the dash, and unmute David. "Next question."

Gabriel's looking at me again. I can see him out of the corner of my eye. I pretend to ignore him as David struggles to find the second question on his list.

"Uhh…would you want to—no, that question doesn't work. Let me change it. Did you always want to be famous?"

Gabriel mutes him again.

I answer first this time. "No." When I was younger, I wanted to be like my mother. Glamorous, with everyone rushing to make me happy. Blissfully unemployed, spending other people's money. Causing drama because I could.

"Yes," Gabriel answers immediately, glancing at me again.

His puzzled expression irritates the hell out of me. "What?" I demand.

"Serious? You didn't want the fame?"

I shrug. I moved to LA because Nic was there. I tried to break into the industry because he was in it and it was something we'd have in common, something that could help bring us together.

It turns out that looking like a thousand other twenty-something blondes with fake tits doesn't make it easy to get roles. Before *Love on the Line*, my career had peaked at Murder Victim Number Two and Angry Stripper.

I'm nearly thirty. The odds of a career breakthrough are infinitesimal, but here I am, grabbing for what I can get. I will make it happen, whatever I have to do.

Gabe frowns. "So, what are you doing?"

"Oh." I wave it off. "I'm here for the death threats."

His face darkens.

I unmute David before Gabe can say anything, punching my finger at the phone in a way that clearly grates him. "Next."

"Okay...I'm setting my timer for five minutes." David pauses. "Tell each other your life story, in as much detail as you can. Ready?"

Okay, easy.

My parents, when they're together, forget I exist and that's been true since I was a baby. When they're fighting, they use me like a weapon against each other. I don't know which is worse.

On top of that, everyone in America hates me, the man I love just married my cousin, and now I have to fake date someone I can't stand.

Oh, and I can't get a job, and believe it or not, I'm not a trust fund baby. The money I get from my parents—I *earn* that shit.

Not that I'll tell him. I don't want Gabriel Sinclair's sympathy. I don't want his sad eyes on me or his big hand on my leg.

He doesn't look at me. He's gripping the steering wheel like he wants to strangle it, his brown eyes locked on the road. His jaw is clenched again, and his words about not having a perfect childhood come back to me.

"I think we're done for today," he says to David.

"But we've—"

"Just get some cameras outside our hotel. I'll do better."

He'll do better. Something tells me I'm about to get chaste kissed again.

"Can't wait," I say flatly.

He ends the call and upbeat music, at a low volume, fills the car. It doesn't touch the silence between us. I'm raw after those questions, so I retreat into my phone, scrolling fast enough to turn every uninteresting opinion on the internet into a soothing blur.

After a few minutes, Gabriel clears his throat. "What roles are you looking for after this?"

Maybe he's trying to distract himself from the memories that the last question dredged up, but it feels like an interview. Are my goals worth his time? Will I pass his judgment?

Can anyone? I'm done playing this game.

"Did your dad fuck his assistant?" I ask as I scroll, putting more boredom in my voice than I probably need. "Or maybe your mom blew the pool boy?"

His silence makes me sit up. Shit, I must be close. And the closer I am to him, the farther away he is to me.

"Did they belong to a sex cult?" I press.

"My *uncle* was Michael Sinclair. He and my aunt adopted me when my parents couldn't raise me. No one fucked the assistant or pool boy."

I grin. "It's a sex cult, isn't it? It's always a sex cult."

The car swerves onto the shoulder and screeches to a halt, and Gabriel Sinclair turns toward me with the full force of his disapproval. "Timothy was right—you don't know when to stop. My life isn't some game of twenty questions to entertain you."

"Oh, no." I deadpan. "Maybe we need fake relationship counseling."

"Is my existence some splinter under your skin pointing out all the negatives you see in yourself?" he asks, thunder in his voice. "I'm trying to make this work, and you're trying to derail everything."

I open my mouth but no words come out, and before I can find them, Gabe turns back to the road, pulls a U-turn, and accelerates. He's speeding as we turn south on the road we just passed, and a few minutes later, onto the interstate.

The sudden shift in him unnerves me. "Where are we going?"

He doesn't glance at me.

"LA."

Chapter Six

Ashley

The relief I feel giving Gabriel's little scenic tour a miss is a full-body experience that lasts until he pulls up in front of the Cleveland Hilton, which feels like an oxymoron. There's no paparazzi, at least. Fortunate, because I'm too worn out to do anything other than pout over how sore my body is from sitting in his damn car for a second day.

Gabriel hasn't said a word since he threw his itinerary out the window and asked me to book a hotel in Cleveland for tonight. Apparently, driving another hour with me to the boutique hotel he'd already booked was intolerable. I happen to agree.

He hands his keys over to the valet, but the bellhop is on a break. Gabriel simply carries all our things himself.

I follow him inside the hotel and it's impossible, as tired and over it as I am, not to notice how easily he carries a cartload of luggage. The man is unstoppable, all bulging muscles under a dark gray T-shirt. The mirrored sunglasses and the thick stubble shading his jaw almost trick me into believing this is Gabe with the muscle car, not Gabriel Sinclair who is beige personified.

My eyes drift to his denim-covered ass as he stops at the counter and sets the luggage down. I picture him in the Warwick costume, those black leather pants tight across his firm, perfectly shaped cheeks. Accentuated all the more by that black corseted vest...

Okay. I can see it. Maybe this is what they were looking at when they picked Gabriel Sinclair to replace Dominic Fontana.

Since I've found his one redeeming quality, I step close to him at the counter only to discover a problem.

"You only booked one room," he hisses at me.

I plaster a smile on my face. "I booked the King Suite." The King Suite has two rooms, therefore two beds. I might have booked it quickly, but I know I read that. I turn my smile at the young woman staring at him with hearts in her eyes and stage whisper, "He thinks I have too much luggage and it needs its own room." I slap my hand to his chest and laugh. "Joke's getting old, babe."

I hate myself right now.

Maybe she senses the affection in my voice is fake and I'm lying. She gives him an apologetic little smile so sweet I want to rip it off. "I'm sorry, sir. The King Suite has one bedroom with a king-size bed and a living room with a sofa bed. We do have a Standard Queen available if you'd like to book a separate room. For the...luggage."

I'm going to claw her face off, but I notice another woman out of the corner of my eye, discreetly filming us on her phone. Shit.

He's about to accept when I place my hand on his arm. "Babe," I say softly but firmly. "Seriously. Let that joke go."

I barely have to glance to the side before he catches on.

He sighs and offers the receptionist a smile. "Extremely high maintenance, this one." He pulls it off naturally, like this really is some private joke between us. "The King Suite will be perfect. Thanks."

"Let me know if you change your mind," the young woman says, and the sudden smile on her face as she hands him the key card makes me twitch.

I hate her. Thanks to this woman, I want to kiss Gabriel Sinclair so she'll know he's *my* fake boyfriend and I would, except...

He won't kiss me back. He'll leave me hanging. I'll be embarrassed, looking like I'm way more into him than he is into me. Can't have that, especially after last night.

I squeeze his arm instead and slip closer.

The look he gives me sends me over the edge. It's little and cold. Like I'm so far beneath him.

And I am. I am a snake in the grass compared to Gabriel Sinclair, Perfect Angel.

I drop his arm and grab the handles of my suitcases before he can take them, striding to the elevator, dragging all my shit behind me. The moment the elevator doors close on us and we're alone, I drop my bags and round on him.

"Are we doing this or not?" I demand. "You can't keep half-assing it."

"Just give me some space," he grits out.

I'll give him space. I wish I could put the whole of America between us, but since I can't, the moment the doors open, I'm off, stomping down the hallway, dragging my luggage behind me.

Waiting for him to unlock the door ruins the whole storming away thing and my face heats.

Once inside, I leave most of my bags by the door and disappear into the bathroom with my toiletries without a glance at the room.

What the hell was I thinking? This is never going to work. Every time I've checked my name, or his name, online, it's been the same thing. After the initial shock of us being together, everyone is claiming it's a badly orchestrated stunt. Or our whirlwind romance is over already and—surprising no one—it's my fault.

This isn't working. I want to stomp my feet and scream and maybe kick the trash can because I can't break this contract and incur the penalty fee, which my agent only included because she knows me too well. I need this to work. Without jobs coming in, my ability to live my life as comfortably as I like is already in jeopardy.

I wash my face and unpack my toiletries instead, breathing deeply and trying to find some sort of calm.

My agent's words ring in my head. *Give it a couple of days and give them something better to work with.*

I'm *trying*. I want to leave this sham of a publicity stunt, but I'm going to claw my way to the spotlight if I have to do it over Gabriel Sinclair's corpse.

To the spotlight and Nic. Of course.

Since Gabriel Sinclair has a way of taking all my attention in the worst way and I'm thinking of it now, I plant a quick seed. A text to Jessie, thanking her for inviting me to the wedding and asking if I can text her again when she's back from her honeymoon. I need to know if she knows what I did. If she doesn't, I want her trust. It'll make it easier to get to Nic later.

Then I square my shoulders and walk into the room.

Gabriel is sprawled across the bed on his back like a damn starfish, eyes closed.

"Oh, hell no. Sofa bed." I point through the doorway into the living room at the less-than-comfy-looking sofa.

He sits up. "*You* can take the sofa bed since you booked this room."

"I'm not sleeping on a sofa bed!"

He gives me an angry little smile. "I'm sleeping right here, *Ashley*."

I join him on the bed. "So am I, *Gabriel*."

He stands, grabs his bag, and disappears into the bathroom.

I exhale and flop onto my back. Fuck my life.

He comes out in midnight blue swim trunks, a towel draped over his shoulder.

Being shameless has its perks, so I sit up to judge. Muscles on muscles, dips and swells worthy of a sculpture of some ancient god or warrior. He pauses long enough to glare at me—I assume. I'm more interested in his Adonis belt. He's no Nic, but he's pretty hot. Pity about his personality.

"Eh," I pronounce my final judgment, but my face goes warm thinking about how I'd accidentally groped him in the car. My eyes linger on the definite dick print in his trunks. He's huge. I wasn't lying when I told him that dick was wasted on him.

He walks straight out the door. Down to the pool where he'll be photographed without me.

Shit. We're losing control of this story. Not that we ever had any control.

I should give him space. I should go to sleep and try to forget about today. But I can't. This is my life at stake.

I put on a white bikini that will get me thrown out of this Hilton if it gets wet, throw a sundress over it, and follow him down to the pool.

My damn luck. No cameras in sight. Just Gabriel Sinclair, cutting a perfect backstroke through the pool. I should go back to the room and take a nap, but before I can turn to leave, he spots me.

"What are you doing here?" he asks, swimming over to tread water in front of me.

I want to leave. The door is right there. He needs space and I do too.

But I can't. If I walk away, he wins and I can't let him, so I pull the sundress over my head and let it fall onto a lounge chair. "Swimming," I say curtly.

I can't swim, but he doesn't need to know that. I'll dip my toe in the shallow end, declare the water too cold, and go sit in the nearby hot tub for ten minutes. If anyone with a camera comes, I'll watch him swim his laps with total adoration on my face, even if that feels like my personal Everest right now.

"Do you have to make everything so hard?" There's something raw in his voice and it triggers one of my baser impulses: I want to grind my heel into whatever pain he feels and twist. I've never met anyone who elicits this response in me like he does.

And it's not fair. I'm not making this any harder than he is, yet I get the blame. I'm defined by the role I played and he's not, because I'm a woman who went on a loosely scripted reality TV show—therefore I am the persona I played—and he's a serious actor. I get hatred for embracing what I am. He denies what he is and everyone adores him.

It would really suck if I wasn't exactly as bad as everyone thinks I am.

The desire to drag Gabriel Sinclair down into the mud with me is so strong it leaves me shaking.

Carefully, I sit on the edge of the pool, slipping my legs into the cool water and trying not to notice how deep it is. If he can't touch, it's deep.

My tits are doing the work of holding up this bikini top, and I adjust it slightly to avoid a nip slip. "What am I making *hard*?"

"Dating you. Getting to know you," he says, ignoring my tits and my reference to his dick as he swims closer.

His dark eyes are unreadable, and I hesitate. Is he telling the truth? Does he want to get to know me?

That's ridiculous. No one wants to get to know me. It's easier to hate me that way.

Except they'd hate me more if they took the trouble to look closer.

I don't like myself all that much today, either, but maybe I'm tired. Fake dating this man is exhausting.

"This is me," I say. The concrete is cool on my hands as I lean back. "That's all you need to know."

He stares at the door for a minute, a dark expression on his face. "This isn't working," he says when he finally turns back to me.

"It's not." We finally agree on something. Miracle. Though I doubt he has a realistic idea of how to fix this.

"I'll take you to the airport first thing in the morning. Get you on a flight to LA, first class. We'll tell them it didn't work out."

Wait, what? He's bailing?

"Just like that?" Panic slips up my spine. Sure, it's been fun thinking about ending this farce, but I have nothing. No job prospects that don't involve refilling baskets of breadsticks. I need this. I'm a shitty waitress. "You're fake breaking up with me?"

"There's plenty of bad girls in Hollywood to wreck my reputation with." His brown eyes bore into me. Shit. He's serious.

"You ass!" I snap, splashing him with a solid kick into the pool and sending a wall of water into his face.

He shakes it off, droplets flying from his dark hair. "Be a better person, Ashley. In your case, it's not going to take much."

That, from Gabriel Sinclair, might be one of the meanest things anyone has ever said to me. He's drifting away as he treads water, and I'm going to splash him again. I scoot to the edge of the pool, gripping it tight, extending one leg as far as I can, the other propped against the pool wall for balance. I don't care that a herd of kids is thundering closer and there will be parents with phones only too happy to catch this moment and make it go viral. I am going to splash the shit out of Gabriel Sinclair if it's the last thing I—

One of the kids slips, slamming into me, and before I can scream, I fall into the pool.

Water surrounds me, pressing down on me as I stare up at the surface while I sink. It's quiet down here. Like the world has retreated, leaving me alone.

Drowning.

Ashley Foley Dies in Hilton Pool, the headline will read. In fucking *Cleveland*.

Not even those fake tits could save her, some asshole will post and go viral.

All the bad choices that led me here line up to make my final moments as miserable as possible.

My aunt's angry face when I plunged her family into a scandal.

Luca's face, when he found out how far I'd go to win a stupid TV show.

Wendy's tears.

What I tried to do to Nic and Jessie.

No. I'm not about to endure this shit. I will survive out of sheer spite. My toes touch the bottom. I push up, flail my arms.

Nothing happens.

My lungs are burning and I have no idea how long I can hold my breath and panic obliterates my shock like a bomb and I become feral, clawing at the water.

I'm dying. I'm going to die.

Something hard wraps around me. Lifts me up and up and suddenly I can breathe.

Thank god.

I sputter water out, suck air in, and cling to him, but he's doing a bad job keeping us both above water and I go under again, convinced *this* time will be the end as I inhale chlorine and kid pee. We bob back up, both coughing up water.

Suddenly, we aren't bobbing anymore. He's crushing me to his chest with one arm, holding on to the side of the pool with the other, and I'm wrapped around him so tight I can't tell where I end and he begins.

I gasp into his neck as I struggle to get closer to him and away from death and I realize as the water drains from my ear he's saying something, over and over again against my hair. *You're okay, Ash* and *it's all right, baby.* Other soothing little nothings.

I cry, not realizing we're moving, or even that he managed to pry my legs off his waist and is cradling me in his arms as he climbs the steps out of the pool.

His feet slap against the concrete and I don't care if he is Gabriel Sinclair, he saved my life. I wrap my arms as tight as I can around his neck as I sob and shake and shiver.

"YOU!"

The shout rips out of his chest, echoing across the room, and I try to burrow into the space it leaves.

"DON'T FUCKING RUN NEAR A POOL, GOT IT?"

The kids don't answer, at least not that I can hear, but Gabriel is satisfied. He pauses long enough to wrap me in a towel and sling my sundress over his shoulder.

I can't stop crying, can't stop myself from shaking, but what just happened?

Gabriel Sinclair—Saint Gabriel, Hollywood golden boy—cussed out some kids.

For me.

CHAPTER SEVEN

Gabe

ASHLEY IS SHIVERING, CLINGING to me like she'll drown if I set her down. It takes me a moment to get the shower on, to get the temperature right, and when she doesn't indicate that I should put her down, I carefully ease the towel off her and carry her into the shower.

Heat floods back into my arms, spreading to my chest and down my legs. I hold her under the warm spray, careful to keep the water away from her face, still buried in my neck as she cries.

We stand like that until the frantic pounding of my heart calms. My arms go numb from her weight. Her sobs disappear and she stops shivering. We just...breathe.

"You can put me down," she whispers eventually, and I do.

I should get out, but I can't leave her. My head is a jumble, caught in the rush of what could've happened. The moment after I swam away, when I turned and realized she wasn't coming up, plays on a loop. My heart slams into the wall of my chest, an echo of that panic. If I had kept swimming away from her, I might not have noticed.

I don't want her to be alone. I don't want to be alone. So I stay.

"May I?" I pick up the expensive-looking shampoo from the little cubby.

She nods, and I shift us so the shower spray is hitting my back. "Hate to think what the chlorine will do to this natural hair color," I say lightly as I squeeze shampoo onto my hand.

She laughs. It's a small one, but there's none of her derision in it. It's nice. Real. I don't know what to think of it.

A soft floral scent fills the steamy air as I run my hands through her wet hair, lathering and massaging her scalp. Her body relaxes, and she tilts her head back for me. Maybe I relax too because now I'm noticing things. I'm hyperaware of the steam rising around us. The strong pressure of the water pounding on my back. The quiet between us. The way her neck curves as she rolls her head in my hands.

Her moan is soft, half-strangled like she tried to catch it. I reverse the movements of my fingers until I hit a spot that makes her moan again.

Christ.

Near-death experiences can inspire a need for physical intimacy. That's all this is.

I force myself to swallow. I'm imagining things. Feeling that same need to fill the space where fear had me in a chokehold.

She nearly drowned, and she doesn't like me. I don't particularly like her. So I shouldn't be noticing the way the water beads on the dips and swells of her body. I definitely shouldn't be wondering how see-through her white bikini is now that it's wet.

Suds run over her shoulders, down her back, down down down...

Of course, her bikini is a thong and her ass is perfection. The kind of ass I could dig my fingers in, with cheeks made for palming. Knowing what little I do of her, I bet she'd appreciate a firm spanking.

But not ten minutes after she nearly died, for fuck's sake.

I snap my eyes back up to her hair. The showerhead is removable, so I take it down and slowly, carefully rinse the shampoo out. Her moans are more like hums and I think I can live with that, but turns out I can't. My cock is rock hard, and I'd give anything to kill this erection.

What would she think, if she knew the direction my thoughts are going? Would she still call me boring? Would she be disgusted? Turned on?

I need to get out of here. I'm about to hand her the showerhead and step out when she pulls her bikini top off.

My pulse throbs, echoing in my cock.

She slides the bottoms over her hips, bending to push them down her legs before stepping out of them.

My groan is out before I can stop it.

She turns and I reach for her, cupping her face and tilting her head up so she can't see my hard-on. So I have to look into her eyes instead of at the water streaming over tits I want to suck.

Her eyes are a dark shade of caramel, and the sorrow they hold is enough to fill me with a deep sense of shame.

I'm better than this. I need to get a grip.

"I—" She bites her lip, leaning into my touch, her hands coming up to grip my forearms. "I thought I was going to die, and I didn't want to watch the crappy highlights reel of my life."

Her admission glues my feet to the floor. Vulnerability isn't something I expected from her. Ever.

I brush her wet hair from her face. "You can make a new highlights reel." I bend down and plant a chaste kiss on her forehead. My lips dip back for a second kiss, drawn closer by the softness of her. On the third, I hold my lips to her wet skin and we stand like that for a while because oh my god do I want to give her some new highlights.

She nearly died. The fact I have to remind myself is more proof I'm not what everyone thinks I am. I hate the reminder.

"I can't swim," she says eventually, and yeah, I kinda noticed she can't fucking swim, but I don't know what to say so I tear my lips from her and nod.

"Thank you." She slides her hands down my forearms to my wrists and gently pulls my hands from her face to her neck. A small smile plays across her face—a shadow of the ones she's given me before. It's not seductive or conniving, just a shade cheeky.

I like this Ashley, but I want the old version back. The old Ashley isn't half as dangerous. This Ashley...she has me sliding closer to my destruction.

"Guess I can't make fun of you for being a real-life boring-ass Clark Kent," she teases.

"There she is." My fingers trail over her arms as she releases my hands, and it takes all my willpower not to follow with my eyes. "I was afraid I'd lost you." *Shit.* I'd meant to say I was afraid I'd lost her sparkling personality or something cutting. Something to get us on safer ground. To get us far away from the urge to fuck it out.

She steps out of the shower, wrapping a towel around her body while I mentally kick myself for being unable to look away. "Oh, Gabe. You never had me."

"Yet," I say, apparently hell-bent on self-destruction.

Ashley bends to wrap a towel around her hair, twisting it and straightening with a smile on her face. Her eyes finally flick down to my cock, straining against my swim trunks. So fucking hard for her. I cover it with both hands, but too late.

"Yet," she agrees softly, the thoughtfulness on her face terrifying. She walks out, closing the door behind her, but not before I catch a glimpse of the only bed.

Dammit.

I shove my swim trunks down and take myself roughly in hand. I need to put temptation as far out of reach as possible. Just...just in case. It's been days since I've jerked off, denying myself because I knew I'd be thinking of her on that chaise in the hotel room. It was safer to keep her out of my fantasies, but now...I need this. Once I get off, I'll be back in control.

I stroke root to tip and it's incredible. I can't even bite back my groan, but my hand isn't enough. I want her to walk in. To see me fucking my fist and get in the shower with me. To lower herself enough to push her tits together around my cock and watch as I thrust against her sudsy wet skin.

Her bikini bottoms are on the floor of the shower. I shouldn't, but I'm not myself, or maybe I'm more myself than ever. I grab them and they're slick and wet when I wrap them around my cock—not the same as her tits, but fuck it's better than my hand and I'll take it. They're warm from the shower, tight in my grip. I don't think she would mind, but I don't care. I'll buy her a new bikini.

A dozen new bikinis.

It doesn't take me long now that I know how those tits of hers feel, wet and pressed up against my chest, separated from my skin by the flimsy fabric that I jack myself with. My release builds, everything pulling tight as my legs start to shake. My cock between her tits, her head bending, the hot wet suck of her mouth…

I come hard with a grunt and it's like lightning breaking free, surging with every stroke, every gasp, every beat of my heart. I keep coming because it's been a while. Because I'm stressed out and uptight. Because I'm thinking about Ashley and this is so wrong, but it feels incredible and fated and electric and I'm left empty and wrung out. The wall holds me up as I catch my breath and find my way back to earth.

I feel like shit after, a sinking disappointment deep in my guts as I rinse my cum out of her bikini bottoms. She nearly died and I'm in here jerking off because I felt her tits on my chest.

I'm no golden boy. I'm not any different or any better than any other asshole. I need to do better. Be better.

I rinse her bikini top too and hang it to dry alongside the bottoms and my shorts. I rinse the walls because I hit those too. When I'm confident the shower would pass a black light test, I turn the water off and get out.

I can't delay forever, so once I'm dry I walk into the room.

Ashley's sitting cross-legged on the bed, dressed in an old T-shirt and a pair of loose pajama pants with unicorns on them. I'd expected silk nighties. Lingerie. Her hair falling in a soft curtain around her face instead of in a simple braid she's woven around her head. She looks alarmingly un-Ashley-like.

Getting myself off was the right choice because something about this Ashley makes me want to find out how soft that shirt is and how she tastes underneath.

She glances up from her phone. "I ordered pizza. Pepperoni and pineapple."

I freeze, pulling a pair of sleep pants from my bag. "How did you know?"

"You did an interview with Leo Wallace."

Leo does all his interviews over pizza in the same green leather booth at Antonio's Pizza Shoppe in New Haven. He roasted me the whole time over my favorite toppings, especially when Antonio refused to put pineapple on our pizza and I had to go in the kitchen, open a can of pineapple Leo's people had brought along, and put it on my own damn pizza. I can't believe Ashley watched the interview just to find out. "You like it too?"

"I'm basically the devil, so…" She laughs her little derisive laugh, but it's weak this time and she shrugs it off, reaching for a glass of red wine on the side table. "Yeah. I do."

The pizza arrives, she pours me a glass of wine, and we eat in silence. David calls after we finish and I listen to him complain about our abrupt change in plans. He'd arranged for a couple of paparazzi to photograph us at the inn we were supposed to be staying at tonight. Ashley pretends not to listen as I try to placate him.

We sit against the headboard and finish the bottle of red wine in silence. It's impossible to shake off this heavy moment we're existing in.

She scrolls on her phone, her eyes unfocused. She must find it soothing. I'm surprised to find watching her soothes me.

I slip on my glasses and pull up the reading app on my phone. The words on the screen—a biography Emma recommended—fail to leave an impression. Ash is close enough that I can smell an expensive cologne on her shirt.

It's a man's shirt, though it's not overly large on her.

It's just a shirt, and she is just my fake girlfriend who I was ready to fake break up with a few hours ago. My fingers twitch and I go back to my book.

Ashley makes no move for the sofa bed. Against my better judgment, neither do I. After what happened in the pool, I want her close, I guess. We go to bed early and lie awake in the dark listening to each other breathe and it's more intimate than holding her in the shower.

I stretch my hand out to hers, resting on top of the comforter between us. "Tell me something real." Something like she did in the shower. The admission she couldn't swim. *Tell me you can be vulnerable again. Tell me whose shirt that is. Tell me why we met. Tell me who you really are.*

Her hand slides away, and she turns onto her side, facing me. In the dim city light filtering through the thick curtains, her expression is wary. "Am I going back to LA alone?"

Is this over?

Fuck, I should say yes. When I ditched the scenic route earlier today, I planned to get some space. Then to put an end to this because I don't need her complicating my life and this is getting dangerous. Not just when she's like this either. I like the bratty bad girl far too much.

But I need this to secure my role from a fandom that dislikes me so I can reach my larger goal of bigger, better roles, awards and prestige, and a reputation worthy of the man who saved me.

The reminder feels more like an excuse than a justification now.

"If we do this, I need you to try," I say quietly. "Being photographed with me isn't going to be enough to make people want to work with you, and I think you know it."

"You need to try too," she shoots back, but with no venom this time.

She's right. I've been acting like a dick in front of the cameras, and it isn't exactly what my team had in mind.

"I'll try," I promise.

"Kiss me," she says softly. "Prove you can kiss me like I'm not some slimy toad."

I hit a patch of ice in my head, sliding, skidding, losing control.

Kiss me.

I shouldn't.

I want it. A real kiss, not some fake angled trick for the cameras or a chaste peck. I want to taste her again, and this time do the taking.

Even though it's a bad idea, I roll on top of her, propping myself up on one arm and wedging my thigh between her legs as I press her into the mattress. Ash's eyes widen as I brush my knuckles along her jaw, my fingers coming to rest on her slender neck, my thumb in the notch of her collarbone. Her pulse is wild, her throat moving as she swallows. Her eyes are dark pools, staring up at me with a burning hunger that could consume me if I'm not careful.

My lips brush hers and I can practically see the sparks. Maybe the dark lets her be gentle, too, because the slide of her lips on mine is careful for once. Our lips part and inexplicably we fit with no awkwardness, no messiness. Even when she licks into my mouth and I lick into hers, the kiss merely shifts into a delicious give and take, and I have to end it because it would be too easy to let it be more. To comfort ourselves in each other. We don't need that kind of complication.

I kiss her one last time and lift my head to study her expression. It's hard to tell in the dark, but I think I put some color on her cheeks.

"Not bad," she says, wetting her lips. Her breathy voice tells me it was better than *not bad*.

"Look at that," I say softly, tilting her chin one way, then the other. "Not a toad at all. Still very much a princess."

She rolls her eyes.

"Tell me something real," I say again, brushing a loose strand of her silky hair back. She's opened herself tonight, and I want to see her, understand her. Know her, even. And not to help make this fake relationship work. I want this piece of her for me.

She sinks her teeth into her lower lip and I can't look away. I want to bite that pillowy lip. I don't want to stop at her lips either. Her breasts push against my chest with every breath she takes, and I haven't forgotten the image of her ass in that bikini.

I snap out of it when she speaks.

"I've never shared a bed with someone before."

She must see the disbelief on my face because she pushes me off her. Thank god.

I land flat on my back, exaggerating the force of her push.

"Obviously I've had sex," she says dryly. "But I don't do sleepovers. You're my first."

"I'm honored." Oddly enough, I am.

"You should be." She huffs. "Now tell me something shockingly filthy."

I laugh and rest my head in my hands to stare up at the ceiling. Welcome back, Ashley.

Something shocking and filthy...I don't need to ask her if she's sure she wants that—it's a command. My arm blocks my view of her, making it surprisingly easy to say, "I used your bikini to get off in the shower after you left."

She sits up. "Gabriel Sinclair, you did *what*?"

I chuckle at how fake-scandalized she sounds, but there's surprise in her voice too. "I wrapped that excuse for a bikini around my cock while I fucked my hand. I'll buy you a new one."

She covers her mouth with her hand, tips her head back, and laughs.

I grin. Two can play this game and she started it with my stick shift.

"You owe me." She punches me lightly in the kidney, lying back with a smug little laugh. She liked hearing what I did as much as I enjoyed telling her. And I enjoyed telling her—I'm painfully hard again.

"Sure." I fake a yawn and rub my ribs.

I dream of her in a moonlit pool, riding me, her wet tits slapping my chest. In the morning I wake up impossibly hard, with Ash's hand wrapped around my cock.

Chapter Eight

Ashley

I'm holding Gabe's cock.

I was asleep and now I'm not and I'm holding his fucking cock and I can't tell if he's awake or not, but I am *freaking out*.

I don't sleep with people in my bed because I move around at night. A lot. So I'm not terribly surprised to wake up using his stomach as my pillow, but I *am* surprised to find my hand curled around his massive hard-on.

He's going to kill me. This is so much worse than the accidental grope in the car. It doesn't look like an accident, for one, and for two, my mouth is watering.

If this weren't fake, if this man wasn't Gabriel Sinclair, I'd blow him awake. He'd pull me onto his face. We might get out of bed before lunch. But this *is* Gabriel Sinclair and despite what he claims to have done with my bikini—I have to clench my legs when I remember his rough voice telling me in the dark—it doesn't seem like something he'd approve of.

His dick twitches and my hand jerks a tiny, tiny bit. I want to stroke him so damn bad. I'm already wet when a small damp spot appears on his sleep pants where the tip of his cock presses and I stare at it, wanting.

If he's not already awake, he will be soon. After everything that happened last night…I want him to want to try to make this work. *I* want this to work.

I want him to kiss me like he did last night, but this time for the cameras.

Maybe I want him to kiss me like that for me, because fuck, what this man could do with a mouth like his...

My hand tightens reflexively and I'm pretty sure that soft little mewling sound came from me too.

"Ash."

He whispers my name but I still jump, my hand squeezing hard enough he gasps.

I bolt to the bathroom, slamming the door.

Fuck, what have I done?

I pace, my hand to my forehead, my whole body on fire. Now I've done it. Ruined everything. This is why I don't let anyone in my bed, tell people I can't swim, or let them get too close to the real me. Nearly drowning scared the shit out of me. That's the only reason I opened up to him, but last night was nice and—

Fuck.

I *care* what Gabriel Sinclair thinks about me. About me accidentally groping him, not about me as a person. Right?

It makes me feel sick to my stomach, so I look around for a distraction.

My bikini is hanging up to dry. I inspect it, but aside from the faint scent of chlorine, there's no way to know if he told me the truth. I want it to be true. I want to think he came all over my bikini while thinking about me. The idea that Gabriel Sinclair has a filthy side turns me on enough that I start up the shower and dig through my toiletry bag for my little waterproof bullet vibrator.

I don't think Gabe can hear the buzz over the sound of the shower, but I can hope. I can hope he hears it and pulls his thick cock out of those thin pajama pants.

My nipples tighten when I pass the bullet vibe over them, and I imagine a different ending to waking up with his cock in my hand. An ending where his raspy morning voice tells me to sit on his face. I can nearly feel his sinful lips on my inner thigh as he pulls me down to his mouth.

Wait.

Why am I thinking about Gabe when I should be thinking about Nic?

Oh, who cares. I nearly died last night. I deserve some release and it doesn't mean anything if Gabe takes center stage this one time.

I chase the path fantasy-Gabe's mouth takes up my thigh, working my way closer as I imagine the feel of his tongue, his lips. The taste of me is too much for him and he pumps himself hard as he eats me like he's never tasted anything so good. He pauses long enough to tell me to suck him, so I do. His cock is silky smooth on my tongue. The tang of him—Christ, I press the vibe against my clit and bite my lip to keep from moaning.

When he finally loses the battle for control, I come so hard I drop the vibrator, crying out so loud he must hear me. There's no knock on the door though. Because Gabriel would never.

The orgasm calms me down. My grabbing him this morning was an innocent, accidental grope. Not something that changes the fact that we need each other.

I get out and press my ear to the door and eventually open it a crack.

Gabe is gone.

Either he heard me and ran, or he left before. I doubt I'll know which.

There might be cameras outside the hotel, so I take care to make my face effortlessly flawless.

When I come out, Gabe is still gone. I dress, pack up, and burn some nervous energy scrolling social media.

A Hilton employee uploaded the security video from the pool, and stills of Gabe carrying me, of my body wrapped around his, are everywhere. People are into it. Plenty of trolls are regretting that he didn't let me drown, but the clickbait headlines are looking good. There's speculation it was a stunt, of course, and me getting knocked into the pool by that kid has already been turned into a meme, but the image of me in Gabe's arms is making people swoon, and maybe...maybe this is going to work.

Gabe returns with doughnuts and coffee, reporting that there are a few paps outside milling about, courtesy of David. He meets my eyes, unembarrassed, so I guess he didn't hear me in the shower.

We don't talk about how we woke up either, and I guess we'll ignore that elephant. We eat in silence, drink our coffee in silence, and the only time either one of us speaks is when he asks if I'm ready.

I'm not ready, but I nod.

Gabe finds a hotel employee to help with my luggage, which is the least they could do since I nearly drowned in their pool.

Just before the elevator doors open into the lobby, he slides his hand over mine.

My heart flutters. What the hell? I was naked in the shower with this man last night. I grabbed his dick on accident this morning, but walking palm-to-palm with him across the lobby fills my body with butterflies?

This is the direct consequence of fantasizing about riding his face. It has to be. I won't be making that mistake again.

He isn't squeezing my hand or holding it tight. This is loose, our fingers entwined, palms grazing as we walk. It's natural. Casual in a way I wouldn't have thought to try.

We walk out into the bright sunshine and I feel oddly naked.

The car. I need to get to the car.

Gabe pauses, but I don't. I let my hand slip free. He can stop for a phone call or to look at the clouds, for all I care. I need the shelter of his car and I need it now.

His hand brushes the back of my neck and I freeze when he grabs me. His fingers bite into my muscles, pinching a strand of hair in his grip, and when he pulls me around, what I see in his eyes blows everything inside me apart. It's the same unwelcome desire I'm feeling, swirling in a storm that even the longest telephoto lens across the street can't capture.

I'm alone in the middle of it. This storm is mine.

My knees betray me and I fall into him. His body is hard against mine. His cologne wraps around me, dark and sweet, calling to mind leather and rum, expensive cigars, and hot salty nights. This is nothing like anything I expected and suddenly I'm terrified I'm in over my head. This man could bare my vulnerable center to the entire world and I'd let him for a kiss.

Our noses brush, his hand tightening on the back of my neck. The tiny bit of pain feels damn good, but not as good as the little hitch of anticipation that fills the pause.

"Where do you think you're going?" he whispers against my lips, his breath minty.

"To the car." My lips brush his as I whisper back. I'm not going to back down, even as I'm inexplicably falling apart the longer we exist in this near-kiss.

His hand at my side moves up until his thumb brushes the side of my boob. "This okay?" he asks roughly. The cameras will be able to see this little PG-13 touch, or he wouldn't be doing it. What's not okay is how hard my nipples get or how wet I am.

I hate how horny this man has me, all from five stupid fingers digging into my neck and one thumb brushing side boob. He's not unaffected either. He's hard against my stomach and my hand remembers the thick feel of his cock.

"I told you," I say, desperate to get on top again. "You can fuck me right here."

"I thought we were saving that for a dive bar," he chides. I think I see the corners of his lips turn up, but I'm losing my mind, so what do I know?

I fist his shirt. "Are you going to kiss me or not?" I can't breathe much longer without this kiss. Lust is shorting out my brain.

He turns us until his back is blocking the cameras. His lips brush the corner of my mouth. "No." It lingers on my cheek and I deflate as he releases my neck and steps away from me.

My gasp for air at the sudden space between us is involuntary. It brings a twitch to his lips.

"Asshole," I mutter before the cameras are back in view. Stupid actors and their camera angles. My lips feel betrayed and I am going to make him pay for this.

I have no idea how though.

I spend the entire day doing the little seductive things that should draw his attention. Like putting my feet on the dashboard to show off my legs. I get his attention, all right. He snaps at me to keep my feet off the dash. I toy with the three tiny buttons—all undone—on the low neck of my pink tank top. He doesn't glance my way.

At a gas station, I wash the windscreen of his car, making sure I'm bent over in my short denim shorts when he walks out. A guy staring at my tits rear-ends the car in front of him, but Gabe just thanks me. I touch his arm, his leg, and the side of his face once when I'm desperate, but he only tenses and brushes me away.

He does let me take control of our social media presence. Throughout the day, we stage little photos. His hand covering mine wrapped around the gear stick, in black and white. The two of us cozied up in a leather booth at a diner in a college town, him feeding me a fry. Unfortunately, other people were also filming us, so we had to stay cuddled up the whole time, which at least allowed us to trade whispered insults. We take a few extras at generic locations or in his car—stuff we can post later. My favorite is when we're in the car, and I lean over and plant a kiss on his cheek. The scrunch of his face is adorable.

After, he adjusts the mirror and looks at the kissed cheek.

"No lipstick?" he asks.

Of course, I'm wearing lipstick. Today it's a sexy little pink shade, slightly darker than my tank top. I pull it out of my handbag and make a show of touching it up.

Gabe rubs his face and frowns at the mirror before starting the car. The roar of the engine revs up my blood, but while I convince Gabe to let me take a picture of my hand on his thigh, and his hand on my thigh, he appears unaffected while I...am not.

Bringing Gabriel Sinclair to the brink of seduction is exhausting, but I'm going to break him if it's the last thing I do.

Chapter Nine

Gabe

Ash finally falls asleep and I can breathe again.

Her perfume still saturates my car, but at least she's not resting her foot on the dash and tempting me to find out how much of her I can see in those tiny shorts.

I know what she's doing. She was more affected by that almost-kiss in front of the cameras than she'd like to be. It was in her eyes, the way her breath hitched when my lips brushed the corner of hers. I made her vulnerable, so she's paying me back.

Unfortunately, it's working. Hiding it is getting hard, but I'm not going to crack. There's no point in imagining all the ways I could make her scream my name because it can't happen. I can't have her. Dating Ashley Foley for real would be a disaster for my reputation in the long run, and having a fling would have god-only-knows-what consequences.

My reputation is more important than getting my dick wet, however inviting the pool may be, so this fake relationship has to stay fake. But I can't stop picturing her sitting in that bed, her armor off, watching my interview with Leo Wallace to find out what I like on my pizza.

I want to know more about this woman who doesn't share her bed, can't swim, and doesn't like looking back at the decisions she'd made. I want to know what her skin tastes like and what gets her off. Driving this boring stretch of interstate doesn't distract me enough to keep me from imagining.

She's a handful now—if that translates to the bedroom, she'd be demanding. Into games and intense foreplay. Hard to satisfy on a deeper level than a handful of orgasms. I doubt anyone has ever been enough for her.

We arrive at our hotel in Nashville and I wake her up, touching her higher on the thigh than before. She shifts under my touch before she fully wakes up. Her fingers slide over mine and she squeezes her legs together.

"I had the best dream." She grins, her stretch moving my hand higher up her leg.

I'm not letting her win after a full day of messing with me, so I squeeze her thigh before removing my hand. "I'm even better in real life."

"Bold claim."

I wink at her and get out of the car while my dignity is still mostly flaccid.

What the hell am I doing? This isn't me, winking and being suggestive. What the hell is she doing to me?

Thank fuck David booked us a two-bedroom suite. Ash goes to her room to get ready, and I go to mine. Tonight, it's showtime. We're going to sell this fake relationship for all it's worth.

And I'm going to wind her so tight she'll have no choice but to run back to her little vibrating friend when we get to the hotel. Oh yeah. I heard her in the shower this morning. Hearing her cry out triggered my release as I frantically beat off under the covers like a damn teenager. It couldn't be helped, considering how we'd woken up. The way she'd touched me, squeezed me before she'd panicked.

There's a spark between us, one she's perversely fed and protected from my efforts to snuff out, and ignoring it is quickly becoming impossible. If we can figure out how to turn it on in public and off in private, we'll nail this and come out unscathed. I'll get that edge I need, she'll soften up.

Tonight's the test.

Ashley's waiting when I walk out of my room and she's aced the assignment. Her dress is subtly sexy, a flowy cherry blossom pink number with a sweetheart neckline and a lower hemline than I've seen on her, hitting just above her knees.

Her pale blonde hair artfully tumbles over her shoulders in gentle waves, her makeup soft and dreamy.

Since sex bomb is her flavor of villain, looking this sweet has to be a trap.

"Not that," Ash says, motioning to my shirt.

"What's wrong with my shirt?" It's a standard white button-up. Perfect for a night on the town.

"It's boring." There's a black shirt folded over a chair and she picks it up. "Wear this one. Lea sorted it out, so let's see if she got it right."

There are no cameras in our room, but she steps up to me anyway, unbuttoning me, her eyes holding mine while she works, a smug little smile widening on her face as she tugs the shirt out of my pants.

I don't know why I'm letting her undress me right now when we need to save this energy for the cameras. She walks around me to pull the shirt off, tossing it onto the floor, and from behind me her fingers gather the hem of my undershirt, and this, right here, is why I haven't stopped her.

Her touch is electric.

Because she can, she slides her fingers slowly up every ridge of my abdomen as she pulls the shirt up. It's excruciating how tight my skin goes, everywhere she touches. Places she doesn't touch too. It's the most exquisite torture.

Her palms slip over my nipples, and I shrug the shirt off, turning to face her, raising one eyebrow to ask where this is going.

She smirks, but there's a bit more color on her face and she reaches for the new shirt and pushes it against my chest. This is going nowhere.

Good. Because that's what I want. Chemistry in public. Not in the privacy of our suite where I'm tempted to take this to her bedroom.

I pull the shirt on and Ash stops me from doing up the last couple of buttons. The short sleeves hug my biceps, just the right side of too tight. She traces a finger down my arm, over the rise of my muscle, into the dip inside my elbow. My cock is already thickening against my thigh.

"You need a tattoo," she says, messing up my hair with her fingers before walking away.

Okay, she wins this round. I have to adjust myself and all she's done is touch me.

I'll win the next one.

I go back into my room to look in the mirror. She's nailed it. This look is edgier without coming off as dangerous or douchy and with her all sweet and sexy at my side...this is going to work.

We leave our hotel, holding hands. Our first stop is a bourbon tasting for a distillery owned by an actress repped by my agency. The place is crowded but other patrons are pushed back to give the photographer space. This is a publicity stunt as well as a chance to show off this fake relationship, after all. We drink and listen, Ash leaning against me, my arm around her. Until the photographer's assistant sweeps her aside, engaging her in conversation while they photograph me.

Our eyes meet, and I see it, and maybe only because she's had a few bourbons, but she's hurt. They don't want her. They want me.

The distiller is talking, pushing another glass toward me—this one is their top-of-the-line, rare collection whatever. The camera fires off shots, but I can't concentrate, the bourbon I've already drank isn't sitting right. I stop the guy with one raised finger.

"Ash? Baby, come try this one." When the photographer opens his mouth, I shake my head slightly, shooting him down. Ashley walks over and I box her between me and the bar, where they can't pull her away without going through me. The distiller doesn't care. He launches back into what he does care about—the bourbon—as he pours her a glass.

Because Ashley is Ashley, she can't let my good deed go unpunished. She pushes her ass against my groin, her hips swaying just enough to set my pants on fire without drawing too much attention to what she's doing.

I'm not letting her get away with it. I grab her hip with my free hand and press against her, letting her feel what she's doing to me.

Her breath catches, her hips stop, and I've won.

Except now I have a fucking erection to hide and the bourbon tasting is over.

Ashley turns, smiling sweetly up at me as her arms slip around my neck. Because we're in public and I get to touch her with no risk of crossing lines

I don't want to cross, I slip my hands around her and, mostly blocked by the counter I have her pinned against, grab two handfuls of ass, palming her good. Paybacks for her grinding on my cock.

The little noise she makes turns my blood hot.

"You thirsty or hungry?" I ask softly.

She doesn't blink, but her tongue peeks out to wet her lips. "Hungry."

"You ready?" I'm not winning this. She's still smugly in control.

Her smile widens. "Are you?"

I jam my hands into my pockets, using the cover of her dress to rearrange myself into a less obvious position before I step back. "I'm ready."

I hold out my arm and she slips hers into it, and we walk out to where the driver David hired for the night waits.

"I'm not sure that worked," she says once we're in the car, without a hint of the coyness from in the distillery.

"What do you mean?"

"They mostly photographed you. After you brought me back in, the photographer stopped." She brushes a strand of hair from her face. "I think the distillery just wanted you."

Shit. I'd been too caught up in the little game we were playing to notice the photographer once I had Ash back at my side.

"What do you want to do?"

She thinks for a minute, pressing her lips together as she stares out the car window. "The restaurant David booked is upmarket—what if we went somewhere else, where the other diners wouldn't hesitate to film us?"

Maybe it's the bourbon on an empty stomach, but I want to throw us in the fire and see what happens. I nod and after a word with the driver, we change course for a BBQ joint famous with locals and tourists alike.

It works. We're recognized. Or rather, I am. Ash is openly ogled by men and women. Only a few people give her dark looks, suggesting they know who she is.

We're seated in a deep corner booth with a high leather back, the excitement our arrival sparks soon settling down to a simmer.

Unfortunately, so does our conversation. People are surreptitiously watching us, a few trying to discreetly film us.

"Get David's questions," she says softly, tapping my phone through the pocket of my pants.

I skim the thirty-six questions for intimacy that David has incorporated into what he calls the Savannah Protocol. "Name three things we appear to have in common."

She furrows her brows and takes a sip of her bourbon and cherry coke. I can't wait to see what she comes up with, honestly.

"We're both incredibly hot," she says, cozying up to me with a smile. "We had shitty childhoods, and we're both dying to know what the other is like in bed."

We're still playing this game, then. All right. I can up the ante.

"We go after what we want," I say, sliding my arm around her and pulling her close. Her perfume smells better than anything coming out of the kitchen, and I press my lips to her ear. "We both like a challenge. And this morning, we both got off fantasizing about what it would be like to fuck."

Her startled laugh cuts clear across the restaurant and she leans back to look at me, color high across her cheeks. I grin at her and the photos taken in this moment, the video—they're viral. They're believable.

"You were right about coming here," I whisper as I cup her face, draw her to me, and kiss her.

It's perfect, like when we kissed in bed. She tastes sweet and meets me slow kiss for slow kiss, pulling away before we cross over into a full-on public make-out.

"Well done," she murmurs, staring at my lips.

I swipe my thumb across my lower lip, but there's no lipstick on me. Something tugs in the back of my brain, but the waiter is here, taking our order, asking for my autograph.

We pick easy questions off David's list as we eat brisket sandwiches and coleslaw. When Ash gets a little sauce in the corner of her mouth, I wipe it off with my thumb. Her eyes go dark when I suck the tangy sweet sauce off the tip of my thumb.

The table cloth isn't long enough, and Ash and I aren't real, but I still think about what I want to do to her under the table. I'd tug that skirt up nice and slow, slipping my fingers inside her thong, running them up her slick center until I found her swollen clit. Rubbing it and watching the color rise on her face as she tries to hold in her moans. No one—including Ash—would expect it of me, and that turns me on too.

I'm hanging on by a single fraying thread.

We feed each other dessert and after, her perfectly painted lips don't smudge on the napkin as she dabs her mouth and places it on the table.

"No lipstick mark," I point out. My heart kicks up a notch. I feel sick to my stomach at finally recognizing the significance.

Ash looks at me like I've lost it. "This stuff is bulletproof."

It was a setup after all.

I take a sip of water and try to sound casual, but a dull roar is building in my ears. The conversations and the clatter of silverware on plates and the skid of chairs on wood floors are jarring when a moment ago they barely existed. "Is that the only kind you wear?"

She shrugs. "Pretty much."

"But not to weddings," I say quietly.

Ashley reels back, her eyes wide.

I still don't understand what happened that night. Nothing makes sense, but I hate feeling like I was a mark.

"Is this what you wanted?" I ask her. "Was it all a con with your aunt to get me here? To save your career? To ruin mine?"

She glances around the bar, and too late I realize I should have waited to confront her until we got back to the hotel. She's gone pale.

"I'm going to get up," she says quietly, her voice firm. "I'm going to go to the ladies' room. You are going to settle the bill and walk out of this restaurant after me like you can't wait the ten-minute drive to the hotel to fuck me. Got it?"

Was she trying to end my career? Hoping to blackmail me?

I'm coming out of this on top, whatever little plans Ashley Foley has for me.

I grab her and kiss her and this time it's hard and a little mean and she bites my lip and pulls away before I can return the favor, but there's heat in her eyes again.

"Go," I whisper. Before we both do or say something in public we'll regret.

She goes.

Chapter Ten

Ashley

The ride to the hotel happens in a blur of cold, hard silence. Gabe leans against the seat, his body relaxed, watching the city go by. He's trying too hard though. Tension is leaking through the cracks. I wonder what role he's calling back, what situation he's pretending he's in. Or maybe it's a muscle memory of a man projecting a calm, quiet confidence.

He must be worried if he thinks this was all about getting into a fake relationship. Honestly, if that was what I'd wanted, I'd have my agent call his. Except his agent wouldn't have taken the call.

And why would I want to ruin his career? I don't give a shit about the Warwick franchise. I care even less about his career.

No, why I did what I did is so much worse than anything he could be thinking.

He'll walk if I confirm his fears, he'll walk if I tell the truth. Either way, my career is dust. I'd do anything to put more miles between us and the inevitable fake breakup and if I'm honest with myself, it's not just my career I'm about to kill. Whatever this thing with Gabe is, I like it.

Today was fun. Pushing each other, testing boundaries. Shamelessly flirting. One bright day of sunshine after a year of clouds and I want that warmth on my skin again, not to shoot down the fucking sun.

Except Gabriel Sinclair is not my sun. He's not important to me. So he saved my life and took my breath away with a couple of kisses and pulled me in at the distillery when the PR people wanted me out. He's Hollywood's golden boy, and I was a kitten stuck in a tree. Now I have to tell him I was in that tree to wreck a nest and eat some birds.

He's going to hate me. But he's Gabriel Sinclair. NDA or not, I know this secret is safe with him.

He takes my hand and leads me into the hotel, like a dutiful boyfriend. Maybe people are watching because he makes more of an effort than I do, bending to whisper in my ear. His words are empty—some actor's warm-up technique. When the door to our room shuts behind me and locks, he turns to me with an expectant look on his face.

There's a bottle of bourbon in the room, so I delay the inevitable and pour us each a glass.

When I turn around, Gabe is sitting on the couch, his ankle resting on his knee. He's undone two more buttons on his shirt, and he's watching me with a dark intensity.

The effect hits me right in the guts—he looks exactly like what I want.

No. This is wrong. I can't want him. I have to burn it all down.

I hand him his glass, then down as many gulps of bourbon from mine as I can take before the fire becomes unbearable. "I'm in love with Nic." I gasp through the burn, wiping my mouth with the back of my hand.

He stares at me, unblinking. Unmoving. No change of expression on his face. No indication of what he thinks of me.

I take another big gulp and barrel on. "It was supposed to be him in that room, but Lea messed up." I can see him connecting the dots, so I look away. "A photographer was waiting outside with a view into the room. When you walked in...well, you look enough like him I figured it didn't matter. A picture of us together, at that distance, would do the trick. No one would know you weren't Nic. The paps at the door weren't part of the plan."

Silence stretches between us. His unblinking stare has me squirming like a bug.

He drains his bourbon and sets it down on the coffee table. "You tried to end your cousin's marriage."

I nod, tears springing to my eyes at the closed expression on his face. "Yes."

"Thanks for telling me." He gets to his feet and with a murmured good night, walks off to his room.

And that's it. That's the end of the fake us, and it hurts like we were real.

I drop into his spot on the couch. It's still warm. I can smell his cologne, and I think I like it better than Nic's, which is not helpful. I sip the rest of my bourbon and stare at the wall, and suddenly, I don't think I'm as in love with Nic as I used to be. He's barely been on my mind since I climbed into Gabe's car.

It unsettles me enough that I sleep in Nic's shirt, hoping when I wake, things will make sense.

They don't.

I'm up early for once. I pack the shirt deep into my suitcase, then piece by piece I slip back into Ashley Foley, Reality TV Villain. A too-short lilac dress, strappy heeled sandals, and a deep mauve lip. Hair perfectly styled. Like I'm ready for a day out rather than a whole day in a car.

Who am I kidding? I'm going home. Even though my attempt at breaking up Nic's marriage isn't public knowledge, I have no doubt the fact that I tried matters to the golden boy.

I think it's starting to matter to me, and the guilt is uncomfortably heavy.

If Gabe couldn't stand my company last night, he won't be able to be in the same car as me and he definitely won't be able to fake kiss me in front of the paps or real kiss me in the dark.

Not that I want him to. Because I don't.

Except maybe I do.

Gabe isn't up yet, or he's hiding in his room, or he left already. I walk out of the hotel, sunglasses on, ignoring the guy who takes my photo from the rolled-down window of a shitty rental car as I cross the street to the coffee shop across from the hotel.

I'm recognized by more people than I expect. I'm not this famous, so it has to be because of Gabe. But there's elbowing and whispering. I want one of these bitches to come up to me and call me names on Wendy's behalf or anyone else I wronged on that show. I'm pretending to ignore everyone as I book a midafternoon flight to LA on my phone. I'm so stressed out when I reach the front of the line, I forget my coffee order.

I order Gabe's Café Americano. Two, because people are watching and at least right now, I'm still in this relationship. And two breakfast sandwiches even though I don't like breakfast sandwiches.

I'll buy him breakfast, I guess, but then say goodbye.

My phone rings. It's Lea, so I answer it.

"Hey, so how badly do you want me to dig into Gabriel Sinclair?" she asks. "I'm hitting some roadblocks, but with a bit more time—"

Shit. I'd forgotten I asked her to research my fake boyfriend's past. Might be good to have something on him, just in case. "Do what you need to. Call me when you're done," I say. I end the call with the awareness that at least half a dozen people are close enough to have heard me sounding like the bad guy in a movie. Nothing about my life has felt real for years. No reason it should start now.

"Oh my god, it's him," a voice somewhere behind me hisses.

There's only one *him* it can be. I can't fake it right now. I'm stretched so thin, one stern, disapproving word from Saint Gabriel will have me in tears and I refuse to cry in public for the glee of my haters.

He steps close behind me, wrapping his arms around my waist and resting his chin on the top of my head. All the stress leaks out of me in one long exhale, and I feel worse about everything.

Of course, Saint Gabriel wouldn't throw me to the wolves in public.

"Hey," he says softly, and that's it. All he says. I lean against him, letting the strength of his body hold me up this one last time.

The barista calls my name, but Gabe holds me back and whispers against my ear, loud enough for the people nearest us—and there are a few more than before—to hear, "You look better than breakfast."

The worst thing happens. I blush.

He releases me to get the coffee, then takes me to a table and disappears again. He comes back with my iced white chocolate mocha, a fruit salad, and a yogurt, setting all three down in front of me.

"What are you doing?" I ask, narrowing my eyes at the food. I want his anger, not his kindness. Why is he treating me this way?

He smiles because people are watching us. "You weren't going to eat this." He picks up the sandwich, and I shudder. "Too much bourbon last night?" he asks for the benefit of our audience, his smile turning impish, popping out his dimples.

"Something like that." I grab my coffee and suck down the sweet, creamy caffeinated glory of it. As soon as we're back in the privacy of the hotel room, he'll put an end to this arrangement. Maybe our agents already have. I check my phone, but there's no call or text, or even an email from Neve. Only one message with a photo of me and Gabe kissing at the BBQ joint last night:

> Holy shit, you two are <fire emoji>.

WENDY

We were. I don't bother to correct her yet.

> Thanks for the notes on my screenplay. As good as you are on camera, I think you'd be amazing behind it. <kissing face emoji>

WENDY

She might be right, but if I have to crawl through the mud of this industry, I'd rather get some fame out of it. Even infamy is better than anonymity. It at least gives the illusion of some form of power.

One brave teenager approaches our table, asking for an autograph and a selfie. Gabe obliges him. It opens the floodgates. Everyone wants a piece of him, a word with him, one of his smiles.

No one bothers me beyond a few dirty or curious looks.

Gabe shoots me an apologetic smile. Maybe he enjoys the attention. I can't tell if he's acting or not, but regardless, Gabriel Sinclair cannot tell these people to go fuck themselves.

If I'm trying to salvage the wreck of my reputation, I can't either.

I eat my breakfast while Gabe's gets cold. He glances down at his breakfast sandwich with a little sigh, but smiles up at the next fan. Because he's a saint.

This is ridiculous. This man needs saving from himself.

I wait for him to say goodbye to the fan gushing at him, then slip out of my seat and stand between him and the next one.

Of course, she's a gorgeous twenty-something and the look she gives me is violence. I glare at her and everyone waiting for a piece. "We're trying to have breakfast. Maybe this can wait until after."

She gives me an obvious once-over and turns to Gabe with a smile.

My fists clench. I want to grab her by the hair and drag her outside, but my self-control is better than that. Barely.

Gabe stands, using his size to create a bit of space around us, forcing the young woman to take a step back. Without a word, he grabs the brown paper bag with his sandwiches and the second coffee with one hand and wraps his arm around me.

"You ready?" he asks me, ignoring the disappointed noise of the fans who haven't had a turn with him. I grab my coffee and nod.

"Stupid bitch," the young woman mutters under her breath.

Gabe hears, turning to glare. "Don't put other women down. It's disgusting."

Her eyes are on fire as she stares at me. "Tell that to her."

I turn away because she's not worth my time. I get this shit like a firehose on social media and maybe I'm not as immune to it as I want to be, but I have learned to at least act like I give zero fucks. Mostly because it's the best way to piss off the haters.

Gabe hasn't learned that lesson, I guess.

"Editors leave a lot of footage on the floor to tell the story they want to tell," he says in a calm, deep voice.

The twenty-something's smile falters and it's clear she's failing to find a way through this that will get her what she wants.

"Don't believe everything you see on TV," he adds, tugging me away. "Let's go, baby."

We head toward the door and I can't resist shooting her a smug little smile over my shoulder.

"I saw that," Gabe murmurs as we step into the sunshine.

"Sue me."

We get back to the room and he reheats his coffee in the microwave, eating his cold sandwich while he waits. Since it might be my last chance in person, I admire the tight fit of his T-shirt and the way his jeans make his ass look so delectable. I'm going to miss fake dating him for the view alone.

"How do you want to do this?" I ask, slumping into a chair.

"Do what?" He pulls his coffee out and turns to lean against the counter as he blows the steam off his drink.

"Our break up. I booked a flight for this afternoon. I can get a ride to the airport. Do you want me to say anything on social media, or should we let our agents handle it?"

"Are you fake breaking up with me?" he asks, incredulous.

"No, you're fake breaking up with me."

His frown deepens. "Why?"

"Are you serious?" I snap. My eyes burn. I've done and said enough in front of this man. I'm not crying again. Not over this. "I'm the worst. I tried to seduce my cousin's husband on their wedding night and used you as a decoy without a single concern about you. How can you stand to be in this room with me?"

Understanding crosses his face and he sits down across from me. "Do you love him?"

I ball up my fist and press it to my mouth. All I can do is nod and wipe away the tear that falls five seconds later. I don't know if I love Nic. My feelings for him haven't changed, but they're smaller than they were. Like something I've outgrown. My stupid heart is still clinging to the idea of him, though, unable to let go.

Gabe reaches for my other hand and takes it in his. "We both still need each other, and yesterday worked really well. As long as it's not public knowledge, I don't think we need to end this yet."

"You're kidding." He can't be this much of a saint. "I tried to break up a marriage. I'm not a good person and I can't be better."

He rolls his eyes and releases my hand. "You aren't as bad as you think you are."

"You couldn't even stand to be in the room with me last night."

"I needed to think about it. You seemed upset, and I thought you might want some space."

My eye twitches. "Seriously?"

He shrugs. "People do extreme things for love. And I think you regret it."

"You'd be wrong." I snap, but I do regret it.

"I don't think so." His sudden grin is the sun breaking through clouds—blinding. "You saw I wanted to eat my breakfast and scared off my fans, even though it's a step back on your reputation rehab." He leans over the table and points at me. "You're actually a kind, caring person."

I gasp. Now he's trolling me. "You take that back."

He smiles and I want to throw something at him. "Nope. You ready to go?"

"You aren't as good as you like to pretend you are, Gabriel Sinclair." I hiss as I go to my room to grab my suitcases.

"I'm well aware," he calls after me.

Chapter Eleven

Ashley

We're staying in the penthouse of an old, allegedly haunted hotel in the Ozarks, which suits my mood. The floor-to-ceiling windows give a melancholy view of rolling, hazy mountains and the feeling of soaring over them like a lonely hawk.

The perfect place to deal with the guilt of what I tried to do and whatever it is that I'm feeling about my fake boyfriend.

He's judged me and found me...not despicable. And I'm relieved? I shouldn't care. I don't care.

Telling him brought the heartbreak back. For Nic, for what I've turned myself into trying to get to him, I don't know. One man showing me a little bit of kindness and compassion shouldn't put me in an existential crisis, but something about Gabriel Sinclair is making me want to be a better person.

I can't—and won't—let him do that to me. I wouldn't survive in my world if I acted the way he does. Besides, no one would believe me capable of being good at heart.

Gabe orders room service, which is a mercy. I don't want to go out, even if the whole point of this is to be seen together. He's been quiet all day like he's giving me space. I don't for a second think he approves of what I did. He might excuse it as a lapse in judgment by an emotional person pushed to the break. He'd be wrong.

I knew what I was doing, and I did it anyway.

It's who I am, who I've always been. I knew when I told my father the secret Jessie confessed to me about Celia that he'd rush off to the tabloids with it. I was nine, but I knew it would cause problems for my aunt and uncle and I didn't care, because what I wanted from my father was more important to me.

There was more to my betrayal of Wendy on national television than anyone beyond the two of us knew, but when I used Luca to get to Josh? I knew I'd embarrass him, maybe hurt him. I didn't care because I needed to beat Poppy.

It's a pattern of behavior. I'll step over anyone I need to in order to get what I want, and Gabriel Sinclair would do well to remember that instead of forgiving it.

After dinner I change into yoga pants and a T-shirt and grab the ice cream room service sent up, taking it to the soft leather sofa. This is what I need to deal with these inconvenient feelings. Praline and a view of nature without having to be in nature.

The mountains are settling into greens, purples, and blacks as the sun sinks low. It's stunning in a melancholy way.

Instead of going to his room, Gabe steps up to me and points at my ice cream with a spoon in his hand. "Can I join you?"

I have a lot more ice cream than I can eat, so I nod. He sits close enough that the cushion dipping under his ass pulls me in to him.

"Can I get a photo?" he asks, holding up his phone. "We haven't posted anything today."

Of course, that's what he wants. We haven't posted, but I do not doubt that we're all over the internet from this morning's café debacle. I haven't heard from Neve, so it must not have hurt me too much. I'm too depressed to care.

"I'm a mess. Here." I stick my spoon into the ice cream and do the same with his before setting the big carton on the table. With my help, he gets a picture that captures the soft sunset behind the ice cream.

I expect him to leave me alone. Instead, he hands the ice cream back to me and digs in.

"Your personal trainer is going to kick your ass." I can't look away as he slides the spoon into his mouth.

He slides the spoon back out, perfectly clean, and shrugs. "I'm basically perfect."

It's so true it makes my stomach turn. "You don't have to be perfect in front of me. In fact, I wish you wouldn't."

He takes the ice cream away from me, ignoring my protest. "My body is perfect because I just finished shooting an action movie. I'm not even close."

I snort. "I tried to break up a marriage. What's the worst thing you've ever done, Hollywood golden boy Gabriel Sinclair?"

"Apart from defiling your bikini?"

Hmm...definitely unexpected, but I'm not accepting it. "I wasn't wearing it at the time, doesn't count. Tell me how one time, when the waitress got your drink order wrong, you complained to management and got her fired."

He's quiet for a long time, digging little crescent shapes into the ice cream. "I got in a lot of fights when I was a kid. I put a boy in the hospital once."

My eyes narrow. "Were you defending the wimpy nerdy kid?"

"No." He calmly continues making his spoon crescents. "The kid made a crack about my mom."

That's right. He told me he was adopted by his uncle and aunt. I'm curious about his parents, but I doubt he'd tell me, so I don't ask. "Not sure that counts. You were a kid. Your brain wasn't fully formed." I tap the ice cream with my spoon. "Something you've done as an adult."

Seconds tick by and he says nothing. Maybe he does have a skeleton or two in that closet. "There's nothing."

"So you are perfect," I say with a deep sigh.

He grumbles something but doesn't push the point, handing me the ice cream so he can pull his phone out of his pocket again. "Let's get a few more."

He takes a video of us as he feeds me ice cream and follows it up with a kiss. His cold lips and sweet tongue send a shiver up my spine. "You can't post this. I'm a mess," I say, eyes locked on his lips. That was so sweet I want to kiss him again. Once I do my hair and makeup.

"You look normal," he says, holding the phone out to show me. "Like any other woman."

"Wow. Thanks," I say dryly. "Can you be more insulting?"

"You should show the world what you're like without all the armor on." He shows me another one. "Be relatable."

Huh. I look like a girlfriend. He's still recognizably Gabriel Sinclair, but I could be anyone, messy bun, T-shirt, and yoga pants, eating ice cream with no makeup. Maybe this makes me more relatable, or maybe this makes me a paper doll other women can imagine themselves as. The only thing I know is that showing my softer side is going to get me hurt.

"Can I post it?" he asks.

I almost say *no*, but maybe he's right. Maybe it would be good for me. The usual trolls will come after me, but they do that when I'm wearing designer clothes and my full face too. And he's right there with me, in the video. "Fine."

"Put the ice cream down, let's get a few more."

We turn the couch into a photo shoot. Our tangled feet as we lie down together. Gabe with his arm around me. It feels a bit like a flimsy excuse to touch each other, if I'm honest. After a day of hurting, having his big, strong body close is comforting, and maybe that's the point.

I don't like how that thought settles over me, warm and comforting. Time to put an end to this and send him running.

"We have enough sweet photos. Let's take a few spicy ones." I say as I climb onto his lap, straddling him.

Gabe laughs, but there's a bit of red in his cheeks. "Okay. Strip."

I gasp, dropping the phone onto his fly, and he winces. It's not a direct hit and I know it because he's hardening underneath me.

"Sorry," I say breezily as I pick the phone up. "I thought I heard you tell me to strip."

His hands settle low on my hips. "I did."

My insides melt into gooey mush as I stare into his dark brown eyes. He's playing with me again. Pushing me when I should be pushing him. Trying to see if I'll break first and make a move. Then he'll reject me because he might be willing to fake date a woman who tried to break up a marriage, but sleep with her for real? He'd run. Even if that dick underneath me is telling me otherwise.

I hold out the phone and touch my nose to his, trying to ignore how close our lips are as I eye the screen until I'm happy. I close my eyes and kiss him just before I take the picture. When his lips move against mine, I break away. Why hasn't this scared him off?

"That'll do." I bolt off his lap and hand him the phone, grabbing the ice cream and taking it back to the freezer. The butterflies in my stomach need to calm the fuck down.

When I come back, Gabe shows me the photo he picked to share, and of course, it's one of the sweet ones. The post is ready to go. *Getting to know this wonderful, sexy woman better. Ash is funny, kind, and honest, and I'm lucky to be with her in a pretty penthouse on top of the Ozarks.*

My face goes hot. It's fake. I know it is, but I can't stop the defensive feeling from taking over. "No one is going to buy that. Write something like 'post-sex ice cream is the best.'"

"I'm trying to help you."

"And I'm trying to help you." I cross my arms, irritated.

He pushes a button, posting it.

I grab my phone and leave my suggestion as a comment.

Gabe rolls his eyes.

"Come on," I say, turning toward the bedrooms. No one will look at him as a gritty superhero if he keeps posting mushy shit.

He follows me without question, all the way into the bathroom.

"Stand here." I position him in front of the vanity and step behind him. "Shirt off."

He pulls it off, sucking in a breath when I place my left hand flat against his stomach.

"I'm not grabbing your dick this time," I say as I slip my hand down his stomach. His muscles tense as I dip my fingers below the waistband of his jeans and underwear. The trail of hair is coarse under my fingers and I wish I was grabbing his dick. Watching him in the mirror as I jerk him off would be priceless.

I maneuver my phone in my free hand around him so I can get a picture of the mirror. In his reflection, his face holds an intense smolder. This could break the internet.

"What should I do with my hands?" he asks.

"Whatever you want." This was a bad idea. My face is pressed against his back and he smells damn good. His skin is so smooth and warm.

His hands go to his fly, undoing the button, tugging the zipper down half an inch before stopping. While he's looking down, I snap another picture and remove my hand from his pants. "That's how you do the man who's playing Warwick," I say, showing him the photo. "Not sweet cuddles on a couch. Hand jobs in front of the bathroom mirror."

I squeak when he grabs me and sets me on the vanity. One tug and he pulls the tie from my hair, sending platinum blonde locks falling around my face.

"You think you can do better?" I ask. His answer is a smirk.

He holds me with one hand on my shoulder, his thumb in the hollow at the base of my throat, and bends to kiss the shit out of me. I barely notice when he lets go, his finger slipping down my sternum. He doesn't have to push me hard. I fall against the mirror and he takes the picture.

I'm dazed, not sure what I'm doing as he holds his phone out to show me. In the photo, my cheeks are rosy, my eyes hazy, and my lips pink and swollen. My pale hair is a tousled mess. I look like I've been fucked senseless.

He grins. "I think I'm doing fine as the man who's going to be playing Warwick."

Holy fuck. Gabriel Sinclair is better at this than I am.

"Don't post that," I say, but my voice is a breathy whisper.

"I won't," he says as his eyes take me in. "But I'm keeping that one. For me."

My heart kicks up as my stomach swoops at his words, and suddenly it's a struggle to breathe. If I ask him to delete it, he will, because he's still Gabriel Sinclair, even if he keeps surprising me. But I don't want him to delete it.

"I'm not perfect, Ash," he says, taking a step back. "Far from it." It sounds like a warning and feels like a promise, and more than anything, I want to make him show me that side of him. Whatever it costs us.

Chapter Twelve

Gabe

I'm losing my grip, my control spooling out the open car window as we speed down a highway under an impossibly big, blue sky.

I'm in trouble.

Ash stepped up for me in that café when she didn't have to, knowing it could set her back on her image rehab. It meant a lot to me.

She tries so damn hard to be this impenetrable bitch, but I've seen a glimpse of the woman inside, struggling to keep her head above water. The woman who told me something real and asked me to tell her something filthy. She kissed me in the dark with an open vulnerability that I doubt she's shown anyone, ever.

I've seen the hunger in her eyes when she glances my way. She wants me.

It doesn't matter if she's in love with Nic. I'm not looking for love. We could never work for real, but the sex...

My brain spends all morning coming up with reasons why casual sex with Ash is a good idea. It would relieve stress. Make this trip more interesting. It's been a while since I've had sex and I really, really miss it.

It would be so fucking good with her.

All afternoon, I shoot holes in those reasons.

Sex with Ash would only relieve stress between the moment of orgasm and the moment she opened her mouth. The odds are good that would be under five minutes.

It might make the trip more interesting, but so would an audiobook. Hell, anything would be more interesting than driving through the plains. Plus, interesting isn't always good, and who knows what the fallout of sex with Ash would look like.

Abstaining won't kill me. Hasn't yet. I can jack off when we get to the hotel. Correction, I will be jacking off when we get to the hotel because this woman is my catnip. I'm jealous of the seat belt pressed against her fantastic tits. If she accidentally grabbed my cock today, I'd come in my pants.

We're still days away from LA and this is trouble. Nothing good can come from sleeping with Ashley.

My resolve holds out until the late afternoon when we're miles from anything. The road is straight and boring and I'm backsliding into bad intentions. I roll my window down, but the fresh air doesn't help. It whips her platinum blonde hair around, the ends of it occasionally brushing my arm. She doesn't care that she's in a whirlwind of hair as she sings quietly to the song on the radio.

Fuck the consequences. I reach over and rest my hand on her bare thigh.

Ashley stops singing and stares at my hand. I squeeze just hard enough for her to catch my intention.

She bites her lip, staring at me from behind her windblown hair, debating the same thing that's been running through my head all day.

I wait to see what she'll do, my heart hammering in my chest.

The song's melody dips low and sultry.

Her smile turns wicked, but her touch, when she slides her hand over mine, is light. Slowly, she slides my hand up her thigh. Under her skirt. Up and up as she spreads her legs wider.

I swallow when the side of my little finger brushes damp silk.

"You used my bikini to get off," she says, her voice husky, barely audible over the music. "I get your fingers."

Fuck yes. I shift in my seat from the unbearable pressure my jeans are putting on my rapidly hardening cock.

"For the next five minutes," she lifts my hand away and places light kisses on my fingers. "These are mine." Her lips part and two of my fingers slip into her mouth. Her tongue is soft and wet and warm. I swallow a moan as she sucks me. Ash slides them out and smiles. "Then we're even."

That's as far as she'll take this. Fine. It's for the best, and I'll still get a taste of her and something concrete to fantasize over when I'm alone in my hotel room tonight.

She's waiting, so I nod, my gaze dropping to where her skirt rests high on her thighs. Yeah, I want this too.

"Eyes on the road, baby," she chides, a slow smile forming under my fingertips.

"Turn the radio off." I all but growl, snapping my eyes back to the road. "If I can't watch you come on my fingers, I want to hear you."

"If you do it right, you won't need the volume down."

Fuck. I hold the steering wheel in place with my knee for the five seconds it takes me to squeeze myself through my jeans.

"Hand on the wheel," Ash says in a stern voice. "And watch your speed. I don't want some state trooper to get between me and this orgasm."

Fine. I'll ignore my cock and focus on the road. As much as I can.

Because she might be the actual devil, she pushes my hand down over her tits, letting me get a quick squeeze while she shifts in the seat and spreads her legs to give me better access. I barely catch the moan in my throat when she brushes my knuckles over her wet panties.

I'm not sure how much control she expects to keep, but she doesn't protest when I slide under the soft fabric and Christ. She's so wet my fingers slip over her. Beneath the thrum of the song on the radio and the rush of the wind through the windows, she moans at my touch. Her hand tightens on my wrist.

I want to pull over onto the shoulder to watch. Instead, I check my speed. Check my mirrors. The road is empty except for us.

Out of the corner of my eye, I watch her head tip back, and what I wouldn't give to suck on the soft skin of her neck. To leave her marked to hell because she's mine right now. My cock hurts for wanting.

Ash pulls her skirt up and her panties to the side and I have to look.

"Eyes on the road," she snaps, pulling my hand away from her hot pussy.

I grumble, but she's not punishing me for not listening. She curls my fingers, straightening my index and middle again. I suck in a breath because she wants me inside her.

Forcing my breath out, I check my speed and risk a glance at her pussy. She's bare except for a neatly trimmed patch. I stare at the road while she moves my fingers up and down from her entrance to her hard little clit. Teasing. Herself or me or both.

Not that she's in control. Something I let her know when I dip my middle finger inside her.

My jeans are too tight for this, but I don't care because Ash feels like heaven and I can't stop glancing at her out of the corner of my eye as I add another finger.

Her eyes flutter closed, her hand tightening on my wrist as I plunge into her tight little hole. My cock aches at how hot and wet she is, her pussy sucking at my fingers.

"Ash." It comes out more of a bark than a growl, but her eyes fly open and I keep moving, thrusting into her. "Look at me."

Irritation crosses her face. "Eyes. On. The. Road."

She's right. I need to stop looking at her. It's not easy, but I do it. She releases my hand and I can feel her fingers move to her clit, circling faster than I could at this angle, all while I fuck her with my fingers.

Ashley's gasping, riding my hand like we aren't flying down the highway at sixty miles per hour. My eyes flick between the straight road and the speedometer because if I don't I will crash.

I steal the quickest glance anyway, and damn. This is how I'm going to remember my time with her when it's over. She's gorgeous, so uninhibited, blonde hair everywhere, pink lips parted, tits bouncing, pussy glistening around my fingers…

A handful of strokes later, she clenches hard around me and falls apart, my name ringing out over the noise of the wind and the radio.

My name.

Her thighs clamp over my hand, but I can still move my fingers, driving her harder, higher. She gasps and pants, swears, and when she finally goes slack, I slide my fingers out and bring them to my mouth. She tastes amazing. I suck her off my fingers, aware of her heated gaze. I need her mouth or her pussy—both, ideally.

But this is as far as it goes. It ends here.

She shifts in her seat, leaning over to kiss me on the cheek. "Thank you for letting me come in your car." She grins. "All over your expensive upholstery."

I give her a quick glare, but I'm too hard to give a shit about the upholstery, and all I can think about is getting my face between her legs.

My fingers are tapping along to the rhythm of the song on the radio, and I'm trying to deep breathe my way through the erection from hell while hoping my leather passenger seat smells like Ash's pussy and wondering if I can find a discreet way to check when she gets out of the car next.

Minutes pass and every muscle in my body is still tense and the need to come isn't going away.

The faintest trace of her lingers on my fingers and she has to know what I'm doing when I keep scrubbing my hand over my face, my fingers over my lips.

After a few minutes of silence, she sighs in satisfaction and stretches out in the seat. "I needed that."

I grunt because if I speak, I'm afraid I'll suggest pulling over so she can suck my cock. Or ride it. Her choice, because I need it too. Then I'll get her off again on the side of the road. Spread her on the hood of my car and eat her out until her screams fill the empty sky.

This is insane.

I'm not this guy. I just broke who knows how many traffic laws without even thinking about the consequences and I'm contemplating breaking a few more.

It feels fucking awesome.

And terrifying, because how did she do this to me? Reduce me to something so primal? How can I lock it back down?

Gabriel Sinclair doesn't lose control and finger women while blasting down the highway. He drives the speed limit and gets them off later, in the privacy of a bedroom, while being in an actual committed relationship with them. Like a gentleman, not an animal.

Except this is what I wanted when I put my hand on her leg. I can't lie to myself about who I am anymore.

Ashley's hand on my thigh is like fire, her voice teasing. "Are you okay, baby?"

I'm not okay, not while the scent of her is on me, making it impossible to think. Making me reckless.

I need to get out of the car, but not out here where we're alone and the chance of this escalating is high.

Ash doesn't want more, and she's right. We can't.

A sign points to a town with a gas station, and at the last minute, I brake hard and take the turn. Ashley's nervous laugh fills the car as she hangs on for dear life. "What the fuck, Gabe?"

I shake my head, my focus on the gas station. On getting some space. On killing this boner, because fucking Ashley Foley would be a big, big mistake.

Chapter Thirteen

Ashley

Gabe slides into the parking space, slamming on the brakes. He's barely turned the engine off before he's out the door. "Stay in the car."

No way am I staying in the car. I'm half-blissed out, half-ramped up, and if nothing else, I need some chocolate. And I might be a little pissed off, and a little impressed he thinks he can go jack off in a gas station restroom when I'd be more than happy to—

No. I'm not going to go there. We're even now.

Turns out, Gabe's not getting himself off in the restroom. When I walk into the gas station, he's perusing the chip aisle. I suppose it's his way of pumping the brakes on this thing between us, and that's good. Definitely...good...

The air inside is thick and heavy, like some kind of dream. Nothing feels real, except my damp panties. I can't believe he fingered me while driving. That's not Gabriel Sinclair. I got a glimpse of the real man behind the golden image and I like it too much. Gabe unleashed...

Distance is good. I'm all about that distance.

I'm such a fucking liar.

He sees me and locks his car with a key fob, even though we're the only people here, apart from the clerk who hasn't glanced up from his phone. We don't say a word and he goes back to studying the selection of salty snacks and I move to the aisle of sweets.

My fingers skate over a row of chocolate bars. There's breathing space between us, but it isn't cooling me down. Five minutes post-orgasm and desire is still pounding in my veins. I don't know if I can fight this. I don't know if he can.

Our eyes meet.

In the space of a heartbeat, we give in. In silent agreement, he moves to the back of the store. I follow him into the ladies' room. The scent of pine and bleach fills my nose as the fluorescent lights flicker on, revealing the surprising gleam of clean, white surfaces.

"Just one time," he whispers as he locks the door.

I nod, reaching for him. One time is all I need.

We crash together—I fist his shirt, he lifts my dress, and our kiss is deep and dirty as he presses me against the wall.

"I can't breathe when I'm around you," he grumbles, and the heat of his mouth on my neck and the cold of the tile against my back battle for the shiver that rips up my spine. "I want you—"

I gasp as he slips a finger inside me.

"—out of my fucking system."

I hold on to his shoulders, hitching one leg up his hip to open myself to him, riding his hand like I didn't come on his fingers five minutes ago. He's fast and hard bringing me right to the edge before pulling out.

"Dammit, Gabe," I bite out in frustration as my fists tighten on his shirt and I shake him. He doesn't give an inch. He might as well be a wall.

"I'll give you more," he growls as he lifts me and sets me down on the edge of the sink, then he's sucking on my neck, pulling down my dress as I claw at his back. My tits spill out of my bra and I'm not worried I won't get mine. His big hand grabs my breast, squeezing, kneading, my nipple going hard against his palm. I arch my back, his head dips and his tongue finds my other nipple. My back nearly blows out, his mouth feels so good. I fist his hair, holding him tight to me and he sucks my nipple so hard I see stars.

I need more, but he's lost in my tits—he's hardly the first to get waylaid by them. I drag his head up to mine, stare directly into his dark brown eyes, and say, "Fuck me. Now."

His kiss has a bite to it, but like a good boy, he pulls my panties off, stuffing them in his back pocket. I won't be getting them back and I don't care.

I reach between us for his pants, but he beats me to it, shoving them down just far enough. His cock is glorious, hard and thick. I wrap my hand around it and the skin is soft and hot and I can't wait to feel the delicious push of him inside me.

The expression on his face goes from desperate to despair as he looks through his wallet while I continue to stroke him.

"Tell me you have a condom," he chokes out, thrusting into my hand with a frustrated groan.

I didn't bring my handbag into the gas station, so no, I don't. I'm about to tell him to fuck me raw—I'm on birth control and don't have any STIs and I'm willing to gamble he doesn't have any either—when his eyes land on the wall. A condom dispenser. He's on it in a split second, feeding it a coin with one hand—how does he have a coin but not a condom?—and squeezing his dick with the other. A string of curses that makes even me blush comes out his mouth when it refuses to give up a rubber.

Gabe rips it off the wall, and it clatters to the floor like an adult piñata, condoms and tampons spilling across the tile.

My jaw drops—did he Hulk-out to get a condom? Gabriel Sinclair committed an act of vandalism to fuck me? This is the hottest thing that has ever happened to me.

He grabs a condom and rips into it, and seconds later he's sheathed and striding back to me. The hunger on his face is all I see.

He grabs the back of my neck with one hand and I whimper against his lips. I need him, but he's fucking with me, sliding the head of his dick through my folds, slapping it against my clit.

"I swear to god—" I don't know where to grab him first but my hands cup his face, his late-day stubble rough under my palms. He doesn't let me finish my threat, one thrust taking my absolute breath away. It's impossible to breathe anyway as he works himself progressively deeper, his hand on my neck squeezing harder when he bottoms out and goes still.

"You're tight," he grunts, thrusting again.

"Stop complaining." I kiss him and hold him against my mouth because I need him to shut up. It's too much. I'm fuller than I've ever been and I want every inch, every plunge, every muscle in his body straining with the effort of fucking me on this counter. Every sensation, every detail—I want to experience Gabriel Sinclair at his basest.

He lifts me and I wrap my legs around him. My back slams into the wall and he pins me. I roll my hips, taking him deeper, grinding against him.

It feels so good—Gabe feels so good—that my eyes flutter closed.

"You'd better not be thinking about him," he growls against my lips.

My eyes fly open and my mind blanks. "What?"

He shifts us, ever so slightly. My left ass cheek stings before I realize he spanked me. My entire body goes warm and suddenly I'm so damn close.

"It's my cock you're going to come on," he continues. "Not his."

Ah. Gabe hasn't left me any room to fantasize about another man, not even Nic. He's taking up all the space I have and more. I think he's pushing me out, taking that place too. "You have to make me come though."

"Oh, I will. And it'll be my name on your lips again."

"Maybe." The way I gasp out that word calls my bluff.

I'm on the counter a heartbeat later. He doesn't pause or stop, but his eyes meet mine, checking in. Like the spanking or his demands might have turned me off. Whatever. I've never been more turned on in my life and I'm so wet he has to feel it through the rubber. I'm already pulling his lips to mine, trying to take him as deep as I can in any way that I can.

It's hard and fast, the slap of skin on skin echoing in the room. He's gripping the back of my neck again and something about it grounds me. We're breathing too fast and too hard to kiss, but our lips still brush anyway. He's staring at me, daring me to close my eyes and pretend he's Nic, but I couldn't if I wanted to. Not with his free hand playing with my tits, squeezing and pinching my nipples. He's driving me wild and I can't get enough and I'm begging—*more, more, more, please Gabe...*

When his hand drops down and his thumb presses against my clit, I come so hard and so loud he has to slap his hand over my mouth.

He doesn't break his rhythm, wringing every last ounce of sensation out of me. There's satisfaction in his eyes, then his head pitches forward, landing on my shoulder as his hips jerk. Deep inside me, he pulses as he comes, his erratic thrusts slowing to a stop as he takes every last second of pleasure in me.

For a long moment, we stay as we are, Gabe draped over me, breathing heavily. In the sudden stillness, the quiet feels obscene. I inhale the clean scent of his hair and hold him to me. I don't want to let go yet.

The moment we walk out, we're going to pretend this never happened. We'll post our pictures and drive for hours and sleep in separate beds, but this time I'll do it knowing how he feels inside me. What he's like when he lets go. I'll know him in a way the rest of the world doesn't. It feels like a secret.

Gabe takes a deep breath, and that's it. He straightens and slides out of me, turning away to take care of the condom.

This is over. Not like it was in the car, but for real this time.

It's cold without his body heat. I shiver and hop off the counter, tucking my tits back into my bra. My dress is ripped a few inches down the front, and I stare at my reflection for a moment, blinking. I hadn't noticed him rip it. Whatever. It's a souvenir of the time Gabriel Sinclair lost control and fucked a woman in a gas station restroom. It belongs in a museum.

In the mirror, I watch him crouch down to pick up the condoms and tampons that spilled out of the dispenser. He piles them on top and sets everything against the wall, frowning.

Gabriel Sinclair is back. I bet he stops by the ATM and withdraws a couple hundred and gives it to the cashier to pay for the damage.

It's a reminder, though, that when I walk out this door, I need to be Ashley Foley. My dress is ripped and I'm not wearing panties, so that's on-brand, but something inside me has shifted. Like Gabe has found a crack in my chest and wedged it open, and anyone who looks at me will be able to see the black hole inside.

He opens the door a crack before stepping out and motioning for me to follow. Like he expects a gaggle of paps or fans to be standing outside, waiting to pounce. The gas station is still empty, the clerk still glued to his phone.

"Get me a water?" I ask quietly, giving up on the idea of chocolate.

He nods and hands me his keys, but his eyes only meet mine for a fraction of a second.

"Thanks for the hot sex," I say loudly, and the clerk finally glances up. His jaw drops as he stares at us.

Gabe looks like he could strangle me for that, but this is what he needs for his image and we aren't going to do it again, so we might as well make the most of this. The surveillance video of us going into and coming out of the ladies' room and the torn-down condom dispenser are going to be all over the internet soon. Hopefully, the twenty-something behind the counter gets some money for this and doesn't give it up for free.

I walk out the door, blowing Gabe a kiss.

Riding without panties isn't allowed in his car, so I open the trunk and pull a clean pair from my suitcase and slip them on right in the parking lot.

A few minutes later he slides behind the wheel, tucking a couple bottles of water into cup holders and dropping a chocolate bar and a packet of wet wipes on my lap. "Eat it before it melts."

He's letting me eat food in his car?

"What will a blow job get me?" I ask, staring at the chocolate.

"A mouthful," he says, then slaps his hand over his face and groans.

I laugh. Maybe Gabriel Sinclair has loosened up a bit.

"Are we okay?" he asks once he's back on the highway. His eyes ask a different question, as they drop to my ripped dress. *Are you okay? Was I too much?*

"Better than okay." I smile and reach over to rub his thigh for a few seconds. "You fucked yourself right out of my system." And ruined me for all other partners, which I am not prepared to acknowledge in this freshly fucked glow-y world I live in. "Am I out of yours?"

He scrubs a hand over his face and frowns, eyes locked on the road. "Yeah."

My stomach drops and I take a drink of water in case it shows on my face. He doesn't look at me anyway.

He's scratched this itch, and he's done and I don't want to be done, but I'm not going to be the one to crack first and beg him for more. A girl's got to have some pride.

Chapter Fourteen

Ashley

I MIGHT HAVE SOMETHING like pride, but I really don't know when to stop.

Since I want Gabe and he's done with me, the next day I put on my sluttiest dress and push his buttons all morning. He takes it with a silent stoicism that only makes me more determined to break him.

If I weren't me, I'd keep my mouth shut. I'd sit quietly or take a nap or play a game on my phone for the millionth time. I'd stare out at the empty landscape around me and not feel the crushing disappointment of being *me*.

But I am me. And I'm tired of never being wanted, of always wanting, whether it's Nic or my parents' unconditional love or Gabe's attention.

I shouldn't even want him. A couple of orgasms should've done the trick—he should be out of my mind and I should be satisfied.

I'm not.

Since he's not taking my bait and I'm getting frustrated with myself and him, I aim to hit him where it'll hurt most.

"I still can't believe they cast you as Warwick," I say with a sigh.

Gabe ignores me.

"Think you'll sink the franchise?"

"I'm a good actor. That's why I got the role." He says it like he doesn't want to engage, but can't let me drag him through the mud either.

"Okay, let's pretend that's true—you do a good enough job, but fandom still doesn't like you. The backlash to your performance is huge. The fans demand Nic back because let's face it, he's Warwick."

His face is like thunder. "He can't act."

"Of course, he can't act! But he put *himself* into that role and made it his. Every broody shot? That's Nic, not Warwick. You have to measure up to that."

"I'll do better than that," he mutters. He's clenching the steering wheel and a muscle in his jaw tics. He takes a hard turn onto a country road and accelerates.

I'm finally under his skin and I don't feel good about it—in fact, it makes me nauseous—but I can't stop the words from continuing to spill out of my mouth. "Worst case, the franchise caves to the whims of disappointed fans. They write out your entire career as Warwick as an aberration, an alternate universe that never happened, no one ever watches your movies, and they offer Nic enough money he can't say no—"

"That's not going to happen. I'm a better actor than Nic."

"Please. Not in this role. He's better than you'll ever be because he's true to himself. He's not lying or pretending to be something he's not so people will like him."

He pulls over, turns the car off, and gets out.

My stomach plummets. Fuck. Why am I like this? Why can't I leave him alone?

He stomps a good ten feet down the dirt road, his hands in his hair. After a moment of staring out at the nothingness around, he strides back to the car, past my door, and to the trunk.

Maybe he's taking a leak. Hurling rocks or kicking a fence post. I don't know. I can't bring myself to look. I should go after him. Apologize.

I jump when he opens my door.

"Get out of the car," he growls, a blanket tucked under one arm and heat in his eyes.

Oh shit.

"Ashley." His voice gets sterner and I don't know how that's possible, but oh my god it's doing something to me.

Anticipation sky-high, I unbuckle my seat belt and slide out of the car. Gabe doesn't give me an inch, and I have to press against his chest while he glowers at me. "Yes, baby?" I blink up at him with innocent eyes when I should be apologizing and telling him I didn't mean it, I don't know why I said it, I'm sure he'll be a great Warwick...well, I'm not sure but I also don't care.

"Get over here." He closes my door and walks around to the front of the car, throwing the blanket over the hood. "Shoes off," he snaps.

I slip them off and point at the blanket. "Is that for wrapping my body up after you murder me?"

He looks unimpressed. "The only one dying is me." He scoops me up and sets me—gently—onto the hood of his car, muttering about dents and spreading my weight out a bit more so it's not all on my ass.

Then he steps back, pulls his phone out of his pocket, and holds it up.

"Really? We're doing social media shit right now?" I ask. On reflex, I push my tits out and find my angle with the sun.

He doesn't say a word. He takes the photo and types something on his phone. I'm too scared I'll dent or scratch his baby to slide off the hood—he can pick me back up and put me on the ground—so I stay where I am.

He hands me the phone. The shot is in black and white, which makes my pale pink dress pop against the darker shade of his metallic car and the much darker blanket. There's a pinup vibe to the photo I like, but when I read the caption, I nearly drop his phone.

Quick lunch stop.

He's posted it too. Somehow, out in the middle of nowhere, he has enough of a signal to *post this*?

I bite my lip and read it again, a hot, tight feeling building between my legs. He isn't going to—

Gabe takes the phone from my hand and tucks it in his back pocket, his hungry eyes drifting down my body.

My knees part about six inches.

He licks his lips. "Gonna need more than that."

I let my legs fall open. He reaches toward me, slow and determined, and grabs me under the knees, dragging me closer.

Giddiness bubbles up into my chest as he flicks my skirt up, holding it in place low on my stomach. The firmness in his touch only intensifies the ache, and by the smirk on his face, I think he knows it. He dips down between my legs and my breath rushes out in a tremble as he nuzzles me. His soft moan buzzes against me, barely audible. The seconds it takes for his fingers to pull aside that little strip of fabric last a lifetime.

I die a little when his tongue finally touches me. He mutters a tortured *fuck* and does it again, adding a flourishing lick and a light suckle when he reaches my clit. He looks up at me before sucking harder.

All the shitty feelings from the day disappear at the heat in his dark eyes. I sink back onto the blanket, murmuring his name, winding the fingers of one hand through his thick hair, and using my other hand to pinch my nipple through my dress and bra. My tits block my view, but I'm going to remember the way he's looking at me.

His tongue is precise, circling and fluttering, licking and sucking to a pattern he reads from my body. There's no sense of urgency, even though we're out in the open and presumably this road is public, but he isn't lazy about it either. He's perfect.

I close my eyes, but the sun still burns behind my eyelids. The heat from the engine, the heat of his mouth between my legs, they're melting me. He moans like he's getting as much satisfaction as I am from this, and that turns me on so much.

"Oh god, Gabe," I murmur, tightening my grip on his hair. A little cry escapes my lips when he slips a finger in, a second quickly following. He's gentler than yesterday, thrusting slowly, curling his fingers while he tongues my clit. When he speeds up, I murmur again. His name, how good it feels, what I want him to do. He does it and some, his fingers hitting just right, thrusting hard and fast while he sucks my clit and I hover on the edge of something huge.

Heat gathers, my legs start to shake, and pressure grows deep inside until the world explodes, turning me inside out and emptying me as I scream his name up into the cloudless sky. Gabe holds me down, pulling every last bit of pleasure from my body as my orgasm goes on and on until I'm a crying, shuddering mess and he finally stops.

Holy shit. I press the heels of my hands to my eyes and take a deep breath, trying to pull myself together.

He doesn't give me the time. He fists the front of my dress and pulls me up. I'm too boneless to complain that he'll rip it. He looks very pleased with himself, and also very wet. His face is dripping.

"Did I—?" Squirt him? That's never happened before.

He yanks my dress down and wipes his face off on my tits. "Sure did."

I wince. "Sorry."

"Don't be," he says as he lifts his head and scoops me into his arms. He puts me into the car, along with my shoes, and pulls the wet wipes from the glovebox to clean us up. I'm too wrecked to do it myself.

After, he folds up the blanket and inspects the hood of the car. I roll my eyes, but god I hope he doesn't have regrets because that was hands down the best oral I've ever received. Either Gabriel Sinclair is blessed with a natural gift, or he's been practicing somewhere the tabloids haven't picked up on.

He slides into the driver's seat and has the car in gear before I can offer to return the favor.

I reach over to his lap and give the lump in his jeans a gentle but firm squeeze. "Pull over."

He keeps his eyes on the road as he lifts my hand off his dick. "I'd rather not."

"Are you sure? I'll blow you while you drive, but I have to warn you—I'm good. You'll want to pull over or we'll end up in a field."

His jaw clenches. "I don't want a blow job."

"You don't like blow jobs?" That's disappointing. I love them. There's nothing like making someone shake and beg. It's a total power trip.

"I love a good blow job, but you don't owe me."

The sinking feeling in my stomach tells me exactly where this conversation is going and I don't want it. But I'm me. I can't stop. "What if I just want your dick in my mouth?" I snap.

His glance is sharp. "I gave you what you wanted—that's why you've been trying to pick fights with me all day, right? But I'm done. I don't want a repeat of yesterday."

Pain slices through my chest. And anger. Red, hot anger. "Are you kidding?"

Gabe glances down and gives his cock a half-hearted squeeze because, of course, he thinks I'm talking about his obvious arousal. He shrugs. "That turned me on. It doesn't mean I want you again."

Tears spring to my eyes. He doesn't want me. No one does.

I need to get away. Now. "Stop the car."

He glances at me in alarm. "Ash—"

"Don't *Ash* me," I snap, brushing the dampness from my eyes. "Stop the fucking car or you can explain to the police and the media why I jumped out of it while you were going sixty."

He slows down and pulls over, putting the car in park. "Be reasonable. We both know—"

I'm already out of the car, slamming the door on whatever it is he thinks we both know.

The window rolls down. "Ash, get in the car."

I flip him off and start walking. There's a town ahead—I can see it in the glimmering distance, maybe a mile away.

Gabe idles alongside me. "Come on. You got what you wanted. Why are you so mad?"

I catch the scream before it has the chance to leave my lips. *Because you don't want me!* I can't say that to him and I hate myself for even thinking it. I don't *want* to want him. And yet here I am, the same place I always am. Wanting someone who doesn't want me.

Thank god it's only sex. If I fell in love with this asshole, after breaking my heart over Nic for decades...

"Ashley, get in the goddamn car."

I flip him off again.

"Fine," he snaps. "You can walk into town. Maybe you'll decide this little tantrum isn't worth it. I'll wait for you there."

He accelerates slowly, and I imagine he's checking the mirror and watching to see if I'll run after the car.

I won't.

He can drive into town and think about how he left me out in the middle of nowhere because he was too stubborn to enjoy a no-strings blow job.

Fucking Gabriel Sinclair. The worst kind of unicorn.

He drives by me a couple of times and he's the only car that does. Both times I ignore him. It's about a hundred and twelve degrees and I'm baking in the sun, but fuck him.

This might be the worst walk of shame of my life.

His stupid car is parked on the outskirts of town, waiting. He's been keeping an eye on me the whole time. The asshole is leaning against the car licking a goddamn ice cream cone when I walk up to him.

As if he can feel the murderous rage rolling off me, he holds out a second cone, melting fast in the heat. "I got you one."

I take it and smash it into his forehead and keep walking.

Chapter Fifteen

Gabe

"There are rattlesnakes out here."

That gets Ashley into my car, but she doesn't say a word and refuses to talk to me. Not that I make an effort—having a melting ice cream cone slammed into my forehead pissed me off, especially after I spent last night fighting the urge to knock on her hotel room door because I *do* want her. That's the problem.

At this point, we're both so keyed up nothing good can come from talking. Ash can have her little tantrum and her silent treatment, and she does. Eventually, she falls asleep. I drive with my thoughts for company and even that's too much.

I wasn't planning on stopping at my aunt's house. I haven't seen Cora since I found out about Michael. I don't want to tell her about his hypocrisy and betrayal, and I resent the hell out of him for turning me into someone who'd lie to her. Christ, if she found out just how imperfect he was—if she finds out how imperfect I am? I don't think I could handle it.

But right now, I need a reminder of who I need to be. Something to firm up my resolution to stay out of something complicated with Ashley Foley. This thing between us...it's too dangerous. She's every bad habit I've avoided, every depraved desire I've suppressed.

I'll lie to my aunt to save myself.

Ash wakes as I turn onto the long gravel drive. "Where are we?"

"Cora Sinclair's house," I tell her.

She mutters something, rubbing her eyes as I pull up to the garage.

Cora's house sits in the mountains outside Angel Fire, New Mexico. It's an eclectic, rambling mix of timber and stucco surrounded by acres of pine, spruce, and aspen. Not the place you'd expect to find the widow of Michael Sinclair, one of Hollywood's most celebrated directors, but it fits her. It's the place she brought me when she plucked me out of my last stint in foster care after my father was arrested. It's full of hard memories—trying to find my place in a world of expectations and consequences was challenging—but lots of good memories too.

I'm going to need all of them to remember who I am.

"I'm not a meet-the-family kind of girl," she mumbles, staring at the house. She looks a little pale.

"No shit." The glare she sends me makes it clear I'm not being helpful.

"Do we need to fake it in front of her?"

I couldn't fake it if I wanted to. The things I'm feeling are too real. "No. I'll tell her. She doesn't watch much TV or read the tabloids, so she probably won't know you."

She doesn't look relieved or disappointed. More like mildly anxious as I lead her through a gate and a small garden to the front door. I have a key, but I ring the bell, and it only takes half a minute for Cora to open the door.

"Gabe!" A smile breaks wide on her face. Her apron is dusted in flour, and her long white hair is pulled into a low ponytail. She's sixty-five, older than my mother by more than a decade. They weren't close as children and that didn't change over the years, but she welcomed me in when I needed a home and gave me a family.

She's glowing with happiness as she pulls me into a hug. It's soothing, being in her presence. I feel better already, despite the guilt hanging around my neck.

Cora pulls back, her eyes kind and warm on me before moving to Ash. "And you brought a friend!"

Ashley's smile wobbles, but she holds out her hand as I introduce her simply as "Ashley." Cora goes in for the kill, wrapping her arms around her before pulling away and staring at her in that way she has. Like she can see into your soul. It's unnerving, but Ashley stares back with a carefully guarded expression.

"Come on," Cora says in a soft voice. "It's past time I opened a bottle of wine and you both look exhausted." The invitation is meant for Ashley because Cora tells me to go get our things and pick whatever bedrooms we want—her way of not being presumptuous.

The house has three levels, built into the side of the mountain, so the main entrance is on the second floor. I take my things around the back to the little studio apartment that makes up the first floor. It can be accessed from the house or the outside and has a small kitchen, a full bath, and a bedroom. It's been mine since I turned sixteen. I open some windows to air it out before heading back to the car for Ash's things.

I put her in the bedroom on the second floor, farthest from my room.

Cora's kneading dough in the kitchen when I walk in. The evening light shines through the windows of the atrium. A quarter of the second floor is a giant indoor garden that opens onto the kitchen. Soft folk music plays over the sound system. I catch a glimpse of Ash in the living room beyond, sitting on the tile floor, a glass of wine in one hand, a string in the other.

"Did you hand her wine and a kitten?" I ask quietly when I pass Cora on my way to get my glass, since she didn't pour one for me. I hadn't pictured Ash as a pet person, but I guess if I had to, I'd pick cats for her.

"I did." Cora nods, blowing a strand of hair from her face. "She needs that more than she needs my conversation right now." Her eyes narrow at me. "Or yours, I think."

I've had about all I can stomach of Ashley's opinions on my suitability for the Warwick role and Nic fucking Fontana. I might be on the way to hating that man.

"No recovering raccoons?" I ask, changing the subject. "Healing hawks? Broken-winged birds?" There's no sign of any other animal in the house.

Cora collects broken things and heals them with love and determination. Stray cats, injured birds...the house can look like an animal rehab center at times. It's partly why living in LA didn't work for her. *If I can't see my husband anyway, because he's always at work, why not live where I'm happy?* In between films, Michael came home, but the house was always filled with her laughter, whether he was there or not.

Maybe there was another reason Cora didn't want to live in LA. Maybe she knew. Or suspected.

Cora always seemed at peace, content and confident about her place in the world. In her marriage. She couldn't have known her husband was a cheating liar.

"There's a sanctuary in town now," she says. "I volunteer four days a week."

I can't remember if she told me the last time I called. My life has gotten exponentially busier recently. The last few weeks have been a vacation of sorts after my last film wrapped. Not that any part of it has been relaxing.

A soft giggle comes from the living room. Ashley doesn't strike me as some-one who giggles easily or often, so I lean back on my stool, trying to catch a glimpse of her.

Cora clears her throat and points to a basket. "Can you go out in the garden? Whatever you can find for a salad."

Like a dutiful nephew, I do as I'm told. Honestly, a salad would be good. Cora's a vegetarian and her salads are incredible. Between her greenhouse, her raised beds, and the atrium off the kitchen, she grows almost everything. When I come back, Cora's in the living room, a bowl upturned over her dough.

"Wash those, please," she calls out. "And start chopping."

Cora is gifted with the ability to see what people need and the perseverance to give it to them whether they like it or not. Right now, this space she's giving me and Ashley—I love it. I need it. The muscles in my jaw and neck relax as I chop tomatoes. I can breathe again, and in the space, memories come back.

It was a lot, coming here after the shabby, run-down house I grew up in, or the foster homes I passed through for a few months before my aunt found me. Her house was a warren. Endless tunnels and chambers, but instead of being dark and shadowy, they were light and airy.

The house even had two *jungles* inside it. Who had jungles in their house?

"They're atriums," she had said in a kind voice. "Go ahead and explore."

I didn't explore. I haunted the house, wandering through rooms like I'd find what I was looking for right around the corner. I wanted to go back home. To see my dad.

I stole, mostly from the kitchen, to see if I could get away with it. Aunt Cora turned a blind eye to my kitchen thievery and slowly lured me out with kind words, sweet treats, and a three-legged puppy. For two whole weeks, I thought maybe this wouldn't be so bad for a while. It was a hell of a lot better than foster care. I could do this. Until Dad got out of prison and brought me home.

Then *he* came home. Michael Sinclair. Tall and dark, like some gaunt villain from a movie I'd once watched—one that kept me up for a week. His face was stern when he looked me over, a sigh escaping his lips like he'd decided I was lacking.

I don't know what made me do it. He'd left a watch on the kitchen counter. It had been easy to slip it into my pocket after I'd raided the candy dish. Dad didn't care when I took things from stores—that was half the reason he took me sometimes. And this watch had to be worth a lot of money. It looked fancy. Maybe I could use it to help Dad.

"Gabriel."

Michael Sinclair stood stiffly, dressed in a shirt with buttons and pants that weren't jeans or sweats, sour disappointment on his face.

"That isn't yours."

"I don't have anything." Lying was second nature. Using my fists was too, but not on a grown-up who could easily beat my ass. Still, I'd hit him if he tried anything.

"Give it here." He held out his hand.

Time crept by, his cool blue eyes never wavering. I was busted.

Would he hit me? Scream and yell? He'd caught me, I might as well find out how things were going to be.

I took the watch out of my pocket, slowly placing it in the palm of his hand and taking a quick step back.

Michael clasped the watch around his wrist, his face relaxing. "Thank you for returning it. This watch doesn't belong to you. It was a gift from your aunt. You stealing it—or anything else—would hurt her."

I didn't want to hurt Aunt Cora. She was kind. If I hurt her, she might get rid of me. Leave me with Michael, or send me back to a foster family.

"You are a Sinclair, now. You will act like a Sinclair, and a Sinclair knows right from wrong. I do not expect perfection from you at such a young age and so soon after leaving your dad. But you will do better. Understood?"

I didn't, not yet. I ran into the living room and down the stairs to the smaller atrium. Down another short flight of stairs was an apartment, but the door was locked, so I hid behind the covered hot tub.

It took the better part of a year before I trusted Michael. A little longer before his lessons started to sink in and even longer before they meant something to me.

Before they meant everything.

Ashley's giggle brings me back to myself, and when Cora leaves the living room for a moment, I take advantage and peek into the room.

The kitten is pouncing and leaping at the string Ashley lazily swings through the air. She's smiling.

I tug at the collar of my T-shirt and go back to my chopping before she sees me. All of Michael's stifling expectations and lofty goals are suffocating when I'm around her. I don't want to be Gabriel Sinclair anymore.

I can't let myself feel this way, not when all I am to her is a step closer to a goal and a warm body that can give her pleasure. She doesn't care about me—hell, she's in love with another man. That alone should be enough to end this fascination. I shouldn't need to come home to look for Michael Sinclair's ghost to remind me that Ashley Foley is exactly the wrong woman for me. She'd push me down to bring herself up and never look back. I can't trust her.

Michael was a hypocrite, but it doesn't mean he was wrong. I can stay on the path he put me on. Ashley's a temporary distraction, a means to an end, and whatever I'm feeling for her doesn't matter.

Chapter Sixteen

Gabe

One night in my old room has me feeling more like myself. Waking up and knowing I don't have to get in the car with Ash, I don't have to pose for pictures with her or fake it in public is a relief. If Cora keeps running interference, I won't even have to see her.

After seven days in the driver's seat, it's good to move too. An early morning run up and down the trails zigzagging the mountains clears my head and puts me back on course. I can fake date Ashley Foley and keep my distance. She's so pissed off at me anyway that I doubt she'll make any more advances. Once we're safely in LA, we'll be down to scheduled public dates.

Cora and Ashley are drinking coffee in the kitchen when I return from my run. Ashley is wearing jeans and a T-shirt and I do a double take. I didn't think she had any clothes other than the sexy dresses, tiny shorts, and tight tank tops she's been wearing. She's not dressed to kill and while I'm sure she's wearing makeup, she's applied it with so light a hand she looks completely natural.

She's powerful as a femme fatale, but like this, she looks like someone who doesn't break hearts for fun. She looks like someone who would stay.

Until she decides to take another shot at Nic Fontana. Or until she decides on a whim to destroy everything I've worked for. I shouldn't have to keep reminding myself how dangerous she is.

"I'm volunteering at the school fundraiser today, and Ashley's coming with me," Cora says as I fill a glass with water. "Want to help?"

"Sure." I down the water and glance at Ash. Guilt twists inside me and Cora's words, whispered to me last night, come back. *That girl's hurting.*

I scoffed. *She isn't hurting, she's pouting because she didn't get her way.*

Cora had given me that look. The *I'm not disappointed in you, I just think you could do better* look.

Then again, Cora doesn't know Ash. Or that we're fighting over a blow job I didn't want. It's not like I tore her heart out.

I stomp downstairs to shower and change, irritated because now I'm lying to myself. I wanted her to suck my cock and turning her down took a massive amount of willpower. She's no good for me. She could destroy my life, and she would, for no other reason than she felt like it.

We needed to stop, I put an end to it. She needs to get over it.

Ashley takes the back seat. I brace myself for a day of pretending to be her boyfriend. Slightly edgier Gabriel Sinclair.

It's getting fucking hard to remember who I am.

Cora turns the music up—classic rock—like she doesn't want us to talk. Like she's protecting Ash. I should warn her that's not necessary. Ashley Foley is a fortress.

But it's a warm summer morning, the windows are down, Cora's singing, and I catch a glimpse of a smile on Ash's face in the mirror. She catches me watching her and her smile withers as she looks away.

The drive to town isn't long, and when I get out of the car, people do a double take. Everyone knows Cora, and I went everywhere with her for years so they know me, too, but I guess I've been away long enough. That and the whole fame thing.

Doesn't intimidate anyone though. They greet me warmly and a few ask for autographs or selfies. Then I'm put to work.

The fundraiser is spread out over a soccer field, spilling into the school parking lot, and half the town is already here.

Cora's busy, gently guiding Ashley and whatever other volunteers land in her orbit. Since I'm setting up chairs and tables near the other food booths, I can't help but notice how Cora pauses to engage her in conversation every so often, trying to draw her out because she's pulling to the edges. Making herself small. The opposite of the woman from *Love on the Line*. The opposite of who she's been in the car.

Unarmored.

"Got another job for you, Sinclair," a firefighter says, beckoning.

I head his way, passing Ashley. Her eyes meet mine for just a second, but I see it. What Cora saw last night: hurt.

It startles me and I stumble. The firefighter chuckles. "Hope you aren't doing your own stunts."

"Not many," I admit, following him toward the field. I turn for one last look, but Ashley's gone.

I have to shake her from my head because too many people want to talk to me and soon my face hurts from smiling for selfies. When the crowd is big enough, I see exactly what my job is going to be for the day. The fire department sits me on a platform above the dunk tank. There are a lot of phones up, taking videos, waiting for someone to hit the target.

A lot of people want to dunk me. I'm surprised Ash isn't one of them. I keep searching for her, but she's not in the crowd.

I finally catch a glimpse of her platinum blonde hair—not by the baked goods, where Cora is selling pastries—but over by the face painting station. She's down on her knees, brush in hand, and a smile on her face as she says something to the little boy in front of her. She finishes and holds up a mirror, and the kid races off to his parents.

Ashley Foley, painting children's faces at a fundraiser. Looking like she belongs. She tips her head back and laughs at something another young woman says to her, and the way the sunlight hits her, she's golden. Happy.

Maybe I don't know her as well as I think I do. Maybe no one does.

Ash turns like she feels my stare. Our eyes meet, and it's exactly like it was at the gas station before we threw caution to the wind. This sense of *rightness*. Of everything falling into place.

Until the world falls out from under me.

Someone hits the target and into the tank I go. The cold water is a relief against the heat of the day, but I shoot to the surface and pull myself up to see her above the crowd.

There's a small smile on her face as she turns back to the little girl now standing in front of her. It hits me harder than the fastball that dropped me into the tank. I miss her. I miss her picking on me and flirting with me and trying to get under my skin as much as I miss the quieter Ash who watches old interviews to find out what kind of pizza I like.

I like her.

I groan and slap my head because this wasn't supposed to happen, and the next thing I know, I'm back in the water as another ball finds the target.

I am drowning in this and I don't know what to do anymore.

We dance around each other for hours. She's everywhere, lending a hand. No one recognizes her, I don't think, but she's a pretty woman in jeans and a T-shirt. As the day goes on, her smile warms.

I haul things around. Beg for another round in the dunk tank when the afternoon heats up. I make a private donation, sign autographs, and pose for selfies. All these pics of me by myself will have people speculating that it's over between me and Ashley, so I need to post one with her.

I find her at the end of the day, sitting on a retaining wall, eating pink cotton candy, and watching the fundraiser wind down. "Hey."

She gives me a wary look. "Hey."

I shove my hands in my pockets, my fingers brushing my phone, reminding me we've got our fake relationship to fall back on. I pull it out and sit next to her.

Ashley pops a piece of cotton candy in her mouth. She's not wearing lipstick, for once, and the natural pink of her lips is so soft and pretty, I get distracted for a good twenty seconds staring while she waits me out.

Right. Fake relationship.

"We need to post a photo together," I say as I wrap my arm around her and raise my phone. She stiffens, then relaxes as she exhales. Without a word, she tears off a chunk of cotton candy and turns to face me. She won't meet my eyes and she's not staring at my lips. Maybe my nose. It's a tiny cut to something in my chest. Pride, maybe, because I broke something real between us. I gave her pleasure, then acted like I was above receiving the same from her, all but telling her I only did it to shut her up.

I take a deep breath and lower my phone. "Ash, I—"

She stuffs the cotton candy in my mouth before I can say anything. It melts away to nothing, but so do my words because she finally looks into my eyes and I can see the pain in hers.

I hurt her. Fuck. This isn't who I am or who I want to be.

She glances away and tears off another chunk of cotton candy. "This time, take the picture."

Cora walks by, shooting me a warning look. I call out to her, handing her my phone when she comes back. "Get a picture of us?" She takes my phone but gives me that *I'm not disappointed, but* look again.

Ashley closes her eyes, squares her shoulders, and takes a deep breath. Her chin tilts up, her entire body shifts, and when she opens her eyes, I'm staring into Ashley Foley from *Love on the Line*. She's slipped back into her armor.

She moves the cotton candy toward my mouth, an impish but fake smile on her face. I search her eyes and find no trace of the hurt, no trace of Ash. She's a phenomenal actress. She stays in character when I grab her wrist and give her my best seductive smile.

The cotton candy hits my tongue, all sugary sweet as the world dissolves around us. I trap her hand, closing my mouth over her fingers. Her armor melts like spun sugar, her eyes going wide. Her lips part in surprise as I kiss her fingertips. She tugs her hand free and balls it into a fist, her teeth sinking into her lower lip, her eyes tight.

"Ash," I whisper. I don't have her hand anymore and I want to touch her. I settle for tucking a stray lock of hair behind her ear. "I'm—"

She brushes me away and stands. "Did you get a good one?" she asks Cora.

"About twenty," Cora smiles, handing my phone to Ash. "I need to help take some stuff down—why don't you two wait by the car? Or take a walk through town."

Whatever Cora hoped to accomplish in keeping us apart must be done. I suspect it was letting me realize what an ass I've been.

"I'll help," Ash says quickly, shoving my phone in my direction.

I grab it before she drops it. "I'll help too."

"Thanks, kids. Gabe, I think Manny could use a hand."

Ash doesn't look over her shoulder as she walks off with Cora.

Something cuts deeper in my chest and I have a long hour of knocking down tables and taking down marquees to think. Ashley cares about me or I wouldn't have hurt her when I turned down her blow job. Maybe this changes some things. Not everything, but enough that maybe we can make this fake relationship a little more real. If she can forgive me.

Chapter Seventeen

Ashley

Cora Sinclair is a witch. The good kind, in a flowy hippy skirt, who sweeps in with kittens and tells me I'm not broken. I'm not bad. I'm whatever I want to be, and I get to decide every minute of every day what that is.

She's magicked me, and when she announces Gabe and I are cooking dinner, I no longer feel like stabbing him with a salad fork. So long as he keeps his mouth shut, anyway. So far, so good. He's been silent since I walked away from him at the fundraiser.

"Try this one," Cora says, pulling the cookbook off the stand, opening to a page, and handing it to Gabe.

He turns the cover my way, raising an eyebrow. "This is Ashley's aunt."

Aunt Celia has been judging me from the kitchen counter since we arrived. Is she following along with the tabloids and social media, watching the carnage she's wrought with her *you two are going to fake date* nonsense? Probably not.

Cora turns and squints at the cover. "Oh. She has a TV show, doesn't she? I've never watched it. A lot of the recipes in there are tricky—if you have any tips, Ashley, write them in." With that, she leaves us alone, the kitten chasing her long skirt up the stairs.

Gabe sets the cookbook down, and I reach for it like a shield. We're making a vegetarian pasta dish. I scan the ingredients and when I feel the warmth of his body at my back, I read them a second time. His hands grip the edge of the counter on either side, trapping me, so I read the list again. If I don't acknowledge him, maybe he'll give up and go away.

"We need to talk," he says softly.

"We need to cook." I correct him, my finger skating over the first step in the recipe. I'm not ready to give up on my strategy of ignoring him, so I try to focus on the words in front of me. The warmth rolling off his body is dangerously distracting. His hair is still damp from his shower and his body wash lingers on his skin. I can't stop myself from breathing him in, as much as I don't want to.

"I thought you were acting like a spoiled brat because I turned you down."

I spin to face him, but I'm not prepared for how close he is, or the pinched look in his eyes. "Thanks, that's so kind of you," I say sarcastically, putting my hand on his chest and pushing.

He doesn't budge.

I push harder and he pins me to the counter. I hate that I gasp, that my eyes drop to his lips, and I want him to kiss me so bad I could cry. Fuck this guy.

"I was wrong," he continues. "I hurt you, didn't I?"

"Don't be ridiculous," I snap, ducking under his arm and striding over to the sink, where vegetables from Cora's garden sit, freshly washed. I can breathe again, but I'm feeling way too fragile to deal with this.

"Don't lie." He takes the veggies from me over to the counter next to the cookbook and reaches for a chopping board and knife.

I glare at the way his T-shirt pulls snugly on his broad shoulders. I'm tired of this. Today was nice. For once in my life, I felt needed and he's taking that away. Reminding me of how much he doesn't want me. "Fine. You want to know? Yes, you hurt me. But that doesn't make you special."

He's silent for a beat. "It makes me just like everyone else," he says quietly.

I don't say anything. Since he's commandeered the veggies and the knife, I put a large pot of water on the stove and resolve to watch it boil while I get my shit together.

Gabe goes to work on the vegetables, and I listen to him chopping, carefully and evenly. He'll be thinking about how I've brought this on myself. How my behavior pushes people away. I know it does, but that doesn't mean I can stop.

I don't want to stop because I don't want to hurt.

Heat prickles behind my eyes.

"I'm not going to cry because you didn't want me to suck your cock." Why the hell did I say that out loud? I take a deep breath and let it out in a loud sigh. "Let's try to get to LA without any more fighting, okay?"

The kitchen falls silent. No more chopping.

I can feel him behind me again. How does he move so quietly?

"I want you," he says softly. "I turned you down because I was afraid I wouldn't be able to stop at one blow job. Believe me, I want to hear you gag on my cock. I want to come down your throat. Or on your tits, if you'd prefer. I want to make you come so many times you forget everything but my name."

His honesty shocks me and the surge of desire his words send through me makes my knees go weak, but the nerve of this guy. I snatch the wooden spoon off the counter and whirl on him. "Don't sweet talk me."

He snatches the spoon and tosses it aside. It clatters onto the counter. "What are we doing, Ash?"

"Faking it." Like we do everything. Gabe and I aren't so different, after all. Both pretending to be what other people want us to be. Him in his golden cage, me in my twisted one, neither of us able to fly through the open doors.

He takes another step closer, his hand tucking my hair back like he did earlier. "I like you."

I blink at him. "Excuse me?"

He smiles, his hand dropping to my shoulder and sliding down to my hand. He laces our fingers together. "I like you. As a person. Not just a walking wet dream."

My heart thumps, but I'm holding on to my anger like it's a lifeline as I pull my hand from his. "And this is how you tell me? *A walking wet dream?*"

He frowns. "Okay, that sounded bad, but—"

"You think?" I snap.

"Not when I'm around you." The smile on his face isn't a happy one. "And that's the problem. I can't get you out of my head. I like you and I don't know what to do about it. We still have an end date. I need to focus on my career, not on a relationship. But we have eleven weeks." His palm presses against my stomach, his fingers curling until he has a fistful of my shirt. One yank brings us together, my hands flying to his chest to stop myself from face-planting into him. "Ash," he says, his voice soft, twisted with emotion. "What are we doing?"

My breath catches. He's asking for more. Not directly, not yet. But he likes me. He wants me. He wants to know what I want.

I grab the collar of his shirt and hold him. "You like me?"

He skates a soft kiss across my lips. "Very much. Everything about you."

What, everything? I'm so stunned I tell him the truth. "I like you too." My throat goes tight. I can't believe I said that.

"I hope so." His hands move to my hips, pulling me flush against him.

The feel of him hardening against me makes me light-headed. I really like this part of him. "The sex is—"

"Amazing," he interrupts, dropping kisses along my jaw on his way to my neck. I bite back a moan when he nips my skin and soothes the bite with his tongue. He's right, we're amazing together.

"You want a fling," I say softly.

Gabe freezes. "Yeah." He breathes a sigh against my skin.

I turn my head to brush my lips over his ear. "You want to spend the next eleven weeks fucking each other senseless while we fake a relationship. You're sure you want to complicate this?"

"I want the fucking," he whispers, and his words make me ache so sweetly. I want that too. The fullness of him buried deep inside me—I want it so bad I clench and the emptiness hurts. "And we're already complicated."

Nothing worth having is ever simple, in my experience.

But.

When I speak, there's steel in my voice. "That option was there when I offered to blow you and you didn't want it. What changed?"

Gabe pulls away, and I let him go. He shoves his hands into his hair, messing it up. "You scare me, Ash, and I don't know what it means that I like it, but I do. When I saw how much I hurt you, I realized you care about me. So maybe...maybe I'm safe. With you. I won't lose sight of who I am."

Understanding clicks, tightening in my stomach. "I won't tarnish you too much." I hate it. I hate it so much I want to scream.

"It's more complicated than that," he says defensively, then sighs because, of course, it's what he means. "This wasn't supposed to happen." He pulls me tight against him. "I wasn't supposed to like you."

"I'm not happy about it," I say into his T-shirt. Because he's right. This wasn't supposed to happen, I wasn't supposed to like him either. It's not supposed to hurt when he rejects me or believes I'll destroy his reputation, but it does.

His arms tighten around me. "We can't be real. You understand that, right?"

"I understand." I do. We're supposed to have an amicable breakup, where he leaves me and I'm brokenhearted but still wish him the best. We can't be friends because people will speculate. Our future is one where we'll bump into each other at a party or professionally. We'll make small talk about the weather, make a polite excuse, and leave the conversation.

Gabe tips my chin up and his dark brown eyes are soft. "Can you walk away, if we do this? Because I want to spend the next three months sinking into you."

You don't know how to stop. My cousin's words, but they're still true. What if I can't walk away? Do I want to risk a future where I trade longing for Nic for longing for Gabe?

But I've walked away from relationships before, when I got bored or when I thought I might have a chance with Nic. There's no reason to think I can't walk away from Gabe.

Hell, maybe I'll walk away from everything. Buy a house on a mountain and get a kitten. Find a life where I don't have to fake date someone to find work.

"You still love Nic," Gabriel says quietly, breaking into my thoughts.

What? My first instinct is to deny it and that shocks me to the core.

I picture Nic. His smile. His voice.

And I feel nothing.

I don't love Nic. The possibility that I have never loved him is too terrifying to contemplate. I have done some shit for Nic and if it has no meaning...

Shit. My entire life has shifted off course somewhere in the last nine days—possibly within the last five minutes—and I didn't notice until Gabe said his name.

Nic has been my end game for so long, and now he's not. It's disorienting, an entirely new world suddenly in front of me. One I never realized was there. I'm not going after Nic, so what am I going after?

I rest my forehead against Gabe's chest. "Fuck," I whisper into his shirt.

"I don't care if you love him," he says softly, and I'm not sure I believe him, but I can't find the words to correct him. It's too new. All of this. His voice hardens as he says, "As long as you aren't thinking about him when you're with me."

"I won't." I doubt I'll think about Nic much at all anymore. "And I can walk away." If Gabe can do it, so can I.

The pot of water starts to boil, and Gabe kisses me. "Stay in my room tonight?"

Dinner takes forever, and the heated looks from Gabe have my blood buzzing with anticipation before the dishes are cleared away. We say good night to Cora, and Gabe takes my hand, leading me through an atrium and down some stairs to his room. I'm half in a daze, my heart pounding and feeling too big in my chest.

The bedroom door barely snicks shut before I push him against it. His dark eyes flare and I can't look away. I don't waste time with kisses—not yet. This man likes me. What was I thinking, admitting I like him too?

The prize I get for that moment of weakness is straining against his jeans, so I unbutton them and shove them down as I sink to my knees to claim it.

Goddamn, he fills out a pair of boxer briefs. I could stare, I could tease him through the fabric. Instead, I free his erection and push the boxer briefs down his thickly muscled thighs.

He watches me with hooded eyes as I wrap my hand around him, stroking him until he's hard. Like every other Foley, I'm competitive as hell—he gave me the best orgasm of my life and I need him to come as hard as I did.

I lick the bead of precum, welcoming his salty taste, swirling my tongue over the wide head of his cock, teasing him where his head meets his shaft, while his soft moans fill the air.

"Ash."

My name comes off his lips like a prayer and I take him deeper, the muscles in his thighs trembling under my hands.

His head hits the back of the door and he swears under his breath as I hollow my cheeks and suck, sliding up and down his length.

He likes me, everything about me. The ugly dark stuff too. I don't know how to feel about that or him. I'm off balance, but right now, blowing Gabriel Sinclair, the world steadies and I'm back in control.

The dim light of the room catches the planes and angles of his face, the dark shadow of stubble on his jaw, and when he looks down at me, his expression is one of surrender. Warmth spreads over me, tenderness I didn't think I could feel with it.

He's beautiful like this—all mine.

I don't know where that thought came from, but I'm not examining it now.

My hand takes over and I pay some attention to the head of his cock, sliding the tip in and out of my mouth, licking and sucking, using my hands on his length. He moans again when I gently play with his balls, and the sound he makes when I tease his perineum is downright obscene. I'm so turned on I can't stop myself from squirming, seeking out whatever friction I can find.

When I take him deep again, he whispers a stream of endearments and praise that make me glow with warmth, punctuated with profanity that turns me on. The way I cling to every word from his lips should terrify me. Maybe it does because suddenly I need this to be rougher. I need him to use me the way I used him in the car.

Gabe's hands are balled into fists, digging into his thighs. He's trembling and the effort it's taking him to hold still is impressive. I slip my fingers over his and his fists relax. When I guide his hands to my hair, his fingers tangle before he pulls me off him.

"I'm close, baby," he says softly, his thumbs brushing across my cheeks.

"Where do you want me to finish?"

"Fuck my mouth." I gather my hair up for him and he hesitates for a heartbeat before taking it, shifting his grip to get it how he wants it. A few hairs pull and the sting makes me moan as I take him in again.

He's gentle, at least at first. Slow, shallow thrusts as he tells me how beautiful I am, how amazing I make him feel, how good I am at taking him. I want to slip my hand down my pants, but instead, I glide both my hands over his thighs, around to the back where they meet his perfect ass. The light press of my fingernails spurs him on. His hand tightens in my hair and he fucks me a little faster, a little harder, and I want more. I want everything from this man.

My eyes water as the last bit of his control vanishes—the light exploration of my fingers might have a thing or two to do with that.

"I'm—"

I know. I can feel it build, feel his desperation in each thrust. I want it as bad as he does. My jaw aches, the back of my throat, too, but I can take him.

"Oh, god, Ash—"

He comes with a strangled cry and I swallow him down. His entire body is shaking, his rhythm turning erratic. I take everything he gives me, greedy for more, taking over as his grip on my hair loosens, milking his cock for every last drop.

"Fuck—Ash. Fuck." With a final grunt, he tugs me off him, letting go of my hair as he falls back against the door. My hair tumbles around me and I kiss down his length, looking up at him as I sit back to wipe my lips with the back of my hand. His smile is relaxed, his eyes dark, and he looks like he's been hit by a bus in the best possible way.

He has to haul me to my feet when I can't stop staring at him.

I cup his cheek. "Told you I'm good at—"

Gabe pulls my mouth right to his, kissing me long and deep, even though he's still trying to catch his breath. In truth, I'm still trying to catch mine, but it doesn't stop me from wrapping myself around him when he picks me up or laughing when he throws me onto the bed.

CHAPTER EIGHTEEN

Gabe

BEING BACK BETWEEN ASH's legs is heaven.

There are probably going to be consequences and when this comes to an end I'll pay for it, but right now, her moans are worth it. Tonight and every night until we have to walk away from each other, I'm going to make sure she knows she's wanted. Ash pulls off her shirt while I slide her shorts down her legs. Her bra and panties soon follow. It does something for me, seeing her laid bare while I'm still dressed.

I pin her legs wide open on the bed so I can fit my shoulders between them. She tastes divine, her fingers tight in my hair, holding me to her as she rocks her hips. I want to take my time with her, but she's too turned on from sucking me, too ready for her release. In less than a minute, she's crying out, her body shaking.

Fuck it. I'm not done. "Give me one more," I tell her when her fingers loosen in my hair.

"I don't think I can," she says with a contented sigh, her arm over her face.

"Ash."

Her tongue peeks out as she wets her lips, a hint of a smile playing there. "Make me."

I grin, slipping a finger into her. Another one. For a few minutes, I thrust into her slowly, admiring her soft skin and the way her body is still hungry for my touch, moving with me, taking my fingers deeper. Her arm slips off her head, and she reaches for the bedframe and holy shit. Her arching back makes her tits look incredible.

"Don't let go." God, I wish I had something to tie her up with.

Ash flips me off, but her hand goes right back to the bedframe.

"Good girl," I murmur, bringing my mouth down to her pussy and sucking her hard little clit into my mouth.

"Naughty boy," she smirks. I give her a light slap to the clit for that, and she moans.

I don't let her come. Not right away. She plays along, holding onto the bedframe for dear life. She doesn't beg so much as complain, but considering she's breathless, I don't care to put her out of her misery yet. Even if I'm already hard again.

"I swear to fucking g-god—"

It's hard to take her threat seriously when my tongue makes her stumble on the last word.

I crook my fingers, fuck her faster, and suck her harder. Ash comes exactly like she did on the hood of my car. I don't let up, drawing her pleasure out longer, until she collapses and releases the bedframe to push me away.

I kiss down her thigh, wiping my face on her soft skin, then reverse direction, crawling up her body. "I love your tits," I murmur, covering them in kisses.

"They're fake."

"Don't care. You wear them beautifully."

She laughs, but her fingers weave through my hair again.

"I'm going to have to fuck them," I tell her, pushing them together and licking both.

"I want that," she says quietly, directing me to one tight bead of a nipple. I bite her gently before drawing her into my mouth. She moans and holds me tight to her. "I want everything," she admits.

I do, too. I work my way up to her lips and kiss her breathless, until she turns her head and murmurs, "You'd better have a condom this time."

"Oh, the condom fairy has visited." I roll out of bed and head for the bathroom. Cora left a box with my toiletries, probably while we were cooking dinner.

Ash laughs when I hold up the value box. I toss it onto the bed so I can pull my shirt over my head and drop my pants and boxer briefs.

"I still feel bad about that condom dispenser," I say, tearing one open and sliding it on. It was worth it, but yeah...I feel bad.

"Of course you do," she says, smiling up at me as I lower myself over her.

This is nothing like our first time. It's slow and rolling, building into something bigger.

I don't know how I'm going to find it in me to walk away in three months. I wasn't lying when I told her she was my walking wet dream—she's everything I've ever wanted. Maybe she's wrong for Gabriel Sinclair, but she's so right for me.

When she clenches tight around me, biting my shoulder to keep from crying out, she drags me with her, making my world go bright. I make an unearthly sound at how good it feels to empty myself into her, how much I don't want to stop.

I collapse on top of her and she strokes my back and makes a satisfied little noise.

God, I needed this. Every last ounce of pleasure wrung from my body. From hers. I must be crushing her, but I can't move.

"Have I ruined you, Gabriel Sinclair?" she teases softly.

I lift myself enough to look down at her, a warm, buoyant feeling stealing over me. "Yeah," I say on a breath, surprising myself.

"It's only fair," she says. Her kiss is soft and sweet and maybe I'm being reckless, but I don't care if she knows she's ruining me for other women.

We spend another day with Cora—who is satisfied we've worked things out—before we hit the road. I wish we could stay longer. I don't see Cora as often as I want, but I have to be back in LA in a few days.

I'm not ready for this trip to be over. Not when Ash is right next to me. When

I can touch her and taste her and fuck her anytime she wants me to. That's going to be harder back home, impossible once my schedule picks up.

My hand is resting loosely on the stick shift, and Ashley's hand slips over the top of mine. She smiles at me but turns back to the road like she wants to touch me without turning it into more.

I spread my fingers to capture hers. "Tell me something about you that would surprise me."

Ash presses her lips together as she thinks. Then she smiles at me. "Wendy, from *Love on the Line*, is my friend."

"No shit." I can't keep the surprise out of my voice. I've never watched the show, but David filled me in. Ashley's fight with Wendy was one of the biggest blowouts of the season. According to him, it cemented her as the villain.

"She needed to leave—a personal reason I'm not telling you—but she couldn't tell the producers or she wouldn't have a shot at coming back in a later season. We planned the whole betrayal thing. Luca was easy to manipulate into sending her home."

"So you became the villain of the season to give her an out?"

Ashley laughs and shakes her head. "No, they cast me as the villain when I walked in the door and told them I was there to win, whatever the cost. It just forced me to out myself sooner than I planned."

"So you didn't get the villain edit?"

She wrinkles her nose. "It wasn't much of an edit." She's quiet for a moment, lost in her thoughts, her thumb sliding along the side of my hand, back and forth. "Honestly, I would have edited the show the same. The storyline was perfect—my rise, my fall. Poppy could have been the villain of the season, but it wouldn't have been as exciting. She was impulsive and bombastic, rather than calculating. The only thing I'd have done differently, if it was my show, would be to make the villain relatable at the end. They didn't even try." She smiles at me, and it's a rueful sort of smile. "Maybe it wasn't possible to give the things I did on that show a sympathetic bent."

I don't want her to dwell on what she did for that show, however scripted or edited it was. Or wasn't. "How did you and Wendy become friends?"

Ash smiles and this time it's warm. "The first night at the meet and greet, I was sizing up the competition when she started talking to me. I thought either she's foolish or way smarter than anyone is giving her credit for. And after that...I don't know. She was a kitten thrown into a shark tank, and when the sharks came for her, like Poppy trying to turn Luca against her, I stepped in."

I have no idea what happened on this show beyond the broad picture David painted for me and I have no intention of finding out who Luca or Poppy are, but I already dislike them.

"We bonded over her situation," Ash continues. "We still talk and hang out, but we have to stick to the story our season told. Viewers can't know how scripted this all is. And she has a good chance at getting onto next season."

"I won't tell anyone."

"I know. What about you? What's something that would surprise me?"

I glance at her. "I'm terrified I'm going to be awful as Warwick."

She lifts our hands from the gear stick, planting a kiss on mine. "I think you'll surprise a lot of people, including yourself."

It's my turn to pull our joined hands close so I can kiss hers. It's not that I doubt my abilities. I don't. But I could give the performance of a lifetime and it might not be enough. Too many other hands will shape the movie into what they want it to be, and fandom will do the same.

"That wasn't much of a surprise," she says softly.

I guess not, since she's already picked up on that anxiety. I want to give her something real, though, because she gave me something real. "I got detention in third grade for making a bong in art class."

Ashley's jaw drops and she stares at me, blinking. "What?"

The laugh dies in my throat. There's no going back if I tell her about my past, but she's signed an NDA, and after the last couple of days, I don't think she'd tell anyone anyway. It's lonely keeping everything inside.

"My dad modified stolen cars to transport drugs." No one in my life knows this outside of Cora. "We used to take these family trips, just the two of us, often with one of his women friends. They weren't vacations though. We'd always leave with a different car."

Ash squeezes my hand and for a while, I'm lost in those memories. My father was pretty good at looking relaxed, at mimicking a working-class dad taking the family camping or visiting the grandparents. We'd always stop at a drive-through just before we got home for burgers and fries, eating in the car. A little celebration for making it without getting caught.

I shake myself and glance at Ash. "What flavor of awful was your childhood?"

"Probably not as bad as yours," she says, biting her lip.

"Doesn't make it better."

"Yeah." She blows out a long breath. Silence hangs for a few minutes, and I imagine Ash is debating the same thing I've been. How much to tell, how much to keep close?

"When I was six," she says eventually, "my dad left. He always left, and he always came back, but this was the first time I realized it was my job to bring him back. Mom taught me the words to say, taught me how to cry, and sent me to him. It didn't work, and he sent me back. My mother didn't speak to me for two months. Not a word. I didn't understand what I'd done wrong—I did everything she asked me to. I don't know how she got him back that time, but she did. Then she ran off, so he took me to Europe with her best friend and promised that if I told her the way he wanted me to, he'd take me to Disney World."

"That's messed up."

She shrugs. "It was better when they were fighting because they both wanted me. And they'd give me whatever I wanted to win me over. When they were together, they forgot about me. They'd go off somewhere and leave me with a nanny or a sitter or sometimes alone and never tell me when they were coming back, or if they were coming back." She squeezes my hand. "Your turn."

I can hear the layer of fear under her voice. It never really goes away. Somewhere inside, that scared kid is still worrying about what happens next, how to survive it, and how it's going to get worse. We're the same that way, even if the worlds we grew up in were very far apart.

"One time my dad disappeared for a couple of days. He didn't say where he was going or when he'd be back. I just came home from school and he was gone." It wasn't that unusual for him to disappear, but usually he left me with someone, a friend or a neighbor. "I lived off of cereal and slept with every light in the house on. He came home, beat to hell, in the middle of the night. Turned all the lights off, yelling at me about the power bill. He took me down into the basement. Our house was shot up a few hours later. It was terrifying, hearing the bullets breaking windows and hitting the walls. Every night for a week we'd hear these cars drive by really slow, but they didn't shoot again." Then one day it stopped. We didn't sleep in the basement anymore and life went back to normal, but for the longest time I couldn't sleep without nightmares.

Ashley squeezes my hand, but it isn't enough for her because a few seconds later, she shifts in her seat to rest her head on my shoulder, both her hands wrapped around my arm.

There must be something about being on the road, about being together or about surviving, because it's easy to talk to her. The rest of the day we trade horrifying stories in dispassionate voices, holding hands and passing back and forth encouraging squeezes as needed.

It's ugly and heavy but by the time we reach the exclusive Sedona resort, I feel closer to her than I have to anyone in my entire life. The door closes and Ash is already kissing me. I take her against the door, hard and fast as her nails dig into my shoulders like we can fuck away our painful pasts.

With her, maybe I can.

Chapter Nineteen

Ashley

Gabe stops at a rest stop, donning a baseball hat and a pair of mirrored sunglasses before heading in the direction of the men's room. I wait until he disappears to get out of the car. It doesn't take long to pull the shirt out of my suitcase, but I stand frozen in front of the car for a long minute, holding it tightly while a hot little breeze tickles the back of my neck.

Nic's shirt.

This worn old thing has gotten me through so many lonely nights, so many days of self-loathing. It never felt wrong to have it, but when my fingers brushed it this morning, that changed. I'm not the same woman anymore. Instead of being a comfort, the shirt is a deep stab of guilt.

Maybe, if he had given it to me, it would be different. Maybe, if that shirt hadn't meant so much to me for years, it would just be a shirt. But it's not. It's my obsession, my desperate need to be loved by a man I don't even really know. A man I now recognize I don't love.

Stone picnic tables are scattered under the trees, and I walk to the closest one. There's no ceremony to it. I set the folded shirt on the table and hope that maybe some random traveler will pick it up. Someone who will never know who this shirt once belonged to.

I walk back to the car quickly, just as Gabe emerges from the men's room. Stretching my arms overhead, like I'm just out here stretching and not saying goodbye to a huge part of my past, I smile at him as he walks up to me. When he reaches for me, though, it's all too much and I dodge him. "Be right back," I call on my way to the ladies' room.

I stop at the sink and splash cool water on my face.

God, if he had any idea...

He'd think I'm crazy if he knew what that shirt was. Christ, I hope he doesn't recognize it and put it back in the car thinking I'd left it by accident...no, I'm pretty sure he didn't see me leave it. There's no reason he'd recognize it as mine.

I do my business, then head back outside. Gabe is waiting for me, leaning against the passenger door. My heart immediately speeds up. He looks too good standing there, that T-shirt stretching across that broad chest, his jeans doing the same across his thighs. What the sunglasses and baseball hat fail to hide is more than enough to tell that he is handsome as fuck.

This time, I walk into his arms. He smiles down at me, and while he doesn't look in the direction of the shirt, I can feel its presence. I ignore it, pulling him down for a kiss just as scorching as the sun beating down on us. "Let's go," I say, pulling back before either of us can reach the point of no return.

He pauses. "You're ready?"

"So ready."

He grins, dimples popping, and kisses me again, quicker this time but no less dirty for the brevity of it. He opens my car door and I slide in. When he crosses in front of the car, my eyes track him and I notice the shirt still on the table, but I don't look directly at it.

Gabe climbs in and starts the car, tossing the baseball cap into the back seat and turning his attention to me. "Sure you're ready?"

What the hell? Why is he so reluctant to leave this rest stop? "Yeah, the ladies' room isn't clean enough for a quick fuck. Let's go."

He laughs but throws the car in reverse. I can't be sure because he's still wearing the mirrored shades, but it looks like his gaze might linger on the picnic table with the shirt for a few seconds. I don't look in the mirror as we drive off. Gabe glances at me, then reaches over and puts his hand on my leg. It's warm and firm and I place my hand over the top of his.

We stop at the Grand Canyon and take selfies like any normal couple would, and it feels so real, this thing between us. So much more than the physical relationship I think we both want to pretend it is.

Talking comes easy between us now. Emptying all our trauma yesterday took away the roadblocks and today we talk about the good times. He tells me about growing up with Cora and her unwillingness to give up on any injured or broken creature. It takes me a little while to come up with any, but the moments are there, in the cracks and spaces in between. Moments shared with Wendy, and with my cousins when we were younger. Even with my Aunt Celia. It makes me long for what could have been. For how many more happy memories I might have had, if I'd done things differently back then.

I don't talk about Nic. Gabe doesn't ask about him.

In Vegas, we let people photograph us having dinner at some trendy restaurant because we're obligated to, but then we go to our suite. I ride Gabe on the sofa overlooking the lights of Vegas until the only name he knows is mine, and everything is perfect.

Chapter Twenty

Gabe

Ashley left Nic's shirt behind, and the next morning, waking up in Vegas with her in my arms, I want to shout, *Fuck yeah—she picked me.*

I don't know if that's true. I didn't even know the cologne-scented shirt was Nic's until I saw her stepping away from where it lay folded on a picnic table. I don't know how she got it or how long she's had it, though it's not big enough to fit him, so I'm guessing it's pretty old. When she never once gave it a second glance—it clicked into place. She's letting him go. Her heart is hers again.

Maybe I should worry about what that means for us and whether she'll be able to walk away when our time together is up, but I can't. Not when she feels so good pressed against me and the scent of her is in my lungs and on my skin.

Fuck, I don't want to leave this bed. So we don't, not for a while. Not until we're both satisfied—Ashley a few times over.

I don't know what gets into me. Maybe it's the way everything feels so right when I'm inside her, maybe it's a moment of madness. Instead of pulling my shirt over my head, I slip it over hers.

Her eyes are round with surprise and panic when I tug it down. Like she recognizes what I'm doing. Before she can protest, I haul her onto the table in front of the huge glass window, push her legs apart, and make myself useful. The T-shirt stays on, even though she's swimming in it.

It looks better on her than his ever did.

Today is our last day on the road. I'm not ready to go home. My car smells like her now, and she looks too good in the passenger seat. I bet she'd look amazing in the driver's seat, but when I ask, she confesses she doesn't know how to drive a manual.

I'm not about to teach her on my baby, but maybe there will be time. I have other cars, ones more forgiving.

"I don't want this to end," I admit before we're even out of Vegas. Meaning the road trip, but our expiration date in a few months is in the back of my mind.

"Me neither," she admits. Her full lips curve into a smile as she looks at me. "Take the scenic route."

We do. I take NV-160 and we drive. Anywhere. It doesn't matter because this is freedom. The open road, Ash by my side. Talking. Enjoying silence. All of it. Nothing's ever going to be as good as this.

The hot wind whips up her platinum blonde hair and sunshine turns it into a glowing halo. Her bare lips curl into a smile at my wild story about *The Last Best Man* wrap party, and maybe it's the warm desert evening or the hum of the engine, but I'm content.

This bubble we're in feels so real.

We drive into Malibu just after midnight, our bubble coming up against Michael's expectations and the lie I have to live up to. Passing through the gate, it pops. Ash feels it too, I think. She lets out a sad little sigh.

Desire to turn around, to go back to driving aimlessly with Ash, hits me, and all at once I'm too hot and too cold. My palms go damp on the steering wheel, but I have to see this through. I'm close to the lofty heights Michael wanted for me.

Besides, I still have time with Ash. My schedule is mostly empty for another week before pre-production starts for me. After that, a quick press tour for the premiere of *The Last Best Man* will take me out of town for a little over a week. Then filming begins. We'll still be fake dating, so I'll still get to see her. Just not as much as I'd like.

It has to be enough.

Ashley's eyes go wide as the house comes into view.

"Holy shit," she says.

The Moorish-style mansion glitters in the dark, palm trees lit from below in the courtyard, the long pool glimmering to our right through the trees as we drive in.

Ostentatious in its simplicity, there's something beautiful but haughty about it. A home for Hollywood royalty, for gods of the screen. Fit for Michael Sinclair, but this house has never felt like home to me. I haven't earned it yet. Something I'm acutely aware of when I look up at it.

"It was Michael's," I say, slowing for the garage door. "He built it years ago. Left it to me when he died."

When I came out to LA to pursue a career in acting, Michael insisted I take the guest house, and while I was welcomed into the main house anytime, I was young and valued my sudden independence. Not that Michael let me stray too far from his vision for me. LA parties were off-limits unless he or a chaperone came along to one deemed an appropriate networking opportunity.

Michael didn't believe in active nepotism. I had to rise on my own merits. Not that the Sinclair name didn't open doors for me, or living in this house and meeting people Michael knew didn't help me in any way. It gave me a considerable boost, but I still worked hard to get where I am.

I grab a couple of our bags and Ash slips her hand into mine as we go inside.

The interior is all smooth, crisp white walls with tasteful contemporary artwork in shades of blue and copper. Rugs with simple patterns in blues and whites. Wood floors, delicate wrought iron rails with filigrees, and arches everywhere. Cora's light touch in a couple of places, but mostly, this house was Michael. Large enough to hold secrets, like the occasional visits of a "family friend."

We leave our stuff in my bedroom and Ash stares out the massive window at the Pacific for a few minutes.

"It's beautiful." Her voice is soft and dreamy.

It is. Ash standing in my bedroom in my T-shirt is even more beautiful. I go to her, wrap my arms around her, and kiss her because I want to and I can and one day I won't be able to. It's bittersweet. "There's ice cream in the freezer," I whisper against her lips and she smiles.

We go down to the kitchen and I sit her on the island and pull out the ice cream. I stand between her legs because I need to touch her and we feed each other spoonfuls until we end up kissing again, ice cream forgotten.

A loud, sudden clatter from the doorway makes Ash scream. I jump.

David's travel mug rolls on the floor as he stares at us, his jaw on the ground. Shit. I forgot about him.

"David lives in the guest house," I say to Ash, who's clutching her chest. I turn to David with a stern look. "And from now on, he'll text or knock."

He nods and quickly picks up his mug. "I'll clean this up and go. Sorry."

Reluctantly, I leave my spot between Ash's knees and pull out some paper towels, tossing them to him.

"I thought you might want to go over your schedule," he says, his ears red.

He emailed it to me and there's nothing about it that needs going over. He's here to ask me how things went on the road, and I guess now he knows.

Ashley slides off the counter and puts the ice cream in the freezer. "I'm going to get ready for bed," she says.

I nod and lean against the counter, watching her walk out the door. Still in my T-shirt.

"What the hell happened?" David asks in a quiet voice, his eyes so wide I'm a little concerned. "You and *Ashley Foley*?"

"Me and Ash," I say firmly.

He stares at me, aghast. "She's using you."

"And I'm using her. That's what a fake relationship is."

"That didn't look fake." He rubs his eyes like he can erase the image of us making out. He should be grateful we were just making out.

I shrug. "It's not anyone's business."

"Right. Because in no way is this going to come back to hurt you."

"I can handle it."

"Christ, Gabe—"

"It's my personal life," I say, gripping the counter lip. "Not your business."

"I've known you for years," he says, shaking his head like he can't believe this is happening. "You never take this kind of risk. This is all my fault. I shouldn't have sent you those questions. They're too powerful."

Maybe I'm too tired, but that makes me laugh. "You did all you could."

David sighs in defeat. "At least tell me this is just a physical relationship. Neither of you is emotionally invested. And please, dear god, tell me you're using protection."

"Of course." Guess the broken condom dispenser story hasn't made it out of the backwaters. "And we're both walking away as planned when we hit the end date." I don't want to talk about this anymore. "So...my schedule."

There are a few changes, although none I needed to be made aware of tonight. We talk for twenty minutes anyway as he catches me up on all the emails I haven't read, and when he leaves, he promises to knock.

Ashley's already in bed, wearing only my T-shirt. I climb in next to her, cuddle her close, and fall asleep holding her tight. Feeling like I've found my home.

Chapter Twenty-One

Ashley

I wake up on my stomach, with Gabe's heavy arm draped across my back, his leg over mine, pinning me down. He's like a weighted blanket. I'm more rested after a few nights under him than I've been in ages. It seems like he enjoys sleeping draped over me too.

"Morning, gorgeous," he whispers in my ear. The brush of his stubble across my shoulder is delicious and I make a contented little noise into my pillow. His lips find my spine and he kisses every bump on the way down before rolling me and spreading me wide.

My fake boyfriend is an oral sex god and I'm smug as hell right now. When he rolls a condom onto that gloriously thick dick and pushes it into me, I want to brag to the world that he's mine. He flips us and I ride him until we're both sweaty and breathless.

Gabe makes us breakfast and we agree to meet by the pool after we call our respective agents. He disappears into his office while I pace around his bedroom, waiting for Neve to call me back.

She does, ten minutes later, informing me nothing's changed. There's still no work, but I'm welcome to go to any open casting call. She's in talks with a fashion brand over a possible endorsement deal, but she won't tell me anything so my guess is it's small.

"The photos from the school fair in New Mexico were great. More of that, fewer references to oral sex on the hood of his car," Neve says dryly before she ends the call.

Quick lunch stop. That was all Gabe's doing, not mine. Not that anyone would believe it.

It's only been two weeks. Not enough time to turn my reputation around. I don't know if the ten weeks we have left will do it, but I want as much time as I can get with Gabe. I'll deal with my career later.

My phone chimes with another message and I take a quick look.

Shit. The reprieve from my parents' distorted version of love is over. They broke up.

Messages flood in. My mother is distraught—my father is the love of her life, how could he leave her for some French socialite? Probably, I want to type back, the same way she left him for a concert pianist six months ago.

Dad flew me to Europe for Christmas, just after she left, for a ski holiday with his twenty-two-year-old Swiss girlfriend. The whole point was so I'd video call my mother to complain while they made out in the background. Oh, and I had to compare the girlfriend to a younger, prettier version of my mother's sister.

It worked. My mother flew over, they fought, then they got back together and took off for Bali. Not before I stole my father's girlfriend though. Checking that box off my list was fun. I've already stolen two of my mother's boyfriends.

That was the whole reason I missed my shot at Nic over Christmas. Although I'm happy with how things have turned out.

My mother's texts continue. Has he reached out to me yet? Have I spoken to him? Can I call him, and let him know that she's miserable and so close to doing something they'll both regret?

It's never just "tell your father" with her though. She'll want me to comfort her, to help her with her schemes. To use me to inflict whatever emotional damage she can on him.

And he's worse. He'll take it, laugh it off, convince me she's using me (to be fair, she is), but that he's the one who really loves me. He'll give me a car or jewelry and send me back to her, where I'll discover that he gave me the things he promised her. That he's better at using me than she is.

The bribe comes in her next message: a trip to Italy and a stay at a villa in Portofino.

I used to take those bribes, milk every breakup for what I could get, and convert what I could into cash to stash for the fallow periods when they'd inevitably get together again and forget about me.

But lately, or maybe since *Love on the Line*, I don't want to deal with my parents. These texts from my mother are exhausting and relentless, little hooks trying to pull me into a life I can't escape and all at once I'm sad. Angry, too, at the person they helped make me.

I don't know if there's a way out, but right now, Gabe is waiting for me by the pool and he cares more about me than what I can do for him. I turn off my phone and slip into my white bikini, thinking of what he did with it in the shower. The fabric feels alive against my skin as I walk through his house and out to the pool.

Gabe is already in the water, swimming laps in those blue trunks. He must be watching for me, because the moment I step onto the sun-warmed stone pavers, he comes for me. I'm powerless to move as I watch him emerge, water sluicing off the hard planes of his body. I forget everything—my job situation, my parents, all of it. His eyes are locked on me and I have no clue what he's going to do when he reaches me and it sends a thrill zipping over my body.

He climbs the steps and in two long strides, he has one dripping hand at the back of my neck and the other on my ass, holding me tight to him. He's wet and cold, but when he kisses me, his mouth is hot.

"You're going to kill me," he murmurs, his hand slipping under the thin strip of fabric between my ass cheeks.

I rub my hips against his. "Remembering how this bikini felt wrapped around your dick?"

"Christ, Ash." Gabe scoops me up, turns, and carries me into the pool. His mouth finds mine again as he carries me out deeper.

My heart is pounding as the water reaches my feet, then calves, the jolt of cold turning refreshingly cool as it closes over my ass, then knees, then my stomach. He sets me down, and the water reaches up to my nipples, which his knuckles brush over.

A little shiver races down my spine at the sensation.

"Ready for your first lesson?"

I laugh, taken aback. "You're going to teach me how to swim?"

"More like how not to drown," he says, his eyes still on his hands as he toys with my bikini top before leaning down to kiss me.

Eventually, we stop kissing and move to waist-deep water, and Gabe teaches me to float on my back. It takes a while. I trust him with my body but I don't trust that I can float, so I rocket to my feet, screaming and flailing, the moment his hands leave me.

He's patient, though, lying me back on the top of the water, one hand supporting me between my shoulders, the other skating from my collarbone to navel before sliding underwater to cup my ass so I can bring my legs up. "That's it. Relax," he says softly. "Arch your back a bit more...there. I've got you."

I blow out a deep breath and this time, when his hands ease off my body, I stay perfectly still. I don't sink.

"I'm doing it," I whisper in awe. "I'm floating."

"Yeah, baby. You are."

The pride in his voice warms me, and I smile.

"Doggy paddle next," he says.

I whip my head up, flail until my feet touch the bottom, and stand. "Doggy style?" I ask innocently.

Gabe growls and tackles me and I shriek, but he's careful with me. He doesn't dunk me or pull me under or even splash me. My legs end up wrapped around him and I cling to his neck as he walks us into deeper water. He's already hard and I take advantage, rocking my hips against him.

"You can still touch the bottom," he says into my ear, but he pulls my hips tight and I don't care if I can, as long as he's got me. "Go on," he whispers in my ear. "I think you've earned a reward. Use me to get off."

His name is on my lips, coming off on a breathy little laugh as I grind against him. His hands slide to my waist and he holds me. I've never felt safer than when I'm in his hands. My nipples press against his chest, the fabric of my bikini rubbing deliciously between us, and this right here, is what I want. Midmorning orgasms with Gabe, in his pool under the hot California sun. Just the two of us in this beautiful place.

He breaks off the kiss, holding me tighter, thrusting against me as I continue to rock into him. One arm bands around me, his other hand sliding between us to grab my breast. He shoves it up and I lean back, supported by his arm, still holding his neck, and his hot mouth closes around my nipple through the thin fabric. He squeezes and sucks and thrusts against me as I grind against his cock and I shatter with a gasp, pushing myself into him because nothing has ever felt as good as Gabriel Sinclair, hard against my body. Except maybe Gabriel Sinclair, hard inside my body.

I collapse forward, onto his shoulder, biting into solid muscle because god-dammit, I'm never going to feel like this with anyone else, ever, and I want to leave a mark on him too. He growls and carries me through the water to the shallows where it's waist-deep, setting me against the edge of the pool.

In a heartbeat, he has my bikini top off. It slaps against the water somewhere behind him as his eyes drink me in. Two fingers land on my shoulder, lightly pushing, and I sink against the wall, watching him because I love the way he watches me.

"There," he says when I've lowered myself enough that the water laps at my collarbone. "Push them together."

I don't need to ask. While he frees his dick from his swim trunks, I cup my tits, lifting and squishing them. He steps closer, straddling me as I crouch, tilting my chin up with two fingers, his other hand stroking his length under the water. "Is this okay? Would you be more comfortable out of the water?"

"This is perfect."

"Tell me if that changes."

It won't unless he shoves me under in his haste to get off, but Gabe would never. I'm safe with him.

As soon as he slides his cock between my tits, his large hands go to the edge of the pool, gripping tight as he tests me with a long, slow thrust. I watch as he does it again, and again a little faster, a little harder, pushing me against the pool wall. The sight of him smothered in my cleavage is hot, even distorted by the rippling water. His abs contract in front of me, water droplets glistening off his chest, falling like rain as he leans over me. I want my hands free to touch him, or maybe myself, but I can't let go. I settle for kissing his abs, trailing my tongue along the salty grooves.

He murmurs my name and within a minute he's gasping it as he comes hot against my chilled skin. When he's finished, he rinses me off in the pool and swims away to retrieve my top, helping me put it back on.

We spend a few minutes kissing and laughing before he teaches me how to tread water. It's easier than floating, possibly because I can keep my head out of the water. When I've had enough, we climb out and spend the next hour dozing in a massive sun lounger.

I don't know what we've done to each other, but he's not the same person he was in New York. I'm not either.

This is a highlights reel I want to replay.

We have lunch on a shaded patio overlooking the Pacific. Salads, because Gabe's diet is strictly controlled from now until filming wraps. We take a few photos and post one on my social media—our lunch, the ocean in the background, our joined hands in the foreground.

"What did your agent have to say?" he asks after a few minutes of peaceful silence.

I pull my eyes away from the ocean, frowning at my salad. "Nothing much. Yours?"

His brows knit as his eyes drift to the ocean. He shrugs. "A couple of scripts to look over. The usual."

"Oh." The guilt in those two words, *the usual*, tells me fake dating is working out better for him than it is for me. Somehow, that's not surprising.

Gabe hesitates. "Maybe I could—"

Whatever he's about to offer me, I don't want it. Not like this, not from him. Time to change the subject. "My parents broke up. My mom left about a hundred messages on my phone." She's stopped, for now. She'll start calling sometime today, I'd wager.

"Does she even know where you are?" he asks harshly.

I laugh. When I told him about my parents, I spoke about my childhood, not about the situation these days. The only thing that's changed is that I'm no longer an innocent pawn.

"I'm serious. They weren't at the wedding, were they?"

"No, there's bad blood between them and my aunt and uncle." Guilt coils in my gut at the role I played, and I let out a breath to ease the discomfort.

"Did they call you after we were photographed together?"

I laugh again. I don't know why I keep laughing like something about the sound turns this into a harmless little nothing. Another piece of armor I wear to remind the world I'm in control. I can't be hurt because I don't care and in that lies power. "No, they were still together, so they didn't need me." If they even saw the photo or any tabloids or clickbait or trending social media topics. "My parents are selfish, narcissistic assholes. Explains a lot about the way I am," I add as a joke, trying to lighten the mood. My parents are a deadweight to any conversation.

Gabe puts his hand on my leg, halfway up my thigh. "You're not that bad." He says it in a light tone with a flirty smile, and I hear the words underneath. I'm not bad at all.

I want to believe him.

We continue eating lunch and he takes control of the conversation, doing his best to make me laugh with stories about Kate Van Sandt on the set of *The Last Best Man*, which is out soon. She's America's Sweetheart, a cross between a young Julia Roberts and Taylor Swift, and apparently, her life is full of magical stories about growing up on a farm.

My phone, sitting on the table and turned on, rings. My mother's name flashes across the screen. I'm about to send it to voice mail when Gabe grabs my hand. "Answer it."

"I'd rather not."

"Is she going to keep calling until she gets to you?"

"Yeah."

"Answer and put it on speaker."

Fine. I'm not embarrassed by my mother and maybe she'll leave me alone if I give her a little sympathy.

Yeah right.

Well-practiced sobs fill the room when I accept the call and I try not to roll my eyes. She's good at crying on demand. I can picture her, cocktail in hand, waiting for me to pick up before transforming herself into Sad Mom.

The sobs are artfully spaced around her list of grievances and for a long time, I don't have to say a word—she can carry this part without any encouragement. I watch Gabe instead. He appears torn between fascination and anger.

"You never called me back," she finally accuses, the sobs tapering off. Here we go, the part where I'll be rewarded for playing dutiful daughter or punished if I ignore her. "Answering my messages is the least you could do after you took your father's side at Christmas. Honestly, Ashley—"

I took his girlfriend, not his side, but history is what she says it is. We aren't even to my cue yet, where I'm supposed to apologize and beg for her forgiveness and ask what I can do so she knows I love her, but Gabe clears his throat.

"Ashley is busy with her own life," he says smoothly, firmly. "You'll have to handle this personal problem yourself. If you keep bothering her, she'll block you."

My mother gasps. "She would never!"

"Then I will for her." He ends the call and leans back in his chair, his eyes on me. "I will. If you want me to."

For a long minute, I stare at the phone, waiting for her to call and demand to talk to me. For her to text me. For her rage and tears to come.

Nothing happens.

I laugh a little and finally look up at Gabe. "Thank you." If I'd known it would be this easy, I'd have done this years ago. A little voice inside me points out that I'll pay for this later because nothing is ever easy, but right now, I don't care.

Gabe doesn't laugh or even smile. His eyes are dark as a storm and when he speaks his voice cracks like thunder. "When she comes back, don't let her in. Not if she's going to use you. Okay? You deserve better, especially from someone who claims to love you."

I don't know what to say, so I stand and wrap my arms around his neck. He tugs me onto his lap and holds me tight. It would be amazing to be someone loved by Gabe. He's protective and loyal. Unafraid to do the right thing, when the right thing is hard. Not that I need any of those things in my life, but...it would be nice.

In the afternoon, we go to an animal shelter for an adoption drive. This is something Gabe arranged for my benefit, I think. He probably figured out fake dating him hasn't been enough to turn my reputation around yet.

Now, more than ever, I need this to work. As much as I hate my parents using me, the money I get from their bribes goes a long way toward supporting me. It's an unpredictable but frequent source of income and I'm walking away from it.

We stop by my house so I can pick up a few things, then head back to Malibu. Gabe gets a call almost immediately and disappears into his office. I pour a glass of wine and step outside to enjoy the cool ocean breeze.

My phone dings.

It'll be my mother. Or maybe my father. I don't want to look, but if I don't, it's going to eat away at me.

It's neither.

> Hi Ashley! Thanks for coming to my wedding. And for texting me—I'd love to catch up. I'm in LA for a few days visiting Lauren—she's living in Timbo's old place. Why don't you stop by?

Jessie

I sink onto the nearest chair, the sudden shock of shame and guilt too much. Fuck.

What do I do? I have zero interest in trying to seduce her husband. I don't even want to see him. I don't want to see her, either, since guilt has become an emotion I feel.

Dammit.

I rub my forehead and try to think. Jessie was hot and cold with me when I was a kid. Sometimes, I was her confidant. Other times, I was invisible to her.

Probably she was living her own life like any other teenager.

As adults, we've hardly seen each other.

Maybe I should try. Forging ties with Jessie will make it easier not to backslide into my mother's clutches, and it would be nice to have some family. I always envied what my cousins had.

After another moment of staring at the ocean, I text back that I'd love to meet up.

CHAPTER TWENTY-TWO

Gabe

I FLIP THE PAGE and take a drink of my cold coffee. The actor who plays the villain in Warwick reads his line and the director stops him with a suggestion. There's a pause while notes are scribbled on multiple scripts. He reads the line again.

I left Ash asleep in my bed, with a soft kiss and a promise I'd see her later. She's been staying with me in Malibu for the last week, but now that my schedule's packed, she's heading back to her place. It's nearly noon. She's probably left already. David was supposed to make sure a car was available to take her home.

My thoughts drift to what she's doing now. Maybe she's lying naked in her bed, surrounded by ten million tasseled throw pillows, thinking about me.

Everyone turns a page and I turn mine a second late. Shit, I need to focus.

This last week has been…

Not sure I have words for it, yet. Just this feeling in my chest, uncomfortable because it's new. It feels deep, though, like it won't be easily dislodged when the time comes.

I won't see her until tonight—we have a public date arranged—but I'm already thinking about her smile, the scent of her skin, and the sound of her laugh. If I could stop there, it might be fine, but I'm remembering the feel of her body beneath mine, the tight, hot grip of her…

My costar Greta's foot presses softly against mine and the room full of people staring at me jolts into focus. My brain spins, panic shocking my heart into a rapid thudding rhythm as I find my line and read it. Fuck, I hope I'm not on the wrong page.

The director is studying me when I finish, maybe thinking I'm more hype than I'm worth. If recasting would be worth the trouble.

I need to salvage this. Make it seem I was thinking about the script and not daydreaming. I clear my throat. "I think—"

"Right. That line's not working," the director interrupts. "Take it out. Let's go back to Greta's last line."

For the rest of the read-through, I'm attentive, tapping my pen on every line as they're read aloud. I get pages worth of notes from the director, who wants me and Greta back tomorrow to go through some changes he wants in one particular scene.

"Don't worry," Greta says as we're leaving. "Nic was a million times worse at read-throughs."

I can't manage more than a weak grin. I need to focus and I don't care if my worst is better than Nic's best. There are people in this room I need to impress with my professionalism and losing myself to daydreams isn't the way to do it.

Walking into Michael's house, I can feel the disappointment in myself through his lens, magnifying my own. Michael Sinclair's nephew does not zone out at read-throughs because he's thinking about the woman he's sleeping with. I'm not some hormonal teenager who can't compartmentalize this shit.

David's in my kitchen and I walk straight past him to the fridge and pull out a beer. He glances at the bottle but doesn't acknowledge my breach of studio-sanctioned diet. "How'd it go?" he asks.

I take a long drink before I answer. "Not great."

His expression shifts to one of concern. "What happened?"

Ashley Foley happened. I stare out my kitchen window at the lush foliage and the Pacific beyond. It's a beautiful, calm evening, the sun on its way down. "I couldn't concentrate." I set my bottle on the counter with a sigh. I'm supposed to meet Ashley for dinner in an hour and a half, but I need to spend time with my script. "Cancel my reservations for tonight."

She's probably all dressed and ready to go. I bet she looks amazing. If I hadn't fucked up today, I'd be seeing her soon. We'd have dinner so we could be photographed together, but then we'd come back here. I need her. To see her, touch her. Make her scream my name.

"Anything else?" David asks.

I push myself off the counter and turn around, rubbing my eyes as I turn away from the brightly sinking sun to my unlit kitchen. "Send her some flowers? Reds and pinks. Expensive."

"On it. Want me to read through your lines with you?"

I shake my head. Having David here might help me focus, but I want to be alone. "Take the night off. Go out and have some fun." One of us should.

David snorts and heads for the door, phone in hand, as he navigates a florist's website. He pauses in the doorway. "For what it's worth, I think getting some distance will help with your concentration problem. This role...it's huge for your career. This is going to show the world you can be more than just the good guy."

I grit my teeth but nod. He's right.

"Your obligations consist of a public appearance once a week. I can book a hotel downtown for your use when you need to...um..." he makes a feeble hand gesture that I guess means *have sex*.

"No thanks." Things would be easier if it was just sex, but it's not. I want more than a quick and dirty hookup in some hotel once a week. I want her in my life.

David leaves and I pull out my phone. I owe her a call, but I can't bring myself to press the button. If I talk to her, I'll want to know about her day. I'll tell her about mine. We'll spend at least an hour talking and I have a script to study.

A text is safer.

> Hey. Rough day today. Need to cancel dinner to work on the script. Raincheck?

I am an asshole. She deserves better than this. I'm about to call her when her text lands.

> No problem. Sorry your day sucked. Anything I can do?

Ash

Pretty sure her mouth could solve all of my problems right now. At least for a few blissful hours. But distraction won't make tomorrow go better.

> Nothing. I'll text you tomorrow.

ME

I type out *I miss you*. My thumb hovers over send, but I delete the three words instead and send a *good night*. Before she can send a reply, I drop my phone into a drawer in the kitchen. I make myself a cup of coffee, hunt down my reading glasses, and head up to Michael's office, script in hand.

This room, more than any other in the house, is where I feel him the most. A trio of Academy Awards sits on the shelf of a bookcase, alongside three Golden Globes and a framed photo of Michael and Cora on their wedding day. A handful of trinkets from travel and film blend carefully into the simple room.

I could always find him here, busy working. Usually sitting in his chair helps me tap into some of his focus, but I find my attention keeps wandering to Ashley, no matter how many times I try to pull it back to the pages in front of me.

Fake dating me isn't working for her. She hasn't said as much, but I could hear it in her tone when I asked if she had any new job opportunities. It's too soon, I think, to know if all the volunteer activities and charity work we've done over the last week will move the needle, but my guess is no. The only solution for Ashley is long-term, sustained change in the public eye. Even then, it might not be enough. The world is shit like that.

I flip a few more pages, skimming the script. Nothing surprising, nothing too difficult inside. There are a few places I read more closely, where I try the words out to see how they feel on my tongue. But my productivity is punctuated by long moments where my thoughts go to her.

When there's a knock at the door, I glance up, surprised to find it's after midnight. Ashley walks in and I do a double take, pushing my chair away from the desk as all my blood rushes straight to my cock.

She's wearing black lace lingerie, and had she been wearing this the night we'd met, my control would've snapped in half. The lace barely covers her nipples, the top looking ready to snap open. Lace wraps her neck. More straps hang from the garter belt accentuating her small waist and the full flare of her hips. Stockings cover her legs and she's wearing shiny black stilettos. Calling the thong she's wearing tiny would be generous. It's more like a thin strap barely covering her pussy.

Ash smiles as she steps between me and the desk, lifting herself to sit on the edge. One shoe finds a home on my chair next to my left thigh. The other next to my right thigh.

I yank my reading glasses off my face and toss them onto the far end of the desk. Doesn't matter how many times or how many ways I've had her pussy—seeing her like this, so shamelessly on display, turns me into an animal.

"I thought you could use a break," she says with a throaty laugh as my hands travel up those stocking-clad legs.

What comes out of my mouth sounds like me choking on the word break, but I'm already pushing her back on the desk and burying my face in her pussy. Her fingers thread through my hair, holding me to her.

"Tell me you weren't walking around LA in this," I growl against her.

"Only your house," she whispers, and fuck I like that. It's scandalous, in this house. On this desk. With the Oscars and the Golden Globes and Michael and his standards everywhere in this room.

Ash cries out my name and I draw her pleasure out as long as I can, but if I can't get my cock inside her, I'm going to explode.

She gasps when I lift her off the desk and spin her around. It turns to a moan when I press her down onto the smooth surface. My hands are shaking as I fumble for the condom in my pocket.

It's a pretty sight, Ash bent over the desk, her skin pale against the dark wood, my fingers wrapped around her thong, and my hard cock pressing between the cheeks of her round ass. So many times we've brought out the worst in each other. Sometimes the best. But something about this, about us...

This is temporary and there is no us, I remind myself as I pull the thong down her hips. Only this damned need.

The more we try to satisfy it, the stronger it grows, and I'm starting to wonder if I'll ever be satisfied. If Ash ever will.

It's hot and punishing, the way we fuck. But after, I carry her to my room and she lies her head on my shoulder and we talk about our day.

"I had a message from my dad," she says, softly. "Mom was so upset she ran directly to him. They're back together. Guess they don't need me to play their games—the idea of me is enough."

I kiss the top of her head as I pull her closer. "They don't deserve you."

"True," she agrees, her fingers tracing over my chest in a pattern I can't recognize. "But it's not always easy to believe, you know? I am what they made me."

I feel that deep into my soul. I'm what my dad made me, what Michael and Cora made me, and what I've made myself. All these parts of me, pieces from different puzzles that won't fit together, jostling for space.

"You're more," I tell Ash softly. "So much more than what they tried to make you into."

My problem, though, is the opposite. I'm so much less than Michael wanted me to be.

She plants an appreciative kiss on my chest. Her fingers continue to draw little circles and spirals over my skin as I breathe in the floral scent of her hair. I should be enjoying the feel of her soft, warm body against mine. I am, but my thoughts are chasing Michael, pulling me away.

"I stole a car when I was eleven." I don't know why I'm telling her this. It's not as bad as the stuff I told her on the road. It's just something that happened, something I did. A step in the life that would have been mine, if things had been different.

Her fingers stop moving. A beat later, she raises her head, looking at me in stunned disbelief.

I comb my fingers through her soft hair and continue anyway. "Drove it home. Parked it in the driveway. I wanted my dad to be proud. I wanted to help because things were getting tight."

Her fingers flatten over my chest and she rests her chin on the back of her hand, her tawny eyes searching mine. "Did you get in trouble?"

My lips quirk. "Yeah." Dad was pissed, worried I'd bring the cops to the house. He got rid of the car, which gave me time to get out of the house until he cooled down.

Ashley's silent, waiting for me to say more.

"Michael took me away from that life," I say eventually.

"And Cora," she adds.

"And Cora," I agree. "But Michael shaped me. Gave me his set of rules and standards and taught me to live like he did."

"Like a Boy Scout." Her smirk is playful, but her eyes are serious. I tug on a lock of her hair and she leans up and kisses me lightly, sweetly.

"He had an affair. Another family, with a son," I say. I shouldn't be telling her this. The only people who know are me and David, and Lilah, the woman he had the affair with. Even their son doesn't know. But telling Ashley lightens the load.

"Wow," Ash says softly. "Cora?"

"Doesn't know." Probably doesn't know. I can't imagine she knows.

"That sucks," she murmurs, resting her head back on my chest.

I stare at the ceiling. Her warm breath fans across my skin and after a few minutes, I sigh. "Michael wanted me to be this pillar of authenticity and goodness. But I'm playing a part, Ash. I've always been playing this part and I'm tired. How can I be what he wanted me to be when he couldn't even be that for himself?" There it is. The question I wanted to find on the open road before

Ashley took over my every thought.

"Because you were a boy who stole a car and whose dad went to prison?" Ash prompts.

My eyes close. "Yeah."

Ash is silent, and the moment stretches between us. I don't know what I'm waiting for her to say. If I want her to absolve me of my sins or tell me to reject the path I'm on or reassure me that I'm doing okay.

"I never knew Michael," she says slowly. "But I know you. And if Michael were alive today and he wasn't proud of the man you've become, then his opinion wouldn't be worth having."

Would he be proud? I have no idea. It always felt like a shifting goalpost, moving out of reach every time I got close.

Ashley climbs on top of me, leaning down so her lips brush mine. "Take it from the villain: you're the good guy, even if you have some nuance."

"You're no villain," I say as she kisses me. "You just like to pretend."

Chapter Twenty-Three

Ashley

"Good news!" my agent Neve chirps on the phone. "I've got something for you."

I freeze, my hand cupping a silky red rose from the bouquet Gabe sent after our canceled date—or had David send, judging by the formal brevity of the card. If I hadn't gotten what I wanted last night, I might be a bit pissed at getting flowers from his assistant, but they're big and beautiful and I left Gabe's house this morning with a smile on my face.

"What is it?" I ask Neve. I don't want to get my hopes up, but I need this to be something good.

"It's *Love on the Line Redemption*," she says brightly. "They're bringing back the notorious contestants, and you're in."

I bring the rose closer and inhale the sweet smell and try to temper my disappointment. "I'll pass."

"Are you sure?" She doesn't sound cheerful now. She sounds exhausted. "Contractually, you fulfilled your obligations. You don't have to take this, but there's nothing else."

"Maybe in another couple of months—"

"It was a long shot, putting you with Gabriel Sinclair, but I think the only way to ride on his coattails would be for him to put a ring on it and get you a job using his influence."

Shit. It's not a surprise though, now that I think about it.

"The endorsement deal with the fashion brand fell through. Your social media has been in a slump since *Love on the Line*. Maybe if you pick it back up, we can secure something..."

I'd been moderately successful as a social media influencer, but after *Love on the Line*, the usual trickle of hate turned into a flood. The gig lost all appeal.

"Are you sure you won't consider *Love on the Line*?" she asks after a moment of silence. "They want you pretty bad. I could negotiate for higher pay."

The pay sucked the first time and won't be much better a second time, and we both know it. "I'm not doing it."

"Okay," Neve says, sounding disappointed. "Call me if you change your mind."

I won't change my mind. I don't want to be everyone's villain anymore, and if I go back to *Love on the Line*, I'll have to be.

A knock sounds at my door, and I know it's not Gabe—he's still at work—but I still hope. And I'm disappointed.

"There's a dude in a gray car with a camera sitting across the street," Lea says when I let her inside.

I glance out the door, and sure enough, they've found me. He'll be here hoping to get a glimpse of Gabe.

Locking the door behind me, I lead Lea up to the kitchen.

"What have you been up to?" I ask, busying myself with making us coffees while she rifles through her messenger bag at the table.

She pauses so long that I stop what I'm doing and turn to look at her. She's staring at me, her expression flat. "You're kidding, right?"

Shit—what have I forgotten? Not her birthday, which was in March. "Uh, no. Haven't seen you or heard from you in a while."

"I was on the research trip *you* sent me on."

I frown. "That I sent you on?"

"You told me to find out everything I could about Gabriel Sinclair. So I did. I've been to New York. Oklahoma. New Mexico. I've researched his entire family tree. He was adopted by his aunt and uncle. His dad's dead, but I went to the graveyard. Mom's dead too. Died of a drug overdose twenty years ago. I have both obituaries. And get this: his name isn't even—"

"Wait, you did *all* this?" Documents, photos. Her handwritten notes are spread all over my table. "I meant like…Google stalk him for an hour."

She blinks at me. "But you could do that yourself."

Yeah. I really could've. I pinch the bridge of my nose while Lea's cup fills with coffee. "You couldn't tell Dominic Fontana from Gabriel Sinclair, but you put together this entire dossier on the man?"

Lea sighs in irritation. "They're tall, muscle-y white dudes with dark hair. They look the same. And this is research, not picking him out of a police lineup. It's easy."

"You should be a private investigator."

"Thinking about a career change," she says, sounding cheerful at the thought. "This was a lot of fun. All the expenses went on the card, of course, but I'll email you the itemized receipts."

Shit. I'm going to have to pay for this. I don't even want it.

"Is this everything?" I ask cautiously. "You don't have any other copies?"

Lea frowns. "No. Do you want me to make a copy?"

I shake my head and make a mental note to buy a cheap paper shredder. "You signed an NDA when I did. That covers everything you found on Gabe." It probably doesn't. I don't know shit about contracts. Lea could find out in two seconds.

She pauses, realization raising her eyebrows in surprise. "You like him."

"Yeah," I admit, looking at the flowers. "I do."

"Then anything I found on him is safe with me."

The relief I feel in that is huge. Lea is good on her word and can keep a secret—she's kept several of mine for years.

After she leaves, I gather up all her research and stuff it into a drawer on my desk. I'll deal with it later. Right now, I need to face Jessie.

I've been to Timothy's West Hollywood house once. My cousin and Nic have always been inseparable, so of course they've been roommates off and on for years. I learned from my past mistake, so the time I stopped by this house, I didn't try to sneak into Nic's bedroom. I knocked at the door. Unfortunately, my information was wrong—Nic was away filming on location, not Timothy.

My cousin made it very clear I wasn't good enough for his friend. He offered me money to stay away. I was young and a bit desperate, so I took it and promised twelve months.

Timothy called me when the twelve months were up. I demanded more. He paid. But I didn't try to avoid Nic. I went to parties and clubs, the places he sometimes went. Our paths crossed occasionally, but my flirting went over his head and he always slipped away. And when Nic married Addison, Timothy told me he was done paying me.

Unfortunately, Addison was a better protector of Nic's virtue than Timothy was. I couldn't get near him. The man went to work, then went home. Anytime he went anywhere else, Addison was on his arm. And she saw right through me.

Jessie isn't like Addison. "Nic is in New York," she mentions so casually I stumble on my way out to the patio by the pool, expecting her to be watching me and assessing what kind of threat I pose.

She's not, and neither is Lauren. We sit at a table in the shade and Lauren pours us all a glass of white wine. I don't know Lauren all that well—she's a few years younger than me, and while I've seen her at various Foley weddings and funerals, I've never spoken more than a few words to her. She always seemed shy, and a bit reserved. Her hair is a soft strawberry blonde and freckles dust her cheeks, but her blue eyes are friendly where in the past they've been cautious.

"So," Jessie says brightly. "Gabriel Sinclair?"

Are we about to have girl talk? I take a sip of the wine. "Yup."

Jessie rolls her eyes. "Come on. You hooked up at my wedding. I deserve some details."

Relief hits me like the first sip of wine, going straight to my head. She doesn't know I was there to seduce Nic. Neither does Lauren, judging by the way she eagerly leans forward.

For whatever reason, Timothy hasn't told his twin. A little voice in the back of my head urges me to tell her, to come clean and maybe this nauseous feeling in my stomach will go away.

I can't tell her. It's nice, drinking wine and talking. It starts awkward, but soon the three of us are talking like we've been friends forever. I'm not going to risk this by telling her the truth.

Maybe I'll get lucky and Timothy will keep his mouth shut and I can have some kind of friendship with Jessie. Lauren too. Her boyfriend, she informs me, is Gabe's personal trainer.

I feel nothing when Jessie talks about her honeymoon. The hardest part of this is the guilt I'm carrying, and while I'm not going to tell her I tried to seduce her husband, I can at least apologize for that other thing.

When Lauren gets up to grab some snacks, I turn to Jessie and drop my voice. "I'm sorry about what I did to your parents."

She waves it off. "I shouldn't have told you in the first place. Besides, it all worked out."

Her parents stayed together, the scandal blew over, and it was years ago, so I guess it makes sense that she'd be over it. I feel a little better, having apologized for my part in it, at least.

Lauren returns with a charcuterie board and asks about Love on the Line. I want to tell them the truth: Wendy and I are friends and I was often playing a part to win. But I don't know if they'd believe me. So I entertain them with gossip about the cast and my feud with Poppy.

We talk for hours and I'm tipsy by the time my rideshare shows up. Lauren and I make plans to go to lunch in a few weeks, and Jessie promises to keep in touch.

I spend the rest of the day watching the clock, counting down the hours until I can surprise Gabe at his house. The drive out to Malibu as the sun sets lifts my already high spirits, and when Gabe meets me in the driveway like he's been expecting me, pulling me into his arms for a blistering kiss, I might as well be flying.

"Let's go for a swim," he whispers.

"That's not what I'm here for," I tease, but he bites my lip and sweeps me into his arms. "I don't have a swimsuit," I protest when he carries me away from the glittering lights of the house and toward the softer lights of the pool.

"Good."

Contrary to that growl, he makes me swim. Not that what I'm doing can be called swimming, but at least I'm not drowning and he's as naked as I am.

I make it to the side of the pool without touching the bottom once. I'm smiling as I stand, turning to Gabe, the lights from the pool and the garden around it catching his every feature.

He's grinning at me, water beaded on his glorious body, and something about the warmth in his eyes fills me with lightness. Like I'm floating. He applauds and something happens inside me. It's warm and radiant and it's because of him.

I touch my fingers to my chest in surprise. What the hell?

It can't be. I crouch down so the water reaches up to my neck, cooling off my too-hot skin.

Gabe swims over, wrapping his arms around me and kissing me. "You did it."

"Yeah," I murmur, glancing down at our bodies in the water. I am naked but for once I feel it—vulnerable like he can see inside me, and it hits me like a wave.

I love him.

A giggle escapes my lips, and he kisses me again, oblivious to the fact that I might dissolve into bubbles right in front of him.

What the hell? How did this happen?

My heart thumps against my chest like it wants to leap from my body into his.

I'm in love with Gabriel Sinclair and I don't think this is going to end well for me.

Chapter Twenty-Four

Gabe

I've taken a pummeling all week. Workouts with my too-intense personal trainer, training with the stunt crew for the fight sequences, and stumbling through the script changes. But knowing Ashley will turn up at my house later, I'll teach her to swim and she'll read through my lines with me, and sometime around midnight we'll tumble into my bed, makes everything okay.

I'm feeling good when I leave Danny's Gym, despite the bruises and screaming muscles from hours of getting my ass kicked by the stunt crew. A car approaches, stopping in front of me, and I slow down.

The window rolls down and Rose's assistant Tomas leans out, calm and professional as my heartbeat spikes. If Tomas is here, something's wrong.

"The boss has been trying to call you," he says, completely unruffled. "Emergency meeting. Get in."

Shit. My phone is in my car. I debate grabbing it, but slide into his passenger seat instead. "What's up?"

"Sorry, you'll have to talk to Rose."

The A/C of his car makes my sweat-dampened skin go cold, goose bumps breaking out over my arms. This is bad. Recast bad.

Twenty-five tense, silent minutes later, Tomas parks outside the office of Dashcombe & Teale. I follow him inside, past the receptionist, to Rose's door. He opens it and gestures for me to step inside. Rose and Emma's hushed voices fall silent as they look up.

Tomas gives Rose a curt nod and disappears down the hall.

"Close the door," Rose says, getting up from her desk and walking over to the drinks cart. Emma once told me Rose keeps three beverages in her office at all times—water for everyday meetings, Champagne for celebrating the good news, and whiskey. The whiskey only comes out when her client is in deep shit.

Needless to say, I've never had whiskey in this office. So when Rose pours two glasses of the amber liquid and grabs a bottle of water for Emma, who doesn't drink, I know I'm fucked.

The door closes with a soft sound behind me.

I sink onto the leather chair next to Emma's. Rose hands me a whiskey, neat, and Emma a bottle of water, before she goes back around her desk and slowly takes a seat in her high-backed leather chair.

I take a sip of the whiskey and grimace. "On the scale of lost endorsement to getting fired from Warwick, what are we talking?"

"Oh, I don't know," Rose says in an icy tone. "Somewhere in the neighborhood of *sex tape*."

"What?" A loud laugh rips free. "Is this a joke?" I have never once taken an intimate video or even a photo. The closest I've come is the content Ashley and I posted on our road trip.

"Am I laughing?" Rose asks, arching an eyebrow.

Emma clears her throat. "You were seen on surveillance footage entering a gas station restroom with Ashley in some Oklahoma backwater, then exiting a short time later. The tabloids are all over it, along with pictures of a condom dispenser ripped off the wall."

My face goes hot and I rub the back of my neck. "Yeah, okay. It doesn't look good, but Ashley and I are supposed to be in this relationship, and the video of us going into and—"

"There's more," Rose says, pointing to my whiskey. "You may want to drink that about now."

More. How could there be *more*? Dutifully, I take another small drink.

"Some people," Rose continues, her calm tone not matching the fury in her eyes, "are perverts. The kind of perverts who hide cameras in public restrooms."

Oh fuck.

I fall back against my chair, but the sensation of plummeting doesn't stop, and I can see the yawning black chasm reaching up for me. Images flash—the way I ripped Ashley's dress, grabbed her tits, and fucked her against the wall, on the counter. Nothing about what we did in that restroom was soft or romantic. We didn't walk out holding hands. I don't think I even looked at her after.

"Deep breath, Gabe," Emma says softly, touching my arm briefly, arresting my freefall.

What have I done?

"Fuck," I whisper, tipping forward, my hands covering my face. One still holds the whiskey and after a moment's hesitation, I take a gulp.

"Lucky for you," Rose continues, "this pervert was more interested in catching people using the toilets than washing their hands. However, enough of you is in the frame to make it very clear what you were doing."

I scrub my hand over my face. "Can they prove it's us?"

"In conjunction with the surveillance video, yes," Rose says with a sigh. "From watching the act itself, it's murkier. The images aren't great and the audio is awful. Yes, I have watched it. Unfortunately, it's my job to see how badly my clients have fucked up."

"I'm sorry." I close my eyes and take a deep breath, trying to move past the crushing shame of knowing my publicist, who I've always had a professional relationship with, has seen me having sex. Aggressive, borderline rough sex. In a public restroom. And she's not the only one. That video will be online, circulating. Fans, directors, fellow actors...they're all going to see this. My hand clenches the whiskey glass. My other one balls into a fist. "What does this mean for my career?"

Emma turns in her seat, her dark brown eyes holding mine, her mouth twisted into something like wry amusement. "You're a white man riding your popular uncle's legacy, so a grainy sex tape with a woman you're in a committed relationship with isn't going to make you toxic. You have to do a lot worse for people to stop wanting you in their films. Hell, you'll probably get more of those nuanced, gritty roles you've been salivating over. It's possible you might lose an endorsement or a charity might drop you for a while, but as far as your career is concerned, this will blow over in a couple of months and you'll be fine."

"It's your image," Rose interjects. "You've always said it was important to you. Fake dating Ashley gave you a bit of an edge, but this takes away that golden sheen you like so much."

The door flies open and slams shut again, David falling against it, his chest heaving. "I got here as soon as I could."

"Help yourself to the whiskey," Rose says, waving her hand at the drink cart, "and take a seat."

David grabs a bottle of water from the mini-fridge and sits on the elegant sofa against the wall, a little apart. I can tell by his face and the way he avoids making eye contact with me that he knows. Worse, I'm pretty sure he's seen the video.

Rose turns back to me. "I need to know what Ashley has on you. Are there any more compromising videos or photos? Especially anything in high definition."

"No."

"Does she have anything on you? Anything at all that might be embarrassing if she sells her story about your relationship to the tabloids?" Rose taps her finger on her desk and gives me a pointed look when I don't answer. "This is why you don't sleep with fake girlfriends. You don't tell them your secrets. You behave professionally and treat them as coworkers."

"She signed an NDA," I protest. "We both did."

"Shameless people are dangerous," Rose adds. "They don't care. If she wants to sell you out, she'll do it. We can sue for violation of her NDA, she can tie us up in court for years, drag your name through the tabloids, and for what? What does Ashley Foley actually have? She'll hardly be worse off than she is now and you'll be in tatters. Your reputation is worth more than she is. She knows it. It's about time you knew it."

"I spoke to her agent before you arrived," Emma says quietly. "She's not getting any work. I don't know her financial situation, but if it comes down to paying her rent or selling you out, which do you think she'd choose?"

"She would never sell me out." She'd have no reason to. I have money. I can take care of her. But dread still curls up my throat. I've told her everything, bared my soul to her. If she wanted to, she could drag me through the mud several times over. She could drag Michael's affair into the open. Throw the spotlight on Lilah and her son. Cora too.

"Really?" Emma gives me a look like I should know better. "Have you watched her season of *Love on the Line*? Ashley Foley would sell her own mother to get ahead."

Pointing out that her mother would deserve it won't get me anywhere.

"You don't know her," I protest. "The way they edit those shows—"

"I know how they edit those shows," Emma says. "I've also read the post-season interviews with the cast and crew. She's the real deal."

"She's not like that."

Emma sighs. "Maybe she's not. But our job is to protect *you*, to look out for *your* interests, and if we assume the worst of her, we won't be blindsided. This isn't personal."

Rose leans back in her chair, eyes wide. "You like her."

I do, but I don't say it. I don't say anything. Like a coward, I stare at the wall.

When I turn back, Rose is giving me a careful look. "Do you want me to rehabilitate your image? Keeping in mind, at this stage, it isn't impacting your career in any measurable, negative way."

I'm already nodding. "Yes." I need to fix this. I can't leave Michael's legacy in tatters, and no future success of mine will mean anything if I can't back it up with a sterling reputation. I have to be better.

"Then you need to do as I say."

"Okay. What do I do?"

"Break up with Ashley," Rose says, but her tone softens a little. "Since you'll be breaking the contract, you'll have to pay her, but maybe the money will keep her quiet about your relationship for a while. Can you do that?"

Every part of me revolts at the idea and I'm scrambling, trying to find an excuse, any excuse. "But her career—?"

"Is dead in the water," Emma interrupts. "You can't help her by posting pictures of the two of you playing with puppies at an animal shelter."

Rose nods her agreement. "Ashley Foley, in my professional opinion, needs to disappear from the public eye, then come back with a new look and a reformed personality. But she's not getting any younger and you know how this industry is with women and age. A breakthrough probably isn't in her future. And with this sex tape..."

Fuck. Up until now, I haven't thought about how this sex tape is going to impact her career. Or her, personally. A ripple of nausea flows through me. No matter how hard I try, I'm not a good person. I'm the selfish, self-absorbed prick I've always pretended I'm not. "So I'm supposed to abandon her?" I ask weakly.

"As per the agreement you signed with her?" Rose says. "Yes."

My head is spinning. "What if she moved in or we got engaged? Could that work?"

Rose steeples her fingers and studies me for a long, uncomfortable moment. "Do you love her?"

My mouth opens, but no words come out. Do I love her? I'm happy when I'm with her, and not just when I'm inside her. I feel better when I can talk to her after a hard day. I've told her all my secrets.

But love?

I haven't let myself think those words yet, but I've felt it when she smiles at me. In the dark of night when I hold her close. Some part of me loves her, but I don't think it's enough.

"If you love her, it changes everything," Rose says with a sigh. "It ties my hands, and it ties you to her. Maybe you both have a happy ever after. But if things don't work out—the usual outcome of these fast celebrity marriages—then we'll have to deal with the fallout and that can be ugly. It will affect your image and it might affect your career, although your lawyers can protect you financially with a solid prenup."

I can't think of a future with Ash, not when I need to focus on my career. This role, the next, the one after. Until the nominations turn into awards. Until, when people mention me with my uncle, they refer to him as my uncle, instead of me as his nephew.

"I don't," I hear myself tell Rose, but I'm at a distance, lost in this future I'm chasing and wondering when I'll accomplish my goals. If I will ever feel like I have.

"Okay, good," Rose says, breathing out a sigh of relief. "You need to date someone else. Immediately. Someone big enough that Ashley becomes an interesting little bit of trivia in your life, rather than the headline. Do you want this?"

"Yes." I don't want this, but I'm taking it. Shame presses down on me. I don't want Ashley to be a footnote in my biography, but she'll have to understand. She can't be more, at least not right now. I drain the whiskey, setting my glass on my publicist's desk.

I think about Michael. About his secret family. He got to keep his reputation and Cora and his woman on the side. He was a success and people celebrate him and talk about him with shining love and admiration. The perfect role model and the man hiding behind that mask.

"Okay." Rose smiles for the first time. "We'll get you back to golden."

I've had about all I can take of this, short of firing everyone, so I get to my feet. "I need to talk to her before you put out that we've broken up."

"They haven't been seen in public together for the last week, right?" Rose asks David, instead of me.

"They haven't," he confirms. "No idea if she's been seen coming to his house every night."

"I'll have someone look into it," Rose says, making a quick note. "For now, we'll assume not. We're going to put the break up four days ago. Amicable split by mutual agreement, you are just too different, et cetera. Nothing to do with the sex tape, which was an unfortunate violation of your privacy as well as a violation of all the other victims of the pervert—who was caught, by the way, thanks to this blowing up. The statement goes out in two hours. Sound good?"

What choice do I have? I spent years holding back, forcing myself into this uncomfortable life, denying myself any chance for the kind of connection I have with Ash with anyone else, and I refuse to let it be for nothing. If there's even the chance I can get my image back, I'm taking it.

"Fine," I say tightly, turning to David. "Take me back to my car?"

He's already on his feet, capping his water bottle.

"You know the routine," Rose calls out. "No comment to the press. Let us handle it—we'll do what we can to get the video taken down from as many sites as possible. And I'll be in touch with Ashley to discuss payment over the broken contract and to let her know what we expect of her—if you have any influence over her, encourage her to go along with this."

I nod stiffly and follow David out of the building.

"It's for the best," David says as we climb into his car.

Doesn't mean I like it.

When David drops me at my car, I climb in and pull out my phone, ignoring the dozens of missed calls and messages from Ash. It isn't hard to find our scandal.

I stick earbuds in and spend the next few minutes watching myself fuck Ashley Foley.

Which Gabriel Sinclair am I? The man in the video, the man I've been telling myself I am, or someone else entirely? I don't know, but there's one thing I do know. I'm no better than Michael, and I'm about to prove it.

There's no one around, but I keep the windows up and the engine on, blasting the A/C as I call Ashley.

She answers immediately. "Gabe. Did you see? I am so sorry—how are you doing? Please tell me you're okay—"

Hearing her voice, even anxious and pleading, immediately calms me down. "I'm okay. You?"

"I'm fine."

She doesn't sound fine, but right now isn't the time to push.

"In a couple of hours, my team is going to issue a statement that we broke up a few days ago, amicable split due to differences, schedules—the usual bullshit. But I'm not done with us."

There's silence on the other end. She had to have seen the breakup coming. She knew this was about roughening the edges of my image, not about creating a whole new, darker one, but her silence feeds the worry returning to my stomach.

"Ash. I want to keep seeing you, but we'll have to keep it a secret."

"For how long?"

I give the steering wheel a hard tap with my clenched fist. "I honestly don't know. But we'd be together. I don't want to give you up."

"I don't want to give you up, either," she says, her voice shifting from soft to husky. "I can be your dirty little secret."

A smile finds its way to my lips and I sink into my seat. "I'm in my car outside Danny's Gym. If you start dirty talking, I'm hanging up on you."

Ashley laughs. "You wouldn't."

She's right. I'd let her talk while breaking every traffic law to get home so I could jerk off to her voice. Which wouldn't help my image right now. "Do you think you can come over tonight without being followed?"

"Mm. I have a few wigs. Maybe those glasses with the fake nose and mustache will help."

It's my turn to laugh. Not ten minutes ago, laughter was impossible. "Yes to the wigs, no to the fake mustache. Why don't you pack enough clothes for a few weeks and hide out at my house? Sound good?"

"As long as I have you."

"You have. But Ash, the only other person who can know about this is David. No one else, not my team, not Wendy, not Lea, okay?"

"Okay."

"I miss you."

"I miss you too." She hesitates. "It's not going to be forever, right?"

"No, baby. Not forever." The lie slips off my tongue way too easily.

Chapter Twenty-Five

Ashley

GABE'S NOT HOME. HE'S busy with work. I don't even know what he's doing today, or when he'll be back. I wander around his huge house feeling like the dirty little secret that I joked yesterday about.

It's not funny though. It feels like shit.

My phone dings.

> I'm so sorry, babe. Want to come over and get drunk? Burn his effigy?

WENDY

Our breakup was announced last night, so I've been expecting this text. Doesn't make it easier.

> Maybe next week.

ME

> Also—aww, baby's first sex tape!! How have you not done one before this?

WENDY

> I don't know, but I do not recommend it. That hidden camera was incredibly unflattering.

ME

Oddly enough, I don't give a fuck about the sex tape. At least the sex we were caught having wasn't the intimate, meaningful kind. I feel less violated, less exposed that way, and I refuse to feel small or shamed over sex.

There are better nudes of me out on the internet—ones I posed for—so I spend a few minutes redirecting my social media to those old links. Let the trolls salivate over that.

What I hate is what this has done to me and Gabe, hurting him and forcing us into secrecy. I can't even tell my secret best friend that I have a secret boyfriend.

I hate that I'm powerless to change any of this.

I love this man. I want to be with him and if this is the only way I can, I should be happy. I've never cared what I've had to do to get what I want, and really, what is he asking me to do? Stay in his palatial mansion so we can spend time together? It's not a hardship, so it shouldn't feel like one.

But it does.

God, who am I? I don't recognize this Ashley Foley, moping around because a man asked her to stay a secret. I've been people's secrets before and it never once bothered me. Am I growing some kind of conscience? Some morals?

That might be going too far. But something has changed and I'm unbalanced and uncomfortable in my skin. This feels wrong.

I want all of him, his public and his private life. I can't change who I am or what I've done in the past, but he could stand by me.

Over a few long, solitary hours, it occurs to me that if he loved me, he'd choose to be with me publicly, regardless of what people think.

Unless he loved me but sacrificed us for this ridiculous notion of perfection he's chasing. That's too tragic to think about.

My phone dings again.

> I'm so sorry, Ashley. How are you holding up? If you want to get out of LA for a while, you can come to stay with us.

JESSIE

Hanging out with Jessie and Nic in their happy home would be the last thing I'd want, were I sitting around brokenhearted. But it's nice of her to offer.

> Thanks, but I'm fine. I need to concentrate on finding some work.

ME

Gabe said this isn't forever, I try to console myself. Just for a while, until things settle down.

Or, it will slide into forever without either of us noticing, because Gabe's goal will keep shifting farther out of reach and he'll never let us be more than this.

Another ding from my phone. Christ, this is exhausting.

> Hey. How are you? Do you need anything? I went to your house, but you aren't home.

LEA

I call Lea back because Gabe isn't the only one who dumped me. My agent cut me loose by email this morning. It doesn't hurt as much as I'd expect. It's freeing.

Given the money I'll get from Gabe breaking the fake dating agreement, I can keep Lea employed for a few months, but she'll need to start looking for a new job. She takes it well. She's more concerned about my heartbreak and what I want to do for revenge.

"No revenge," I say.

"We have that dossier," she points out. "It would be easy if he's so squeamish about his reputation. He was practically a juvenile delinquent."

Shit. I forgot to shred that. It's still in a drawer in my desk. "We signed NDAs, Lea. He'd sue us into oblivion." Also, I'd never betray his trust, but Lea doesn't need to know how deep I am in this man. "I think the best revenge is to go out looking hot as hell. Which I'll do soon. I promise."

A part of me does want to go out and show him what he could have if he'd get over himself, but the part of me that loves him is too hungry for the time we have together to waste a single hour.

Lea makes me promise to call her if I need anything.

Since I have nothing to do, I spend the day thinking about what I want. I don't feel like updating my headshots and standing around all day trying to get cast as Blonde Victim Number Two in slasher flicks. I don't want to be in front of the camera at all.

Maybe what I want is to be behind the scenes, controlling the narrative. Picking the stories that get told. Shaping them. I don't have the kind of money to produce films, but I'm pretty good at helping other people spend theirs when I want to be.

It's an idea, anyway.

When Gabe comes home late in the evening, all the bad feelings of the day go up in smoke because his arms are around me and his lips are on mine. They come back the next day when I wake up and he's gone. I stay because I want to see him. Because soon he'll be leaving for a brief press junket ahead of his rom-com release and after that, he'll dive straight into filming Warwick. He'll be busier than he is now. I don't want to miss a moment since I'll be missing so many.

Watching Gabe dress for a formal charity event is the worst torture. Lying on his bed, still a bit sore from how hard he railed me thirty minutes ago, I drink in the sight of him buttoning his white dress shirt, missing him already. I got an hour of his time today and I'm starving for more.

I'd murder someone to accompany him tonight. It's not even putting on a pretty dress and going out. It's him. I just want to be next to him.

He's relaxed and at ease, everything I'm not, as he swiftly ties his tie, slips into the black suit coat, and does a little turn for me.

"Very sexy. Come back to bed and play with me," I say. We both know he won't.

"I can't," he says, though he genuinely sounds like he wants to.

But he'd never.

I leave him with a blistering kiss, and suddenly the next four or five hours loom long and dark.

There's a bottle of white wine in the fridge, so I take it up to the master bath, downing a glass while the tub fills. Then I soak, scrolling social media on my phone, trying to relax.

My arch-nemesis from *Love on the Line* has been busy. Poppy has tagged me in several social media posts over the last week, calling me trash for having sex in a public restroom. She's relentless. I've been trying to ignore her, but fuck it. Let's go, bitch.

I haul myself out of the tub to put a touch of lipstick on. I debate a smoky eye but opt to go natural.

I have to refill the tub a bit and tip more bubble bath in. The lights are too dim, so I turn them up a little, then climb back into the bath. There's nothing about the white tile wall behind me to indicate I'm at Gabe's house, but I still double-check, carefully framing myself so it's obvious I'm luxuriating in a huge tub somewhere fancy. My white blonde hair is piled on top of my head and my cheeks are naturally pink from the heat of the water. My favorite filter smooths out my skin. I'm so ready for this fight.

The video I send out is short and quick, as I smugly call Poppy out by name and mention I know what she offered to do to Luca. In the kitchen of a swanky

Italian restaurant, no less. "Talk about adding something to the Carbonara," I say behind my sudsy hand.

As usual, I get an avalanche of hate. There are a few people on my side, mostly shit posters who enjoy trolling my haters.

Poppy responds with a photo. It's Gabe and Kate Van Sandt—the actress who starred opposite him in his last film, the rom-com that releases soon—looking cozy at the charity event.

Ashley Who? Poppy says. I can imagine her smug smile as she flips her long, dark brown hair over her shoulder.

I drop my phone onto my towel and slide deeper into my bath.

He warned me his team was looking for his next fake girlfriend, but the idea that Kate Van Sandt, America's Sweetheart, would be in the market for a fake boyfriend is ludicrous. Not only that, but her reputation is pristine, and I thought his people wanted to give him a little bad boy flair. Guess getting caught having sex in a public restroom took him too far over to the dark side.

I bite my lip and scoop up a handful of the rapidly disintegrating bubbles, letting them drop back into the water.

He should have told me it was Kate. On paper, they're perfect for each other. As sickeningly sweet as the trailer for their romantic comedy suggests. In reality—I don't know. I don't think Kate's the type Gabe wants. I'm confident their fake relationship will stay fake, but I don't like it.

If he were any other man, I'd post a photo of myself that would make it damn clear that I'm the one in his house, waiting for him to come home. I'm the one he fucked hours ago and will fuck again tonight. I'd knock out Poppy and Kate in one blow.

"You're lucky I love you, Gabriel Sinclair," I whisper into the bubbles. It makes me feel better. A little more like some internet revenge is something I'm still capable of. Like I'm choosing to set down my sword because I love him instead of laying it down because I can't pick it up anymore.

Chapter Twenty-Six

Ashley

"I can't meet you at a hotel," Gabe says three days later in a gentle but firm tone. "We can't be seen together."

I sigh, peeking out from my curtains. I'm back at my house. Another day alone in his mansion and I'd have lost my mind, but now I have regrets. His press junket kicked off yesterday here in LA and he's off to New York tomorrow to promote his new movie with his new fake girlfriend. Then London and Tokyo. I miss him.

From my window, I can see the two cars that don't belong parked across the street.

I was spotted in Malibu. Thankfully, not in the act of leaving Gabe's gated neighborhood. Someone snapped me at a Malibu gas station at eight a.m. because I'd forgotten, in my haste to get to Gabe last week, to fill the tank. Before I made it out of his driveway, the light had come on. I didn't have a choice.

It was enough. Just a whiff that something might still be going on with me and Gabe when he's become even more publicly linked with Kate Van Sandt, and now we're being watched. Closely.

I let the curtains flutter closed. "You can't come to my house, I can't come to yours, we can't go to a hotel...I want to see you before you leave."

"I want to see you too."

"Do you?" I ask. Sleeping without him is impossible and the bags under my eyes have their own bags. I miss him so much and this is ridiculous.

"You know I want to see you." He sounds irritated. He's been so busy we've barely spoken since I left his house.

I sigh into the phone because I'm being a selfish, petulant child about this. I need physical reassurance, not empty words and promises about *one day* and *after the press junket is over.* "Then why can't we check into some hotel under an alias? Have David book the room and bribe someone to sneak us in—separately."

"Ash, they're following me. I can't shake these guys, not when they're trying to get photos of me and Kate."

I can't hide the rising panic in my voice. "Seriously, we can't see each other before you leave?"

"Time will fly," he promises.

I look around my darkened room and recognize that as a lie. Time will fly for him—he has a pretty woman smiling at him while he promotes a highly anticipated rom-com. For me? I have nothing. I can't even go on social media without seeing Poppy gloat over my breakup.

"We can video call every night," he says, and I'm sure he's trying to assuage me with that seductive voice and the promise of dirty talk, but I'm not in the mood. It's another lie anyway. After hours of promoting his movie and answering the same questions a million times over, with all the travel and time zone changes...he's going to be exhausted. I'll get a text like last night's. *Too tired to talk, miss you.*

It's so predictable it's boring, and I can see the ticking clock behind each word. Our time is up. He's moving on, even if he doesn't know it yet.

"Ashley," he says in a softer voice. "I miss you."

"Then fucking meet me halfway," I snap, dropping onto the couch. It knocks a soft sob out of my lungs. If he loved me as much as I love him, he'd be willing to risk it. He'd find a way.

He won't even consider it.

"I can't." His voice is pained, at least. He cares enough that it hurts.

I can't talk to him anymore. I end the call, dropping my phone onto my coffee table and my head into my hands. We're done. I know we're done because I'll never fit into the life his dead uncle wanted for him. Hell, Gabe will never fit in that life, either, but he'll never stop trying.

My phone rings and for a moment I consider letting it go to voice mail. Some broken part of me can't let go, though, so I accept the call without looking at the number.

"Unless you changed your mind, I don't want to talk to you," I say, putting my feet up on the coffee table and leaning back because I want to talk to him. I want him to make everything all right.

There's a long pause. "Um...Ashley?"

All the air leaves my lungs. I know that voice, though I've never heard it on my phone. "Nic?"

"Guessing you were expecting someone else," he says with a little laugh. "How're you doing?" His voice softens with the question, and I know he knows about the breakup.

I frown at my toes. I've painted them twice today, and it's not even noon. I'm unemployed, directionless. The man I love won't see me. Even my best friend is a secret.

"I'm good," I lie. "You?" Shit, I should say something about the wedding. "Um...congratulations, again." I never told him congratulations in the first place, but I doubt he'd remember.

"Thanks. Hey, I'm calling because Jessie mentioned you were looking for work, and long story short, there's this project that might be perfect for you—I'm in LA to meet with the creators tonight for dinner if you want to tag along."

"Yes, I'd love to," I all but shout into the phone as I leap to my feet. I need to get out of my house and out of my head. This project, this opportunity, could be worthwhile.

Nic gives me a time and promises to send a car. I spend the rest of the day primping and finding the perfect outfit to impress—a sleeveless jumpsuit with a deep V-neck, a sweet apricot yellow at the top, deepening to the color of a ripe peach down the flowy legs. I pair it with strappy heeled sandals and leave my hair in long, sleek waves.

I have no idea what this job is, or if I even have a chance, so maybe I'd be better in something more professional, but I'd be less me. I'm sick of feeling less myself right now. Old Ashley had confidence. She knew what she wanted, and she went after it.

She didn't sulk around her house because she couldn't have the attention of the man she wanted. She went out and lived her damn life.

When the car pulls up and I step outside, I don't care about the cameras. I even smile, a secretive little smile all my haters can choke on. Poppy can choke on it. Gabe...my smile falters, but he won't ever see the photos that will end up online. He's too busy with his own curated life.

The restaurant is swanky and I'm early, but Nic is too. We sit at the table and order drinks. When the waiter leaves and Nic smiles at me—politely—nothing happens to me. No butterflies, no heat between my legs. He's still handsome—his bone structure won't ever let him be anything else—but not in the all-consuming way I remember. He's just...a guy I knew growing up.

"Jessie put you up to this?" I ask, twisting the bangle on my wrist.

"Yeah. Timothy wants me to back this project. I read the screenplay on the flight and thought about you."

"That's kind of you," I say. The waiter sets my glass of wine on the table and I thank him. Nic accepts his beer with a head tilt and the waiter leaves us in uncomfortable silence.

Nic inspects his beer label and I can't believe I ever imagined myself in love with this guy. His reserve is irritating.

"So you told Timothy you'd ask me along to this meeting?" I ask, mostly to fill the silence. Okay, because I'm dying of curiosity.

He shakes his head.

Fucking hilarious.

He has no idea he's bringing the wrath of his brother-in-law down on his head.

A part of me wants to tell him Timothy did everything in his power to keep me away, that not a single person in my family offered me an ounce of help or support—that Nic never offered me anything until now—but I don't.

Not that this will stop me from taking what I suspect is the job he's buying me. If I want it, that is. Honestly, it better be good. I deserve something good right about now.

The people we're waiting for arrive and they're an eclectic mix of eagerness and experience. They smile at me when Nic introduces me.

The movie they want money for is a family movie with slightly more adult humor. An action romp they compare to a few films from the eighties, but updated. I try to pay attention as they talk about it, but I can't stop my thoughts from turning to Gabe. Anxiety pinches my stomach, and I feel sick at the thought of never seeing him again.

"I think Ashley would be perfect for Brittney," Nic says in a tone that, at least to the experienced at the table, suggests his backing demands it. "She's the bad guy," he says to me.

Of course, she is—probably the gold-digging stepmom—and of course, I'm perfect to play her. I smile, but my face feels like it's going to crack. I'm so fucking sick of being the bad guy.

One of the screenwriters nods, but the director, a wiry girl who barely looks like she can legally drink, has a thoughtful expression on her face. They promise to talk about it, Nic promises to think about how much he's willing to put in.

I make no promises. The role is big enough to tempt me, but I don't want to be the bad guy. I don't think I'll take it. Unless I'm desperate.

The problem is, I don't know if I'm desperate. That sense of situational awareness I've always had is gone, and it's terrifying.

The rest of the dinner passes in pleasant conversation. Everyone is nice enough to me, but I can't kick Gabe out of my head. I want to know what he's doing, what he's thinking. If he'll call me back. If he's done with me.

Dinner is cleared away and everyone gets down to business over drinks. This doesn't involve me, so I pull out my phone. Nothing from Gabe.

Why does everything have to be so damn complicated with him? Or maybe it's not complicated at all. I don't mean as much to him as he does to me. He's living his life and I need to live mine.

Nic picks up the bill and promises to be in touch. He leads me out to the car, climbing in after me.

When we arrive at my house, I'm so ready to be home where I can relax and not worry about what my face is doing that I practically jump out before the car stops. "Thanks, Nic, for everything tonight."

He brushes it off.

"Oh," he says as if he's just remembered, turning to motion down the street. "I share an agent with Celia, so I had a few calls placed in your name on her behalf. Hopefully, the bloodsuckers will leave you alone, but if they don't, let me know."

I glance, and sure enough, no one is parked up watching me with a camera or phone in hand. Celia went to war with the paparazzi after they published stories about her affair back in the day, and won—they won't go near her now. "Thanks."

He has the driver wait until I'm inside before driving away.

All at once, I'm exhausted. Today has been too much. I want Gabe's arms around me. I want to hear his voice, feel it buzz against my skin. I want to tell him how tired I am of the barbed wire cage I thought I could escape.

And I can't.

Can't leave the cage behind, can't talk to Gabe. He didn't call me back after I hung up on him. We're done.

My phone rings and it's the number of the director from tonight.

"I don't want you for Brittney," she blurts out.

"You don't?"

"I can't make any promises, everything is still up in the air, but I think you'd be better as Clare." She tells me more about the role. It's just as big, but the character isn't the bad guy. "It's about subverting the expectations. And tonight—you were completely different from your role on that TV show. I think you can more than handle Clare. Would you still be interested?"

"Yeah, I think I would," I say, glancing at my curtain-covered window as a motorcycle roars by outside.

She promises to keep in touch, and we end the call. For a while, I just stare at the wall. This is closer to what I want, but it still isn't what I want. Should I take it?

There's no real decision to make yet. The whole project could fall apart anytime.

A second motorcycle thunders down my road, or the same one again, two minutes later. Slower this time.

My skin prickles.

I race downstairs to make sure I've locked the door behind me.

No one has ever bothered me at my house before, paparazzi down the street aside, but there's a first for everything, so I dip into the garage and pull out an old baseball bat.

After a third pass of the street outside, the motorcycle stops and unless I'm mistaken, it's in my driveway.

Shit.

I peek out from the curtain as a man drops the kickstand and climbs off.

My heart leaps. I know those thick thighs, but he shouldn't be here. He made it very, very clear he wasn't willing to take this risk for me.

But Gabe is here, now, walking up my driveway in a leather jacket and dark denim jeans, pulling the helmet off his head after one final look up and down the street.

He could lose anyone following him in traffic on a motorcycle. He's not recognizable with a helmet on. And who would expect Gabriel Sinclair to even have a motorcycle? No one.

It's a brilliant plan and a stupid gamble.

He barely knocks and I toss aside the bat and rip the door open, pulling him to me. His hands are everywhere, his mouth desperate and hard on mine, and we're not done.

Not even close.

Chapter Twenty-Seven

Gabe

By the time I kick the door shut, I have the top of Ash's pantsuit down to her waist and one hand palming her magnificent tits while the other helps her remove my jacket. I can't stop kissing her and she doesn't stop kissing me. Not until I let her pantsuit drop away and lie her down on the stairs. She lets go of my face and I bury myself between her thighs.

It's my name she cries out when she comes. Still my name. Not his.

The ground floor of her house has an office with a couch against one wall. I scoop her up and lie her down on the soft leather, kneeling between her open legs.

"I missed you," she whispers, while I pull the condom out of my back pocket.

There's no time to get undressed. I push my jeans down and sheath my cock. "I missed you too." More than she can ever know. Going without her the last few days has been like living without a layer of skin, and now that I'm here with her, the pain is gone.

"I need you." Her voice is soft, vulnerable. I need her too. Need to touch her, claim her, and make sure she knows she's still mine. She gasps when I grab her hips and pull her close, pushing her legs wide so I can fit myself between them. She's still wearing her thong, but I need her now so I yank it to the side and plunge into her. The noise she makes sends tingles down my spine and I watch my cock as I fuck her, long and slow. Ash is watching, too, up on her elbows.

Seeing the connection between us as we move together helps knock those little doubts from my head. The way she looks at me when our eyes meet—she's as much mine as I'm hers.

"Harder," she urges as she lies back, her fingernails raking down my chest, biting lightly into my skin. The last shreds of my self-control blow away at that and I grab her legs, bringing them together and placing them both across my chest and over my shoulder. She's so fucking tight like this, the thong I pushed aside dragging against my cock. Leaning against her, pressing her knees into her tits gets me so deep I think I might be lost. I want to be lost with Ash, down some sunbaked highway where the rest of the world can't find us. I don't want to come, I don't want this to be over, but I can't stop the inevitable. Coming inside her...it pulls the tension out of my body, filling me with relief and a sense of rightness.

We make it upstairs eventually and Ash reheats some takeout and I insist she sits on my lap, completely naked while I'm still dressed. The food doesn't make it out of the microwave before I have her spread on my lap, my fingers in her pussy.

After, we lie in her bed, my head on her shoulder while she runs her fingers through my hair. Her skin is soft and warm and I breathe her deeply into my lungs. The urgent, primal force that drove me here fades because this, not the sex, is what I needed.

"Your house is nice," I murmur.

She laughs. "Did you see any of it?"

"No." My eyes were on her. I got the impression of a small rectangular house, the short end near the street with a garage in the back. An office on the first floor, with the leather couch I fucked her on. The kitchen, dining room, and living room on the second floor, her bedroom, and presumably another bedroom, on the third. Simple décor, warm but neutral colors. Tidy but lived in. Small.

"I have a little rooftop patio. Want to go up?"

"Better not." There weren't any paparazzi anywhere on her street—I drove by a few times, just to be sure—but that doesn't mean there aren't now.

Ashley draws in a deep breath and lets it out slowly. "Gabe, what if we just…took our relationship public?"

I lift my head to look into her eyes. "You know we can't. Not now."

The corners of her lips tighten. I bend to kiss the tension away.

"Would it be so bad?" she asks. "We'd be able to see each other anytime. No more sneaking around."

"I'd love that." I trail my kisses down her jaw to her neck. "But we can't." I suck lightly in the spot that usually makes her moan, but she doesn't respond.

Fuck.

I don't want to do this, not tonight. A groan escapes, and I bury my face against her neck. "Ash. Can we talk about this later?"

This is the last chance I'm going to have to see her for a while. I'm leaving tomorrow evening for the press junket for *The Last Best Man* before filming begins on Warwick. Filming should take three months, maybe four, then I have a break and I'm going to tie her to my bed and make up for all the time we've missed.

When she speaks, her voice is soft and I can hear the fear beneath the careful words. "We were fake dating, then we were sleeping together and it was meant to be temporary. Is that still what this is?"

I lift my head. "No," I say, brushing a lock of silvery blonde hair from her face.

She's silent as she watches me. Waiting for me to elaborate on what this is—what she is—to me. I don't know how far, how deep this thing between us goes, but I do know I don't want it to end.

"The only time I feel like myself is when I'm with you," I tell her. "When I'm not with you, I'm thinking of how much I want to be with you. This isn't temporary."

Her hand comes up to cup my jaw. "I'll be your secret for now, Gabe, but this isn't what I want."

"It's not what I want either." I pull her hand from my face and kiss her knuckles.

We shift, so Ashley's lying with her head on my chest, and soon enough, she falls asleep.

I reach for my phone.

A quick search of my name turns up nothing new, and I breathe a sigh of relief. As much as I needed her tonight, coming here was a big risk. In the back of my mind, I knew nothing was going on between Ash and Nic, and my mad dash through LA traffic on my motorcycle was foolish. But all I saw, after the alert I have set to her name went off on my phone, was pictures of Ashley looking gorgeous with the man she once loved. A man she was willing to destroy her cousin's marriage for.

She'd hung up on me before going out with him. I had to see her.

I need her to wait for me, until this thing with Kate is over, until filming wraps. Until I get that Oscar-winning role. Until not even Ashley Foley can tarnish my reputation.

There's no one in sight the next day when late afternoon rolls around and I have to catch my flight. We kiss in the doorway until I have to pull myself away. Ash folds her arms over the T-shirt she's wearing—one of mine—and tells me to be careful on the drive and call her when I get to my hotel. I can't kiss her again or I'll never stop. The part of me I've locked down begs me to do it. Throw all this away. Get Ashley on the back of the motorcycle and drive up to Canada or down to Mexico. I can't help but think I'd be happier.

Chapter Twenty-Eight

Gabe

David and I arrive in New York in the early hours of the morning. I check into my suite and, since I slept on the flight, I head to the gym.

Press junkets are exhausting. Answering the same questions over and over, trying to be engaging and authentic but concise, is surprisingly stressful. The heat of the lights and too many bodies crammed into a luxurious but still too-small hotel room make the experience uncomfortable.

And there's Kate. She's a ball of sunshine and her career has followed the same path as mine, with the press dubbing her America's Sweetheart. We got along great on set. The stories she told about life on her family farm—particularly those involving a notorious goose named Charles—had the cast and crew in stitches.

But fake dating her is another story. Any chemistry we might have had on set ended when filming wrapped. At the LA interviews, she laughed and smiled and touched my arm, but every time I smiled back at her, I saw Ash. It felt like a betrayal.

I made it clear to Kate and her team that while Kate and I shared a few kisses in the movie, we won't be doing it now. Kate agreed.

My workout helps burn off some of the frustration and nervous energy, and I'm even feeling good after my shower. Like I can do this. Fake it with Kate and keep Ashley happy. Do the job I need to do on set. Be Gabriel Sinclair in public and myself in private.

I dress in the dark-washed jeans and cream-colored Henley my stylist picked out for me, fastening Michael's watch—the one I once tried to steal, which he gave me with Cora's blessing for my eighteenth birthday—around my wrist for good luck. He believed in making a good impression during interviews. Putting people at ease and being genuine.

For the next two days in New York, and for two days after that in London, and two more days in Tokyo, I have to be America's golden boy, star of the heart-warming rom-com *The Last Best Man*, and possible love interest of America's Sweetheart Kate Van Sandt. Definite love interest, according to everyone.

My relationship with Ashley, and my relationship with Kate, thank god, are both off the list of approved topics for the interviews. Not that a few entertainment reporters won't hint around it, but these people aren't the paparazzi. They want to be invited back to the studio's press tours, so they'll play ball.

There's a sharp, impatient rap on my door and I open it to a visibly panicked David. He pushes past me, slamming the door and handing me his phone. "We have a problem."

I glance down at the screen and my blood goes cold.

GABRIEL SINCLAIR CAUGHT CHEATING WITH EX.

A close-up from a long-range lens of me, kissing Ash in her doorway, my hand the only thing covering her breast after I'd tugged the top of her pantsuit down. A photo insert in the bottom corner of me still on my motorcycle—it's hard to tell that's me, except I'm wearing the same thing they caught me leaving in. And boy did they catch me leaving, Ash watching me walk away. That photo is close enough to catch the satisfied smile on my face. The unhappy look on hers.

"So this isn't great," David says in the understatement of the fucking century, helping himself to a bottle of water from my mini-fridge and taking a long drink. "And I can't get a hold of Rose."

The story broke ten minutes ago. Christ.

"We need Kate," David says, putting down his water and pacing the room.

"We need the two of you in photographs together like nothing is wrong. Then we need her to keep being that happy sunshine person throughout this whole junket, and—"

I'm not listening anymore. The words in the article etch themselves into my skin like acid. *Cheater. No golden boy. What else is he hiding?* My stomach roils, empty and burning. Everything I've worked for, everything I've built, and it's all crashing down. Now the bastards are looking critically at me and my closet is full of skeletons. Mine. My uncle's.

I take a deep breath and pinch the bridge of my nose. If Emma was right before—and she's always right—my career will be fine. But what's the point of winning an Oscar if I can't hold it with pride? Michael would—

A new alert pops up.

Kate, sitting in a café, shoulders hunched and crying while her assistant gently comforts her.

KATE VAN SANDT'S BROKEN HEART.

"I'm fucked." I drop the phone back into David's hand and sink into the nearest chair, cradling my head in my hands. Kate is loved by everyone and her fans—SuperVans—are a force of nature. Thanks to the lies we sold them, it won't matter that Kate's not my girlfriend and Ashley is. They'll come for me.

"Oh, this is not good." David says, staring at the screen. His phone rings and the circus begins. He thrusts it to me. "Rose."

Rose is already talking as I hold the phone to my ear. "I told you to break up with her. If you can't hold your side of the bargain, I can't help you."

"I'm sorry. What do we do?"

"Gabe, you didn't just cheat on a girlfriend," Rose explains, the patience in her voice thin as paper. "You broke the heart of *Kate Van Sandt*, America's favorite actress, so you could fuck your ex, who happens to be America's most hated bitch."

I bristle. "Ashley's not—"

"That's how the public sees her," Rose says. "The truth of who Ashley is doesn't matter. She isn't my client. You are. So this is what we're going to do. We're putting out a statement that you and Kate enjoy a close friendship and the flirty nature of it was turned into something it's not by the press and fans. She was crying because she just found out from her mother that her dog is unwell. It's true, I just got off the phone with her publicist. Kate's going to issue a statement, and post her dog's recovery on her social media."

"What do I need to do?"

Rose hesitates, just for a second, but it's enough to tell me there's nothing I can do. "I want you to take some time and figure out what you want. Because it looks like you want Ashley, and if you do, I think we need to stop tilting at windmills and let this go. Okay?"

"Yeah," I manage.

"It's going to be okay, Gabe. Put this out of your mind and get through the next few days. We'll do our best to clean the mess."

Clean the mess. They've never had to clean my mess because I've never left one before Ashley.

There's a knock at the door, and Kate walks into my room, tears streaming down her face, apologizing. I hug her and reassure her everything will be okay. But when I ask about her dog, she bursts into loud sobs. Her assistant and entourage follow, and we're joined by several reps from the PR firm running the junket. Everyone is talking, trying to put out fires, all while I stare at the coffee David hands me.

The day is, unsurprisingly, a shit show.

I'm on autopilot, unable to escape dissecting how this disaster happened. Where was that camera-toting bastard hiding? I checked and there was no one on Ashley's street.

Kate's statement about her dog backfires. Her fans go rabid, believing I was fucking my ex, while Kate was caring for her sick dog.

We get updates from our people throughout the day, and I can tell from David's face that I do not want to see what's being said about me online.

The dog is expected to make a full recovery, but Kate smiles through watery eyes and even the makeup people can't hide that she's been crying. Every single reporter gives her the softest look before giving me a cold glare. Not one asks us about it since the topic is off-limits, but I can see what they think.

By the end of the day, I'm easily the most hated man in Hollywood.

"Well, today was a total disaster," David says, letting himself into my suite with a twelve-pack of beer and a pizza. I'm not willing to go out in public—not until this dies down a bit. "Have you talked to Ashley yet?"

I rub the back of my stiff neck. "No." I need to call her. She's blown up my phone.

David puts the pizza down on the table, opens the box—pepperoni and pineapple—and pushes it toward me. "You cannot tell your trainer I enabled you."

"Fuck Jax and the studio," I grumble, grabbing for the beer that also isn't on the list of approved foods. They can deal with whatever one pizza and half a pack of beer is going to do to me.

David sits down and takes a beer for himself. He must drink half of it before he sets it down with a satisfied thump and asks the question he must know has been plaguing me all day. "Do you think Ashley set you up?"

"No." I don't, although the similarity to the day we met is impossible to ignore. But when I left her house she was happy, satisfied.

Except in the picture that dickhead captured. She looked sad.

"No," I say again, louder. "She wouldn't do that to me." Except she did that to Nic, and she loved him. She doesn't love me and right now, I fucking hate Nic.

David isn't convinced, but he shrugs it off and grabs a piece of pizza. "So...how do you want to play this? You're back with Ashley? Or—"

"I don't know."

He leans forward, elbows on the table, eyes on Michael's watch still fastened around my wrist. "Can I be honest?"

I nod, although I doubt I want to hear this.

"You're not Michael."

It lands like a truck.

David opens his mouth to say more, and I cut him off. "I'd like to be alone, if you don't mind. I have a phone call to make."

Hurt crosses his face, but he shakes it off. "Call me if you need anything." He takes his half-eaten slice of pizza and half-empty beer and walks out the door.

I push the pizza box away, drop the heavy watch on the table, and finish off my beer.

There's a part of me that doesn't believe any of this is real, and another part of me that knows this is the consequence of not thinking with my head. I shouldn't have gone to her place. Probably shouldn't be seeing her at all.

I pull out my phone and dial her number. I don't know what I'm going to say, but I want to say it before the anger gluing me together fails.

"Hey," Ash says softly, answering immediately, "I was getting worried."

I glance at Michael's watch. It's nearly midnight here. Not so late in LA, but she's been expecting me. "Did you do this?" I ask tightly.

"No." That's all she says, but there's disappointment in that one word. She doesn't need to say more. She's hurt I had to ask.

And I believe her. She didn't do this, but she's also not dealing with the fallout like I am.

"You think I would do this to you?" she asks after a long stretch of silence.

I sigh, reaching for a second beer. "No. I'm just tired and pissed off."

"In a few months, no one will care."

"I will."

She makes a disgusted sound. "So you aren't this perfect golden boy actor. You're something better. Or you could be if you'd embrace who you are."

Who I am needs to remain buried. "You don't get it."

"Neither do you," she says, all the soft concern gone from her voice, replaced by cold steel. "Michael's dead—you can't gain or lose his love and esteem now. And frankly, he wasn't that great."

Irritation flares because that man saved me. "You didn't know him."

"I know you."

"No, you don't." If she knew me, she'd understand why this is so important to me. Maybe she wasn't listening, those long hours in the car, or when we talked late into the night. Michael saved my life and all he ever asked in return was that

I live up to his ideals.

Ashley sighs. "I don't want to fight with you, okay? Can we just talk?"

"Talk."

"Gabe—" There's a whine in her voice, but it breaks in a sigh. "What happens now?"

I have no fucking clue. I'm such a mess, but seeing her isn't going to help me fix this. When Warwick starts filming, I won't have the time or energy to do it. "I need some time alone. A few months to get my head on straight. We can come up with a plan. I'll talk to my team about rehabilitating your reputation, too, and eventually—"

"—we can be together?" she asks with a dry laugh.

I rub my eyes. "Yeah." I don't believe it though. I don't see a world where Ash can stand in the spotlight with me without dragging me down more than she already has. She has to be my secret, just like Lilah was Michael's, if my accomplishments are going to mean anything. And they have to mean something. I can't throw away everything Michael gave me.

There's a long moment of silence. "No."

My heart sinks. "Why?"

"Gabe, I've—" her voice breaks off into a strangled, frustrated sound. "I've been trying to be a better person, without becoming someone I'm not. But no one wants to see me any other way, and honestly? I don't give a fuck. And neither should you. Just...be with me."

"I can't."

"Try. Be yourself and you might be happier. Stop caring what the world thinks."

"Easy to say when the world hates you."

There's a long moment of silence and I grip my hair, mussing it up in frustration. I shouldn't have said that, but I'm mad enough that I meant it.

"It's not easy," she says, her voice tight as she struggles to keep control. "It has never been easy. I hate the death threats and the internet trolls. I hate that I've hurt people I love, that I can't get close to anyone. I hate how everyone sees me as a caricature, and maybe I deserve it because I played up the role I've been cast in since I was a child, but I don't want to erase my past or hide behind some persona. I want to be myself, and when you ask me to wait until I'm somehow good enough for you? I love you, Gabe, but I can't."

I prop my elbow on the table, my head in my hand. "Ash. It's only for a few months while I'm filming Warwick." Christ, she waited years for Nic, why can't she give me a few months? If she meant it when she said she loved me, she'd wait.

"I'll be just as toxic as I am right now. Nothing is ever going to change enough for us to be together."

A part of me recognizes that she's right. Our relationship should've stayed fake, we should've kept things professional, because this is never going to work between us. "Ashley—"

"I'm not going to be your shameful secret, Gabe. I want everything and I won't settle for less. So what's it going to be? Me, or your golden cage? Because you can't have both."

Something in her voice ticks me off. It's the bravado—not even a quiver or a hint of uncertainty. She thinks she's got me.

"You're giving me an ultimatum. Are you sure about that?"

"You've given me no choice."

"I gave you the choice to wait, but you're forcing me to pick my career."

"Gabe—"

"I choose my career," I say, my voice rising into an angry shout. "I choose my name and everything it stood for before you came into my life and everything it will stand for again one day."

The sound she makes is half laugh, half sob. "One day you're going to regret me, Gabriel Sinclair. Maybe even as much as I regret you."

CHAPTER TWENTY-NINE

Ashley

I END THE CALL. Gabe made his choice, and it wasn't exactly a surprise. I'll cry about it later. Right now, I have a more immediate problem on my hands. There are about twenty SuperVans—fans of Kate Van Sandt—outside my house, and they don't appear interested in going home. Not one of them looks violent, but anyone deep enough in a parasocial relationship with their idol to find my house and sit outside with glittery signs calling me a homewrecker and a whore can't be trusted to remain peaceful.

Worse, I have to sit with the uncomfortable knowledge that my relationship with Nic before Gabe entered my life was not all that different from what these people have with Kate.

I called the police. They said someone would come around. That was hours ago, and it's getting dark. I'm not comfortable sleeping here tonight with them outside.

They aren't buying the statements Gabe and Kate put out earlier about never being exclusive or serious or whatever. I don't plan to stick around to find out what their intentions toward me are. My bag is half-packed when I finally get through to Lea. She agrees to pick me up in thirty minutes a block away from my house.

I'll be going over the back wall and through a vacant lot. Something I'm not happy about, but I'd rather not go through the SuperVans and have them follow me to a hotel.

I bet the police would take an interest in them loitering around a hotel though.

My doorbell goes nuts, like someone is holding it down. The pounding on the door starts immediately and I'm creeping up to the peephole, baseball bat in hand, when I hear her voice.

"For fuck's sake, Ashley let me in this instant. These people are not friendly."

If this is what I get for trying to be good, I'm going back to villainy.

I unlock the door, open it enough to yank my mother into my house and slam it shut, quickly turning the lock.

"What are you doing?" she hisses, her hands fluttering to smooth out any wrinkles I might have made when I rescued her. She's beautiful, like always. Dressed for a night out in a stunning little black dress.

"Why are you here?" I demand.

"You blocked my number after that awful man—was he the one the tabloids said cheated on Kate Van Sandt? With *you*? I suppose he left you too."

I pinch the bridge of my nose. "What do you want?"

She huffs. "Your father's an asshole."

Of course. She's not concerned about the mob outside my house or my broken heart. She wants my sympathy for her problems, and soon enough, she'll want me to help her get her revenge. Or get him back. It's the same thing at this point.

My phone chimes.

> They're still outside. You ready?

Lea

I grab my bag from the stairs and head for the door to the garage. My mother follows, listing out all the ways my father has wronged her this time.

Ready.

ME

Twenty seconds later, an unholy amount of noise erupts at the front of my house. I press the button, raising the garage door and ducking out, holding back a laugh when my mother does the same without questioning what we're doing. She's too caught up in her story to notice the horn blaring or the shouting from the front of my house.

I close the garage door. "Come on. Tell me what he said next." I'm not listening, but it's as good a prompt as any.

"Your father had the nerve to suggest a new doctor—"

My mother has the youngest face money can buy, but she's insecure about it, so the man she professes to love more than anything uses it to hurt her. She's just as bad with his insecurities.

The noise out the front disappears as I put my bag on the waist-high stone wall and pull myself up.

My mother finally takes notice of something other than her scheme. "Ashley, what's happening? Where are you taking me?" She gasps. "Are you going to murder me?"

"Thinking about it," I murmur, swinging a leg over to straddle the wall. "Give me your hand, I'll pull you up."

There's enough light left in the evening I can see her shocked face. "Have you lost your mind? This is a Versace."

"Then turn around and go back out the front. But I'm leaving."

She gasps again, mortally wounded by my lack of feeling for her or her dress. "You wouldn't leave me here, all alone in the dark, with those people outside your house? Isn't it enough I have to come into this part of LA to visit you?"

Yes, my solidly middle-class neighborhood is the worst. "Then give me your hand."

"You always were a selfish child," she snaps, crossing her arms and pouting.

"Okay. See you later." I swing my leg over and she breaks.

"Wait, fine. I'll climb over this huge wall in this expensive dress—which was a gift from your father, by the way—and when I fall and break my neck—"

I tune her out, but I can't pull her over the wall. I have to climb back down and give her a lift. The whole thing takes way too long, she's way too loud, and her dress does not come out of the ordeal the same as it went into it, but somehow the SuperVans out the front don't hear. Which is good, because I left the baseball bat in the garage. We're defenseless.

I lead my mother across a vacant lot, along a narrow alley past other houses, and onto another street. She's still complaining, her voice rising at how I'm just like my dad, cold and unfeeling in my mistreatment of her.

I am anything but unfeeling. She's lucky I'm keeping everything locked down tight or only one of us would make it out of here.

Lea's car is waiting down the street, engine idling, and the lights flick on and it springs to life, stopping in front of us.

My mother freezes. "I'm not getting kidnapped by someone driving a Volvo."

Lea's car isn't a Volvo. It's a Toyota sedan of some type. Maybe ten years old. "Should I put you in the trunk?" I ask sweetly. "I didn't bring zip ties or duct tape, unfortunately."

"Ashley!"

I open the back door. "Then get in."

"Hello Mrs. Foley," Lea says darkly, sounding exactly how I'm feeling as I slam the back door and get into the passenger's seat.

"Hello, Lily," my mother says dismissively. "I don't know what's going on, but please take us somewhere with alcohol." She lifts an old burger wrapper from the back seat by the corner. "Lots of alcohol."

"To the hotel," I say quietly. "She can have my room."

Lea nods.

The drive could never be silent. Not with my mother in the car. She immediately launches into her grievances, taking Lea's occasional disgruntled murmur as interest. I stare out the car window, the lights blurring from the tears in my eyes. I brush them away. I have never cried real tears in front of my mother and I'm not about to start.

When we get to the hotel, Lea changes the reservation. While she's gone, my mother directs all her impotent rage about my father at me. I ignore it. Finally, Lea's back, and my mother—lured by the hotel bar—gets out of the car. "Well?" she says impatiently. "Come on, Ashley. I'm not standing out here next to *that* all night." She motions to the car.

I twist to lean out the window. "I'm not getting out. I'm not going to have a drink with you or help you with whatever drama you're whipping up. My life is a dumpster fire and right now, that's all I can handle. You're on your own."

"Ashley! I can't—"

I turn to Lea. "Drive. If she jumps on the roof, keep going."

Lea throws the car into gear and steps on the gas. The tires squeal, the car shoots forward, and the sudden unexpectedness of it combined with the shocked expression on my mother's face in the mirror brings a peal of hysterical laughter out of me.

Lea laughs, too, slowing down to merge into traffic. "Can you imagine her on the roof?" She cracks up again, and so do I. The image of Rachel Foley in her little black Versace dress, golden hair flying wildly as she screams and ruins her manicure trying to cling to the roof of Lea's sedan is too much.

I brush the tears out of my eyes and realize, as Lea's laughter fades, that I'm crying. It only gets worse, great big gasping sobs, because now that I'm safe, I have to face the fact that Gabe is out of my life.

The city is a blur as Lea drives. She doesn't ask me where I want to go and she doesn't give me empty words of sympathy. Not that I'd hear them over the pathetic noises I'm making. At a red light, she hands me a box of tissues, and later, when I've settled into hiccups and silent tears, she hands me a mini bottle of vodka from her handbag.

"I emptied the hotel minibar." She gives me a small smile. "And since your mother is a regular guest, I had the room charged to her."

"Thank you," I say with a sniffle, twisting the cap.

Lea takes me to the one corner of the world where no one would ever find me—Wendy's beach house. The house was a gift from her father to her Brazilian mother before Wendy was born, and Wendy's been living here while working on screenplays and novels. The tiny seaside town is a safe place I can visit her without worrying about us getting photographed together.

Wendy greets us at the door, pulling me into a hug, and I cling to her. There's still too much roiling inside me, and I can't keep it in any longer. "Beach," I say. Wendy knows what I need. She and Lea walk me down to the cool sand, standing a little back to give me some space. We're alone, and in the dark, I scream my hurt to the waves until my voice fails.

Heartbreak was my friend. I knew how to make armor out of my pain. I did it for all those years with Nic.

This...it's naked. Raw.

I hadn't known heartbreak at all.

I wish Gabriel Sinclair had never set foot in that room at the reception.

Before he came into my life, I would've had my tantrum, brushed myself off, and gone back to work with the end goal—happy ever after with the man I loved—in mind. This time, there's no way forward and I'm so angry because I can't go back to who I used to be. He's left me vulnerable and I'm going to have to learn to live like this in the bad times now that the good times are gone.

I hate him.

I wouldn't take Gabe back if he came crawling on his knees. Over broken glass. With sunburned legs.

I love him.

He's in my blood and under my skin. More a part of me than I am, if this ache is any indication.

He didn't believe me. All the time we spent together, all the secrets we shared, and he still had to ask if I'd planted that paparazzo to catch him. It hurts more than him choosing his reputation over me. He could love me and still choose to sacrifice us for his goals, and it would hurt. But thinking I'm still the woman I was the day we met means he doesn't love me. He never did and he never will because he'll never see me and that's what's gnashing at my heart.

"Come on," Wendy whispers, her arm going around my shoulders, and I realize I'm on my knees in the wet sand. The frothy edges of a cold wave kiss along my legs and I let Wendy pull me to my feet.

Back in her house, wrapped in a blanket with a glass of wine in hand, I'm empty enough that I can finally talk, so when Wendy tells me to spill, I do.

I trust Wendy. I know her secrets, she knows mine, and if mutually assured destruction isn't a strong foundation for a friendship, I don't know what is. And Lea—she signed an NDA before she started working for me, but I trust her anyway.

So I tell them how I fell in love with the worst possible man for me. How our fake relationship turned real turned into a secret. How he doesn't see that I've changed.

"To dickheads," Wendy says when I run out of words, raising her wineglass.

I raise mine, and Lea raises hers.

In the morning, I walk to the beach and hurl driftwood, pebbles, and shells back into the ocean. I imagine each one is a piece of my pain, but it's not that easy. The tide brings the feeling back and my arms get sore, so I do the next logical thing and glare at the water.

How dare that man make me love him?

Gabriel Sinclair is a jerk.

I write it in the sand, kicking out the letters. The rising tide eats it not long after I'm finished, and I do it again. It's cathartic to write insulting messages to Gabe, letting the ocean carry them away.

The man I love doesn't love me. Again.

Why does this keep happening to me? I tried to be better. I tried so fucking hard, and for what? Gabe, the one person I thought could see inside, only sees rot in me. I don't deserve this. I deserve...

I have no idea what I deserve or what I've earned. Maybe I haven't done enough. Maybe nothing is ever going to be enough.

Back in Wendy's house, I search for Gabe on social media. He, or more likely his team, has issued a statement saying he was never romantically involved with Kate Van Sandt. They remain close friends. His visit to me was a lapse in judgment and he'll be spending his free time focusing on his upcoming roles.

When I start to cry, Wendy plucks my phone from my hand. "No internet stalking your ex. You know the rules."

It doesn't stop Wendy and Lea from stalking him and gleefully sharing every post tearing him apart for breaking Kate's heart—and there are a lot of those. The ones questioning what else he's hiding set my nerves on edge. Does he trust me to keep his past a secret? I'll never tell anyone, and there's the NDA, but he must be anxious.

Let him stew, then let him see I'm not the person he thinks I am.

By the end of the week, I feel better. Enough to go home. My heart is still broken, but the pain has dulled to something I can learn to live with.

"Here," Wendy says, slipping a bound manuscript into my bag. "I finally finished the script. Thank you for the notes. Read it if you need a distraction."

I hug her tight and promise I will. Her screenplays are hilarious and this one is about a reality TV show gone wrong—it's the reason she went on the show in the first place, for research. "Thank you for everything. I'm so glad you're my secret friend."

Wendy freezes. "Oh, fuck. We're fixing that. Right now." Her phone is already out, our faces filling the screen.

"Stop!" I duck away. "I look awful! And what about *Love on the Line?* The Girl Next Door can't be seen hanging out with the Biggest Bitch of All Time."

Wendy gives me a gentle push toward the bathroom. "Go fix your face, we're doing this. And fuck *Love on the Line.*"

"You don't have to do this," I say, once I've fixed myself up, so I look a smidge less like I need a trip to rehab.

"You were there for me," she says. "I should have been there for you. From the start."

The pre-show pregnancy tests didn't catch Wendy's positive. She didn't know until morning sickness hit a couple of weeks into filming. She needed to get off the show before anyone else figured it out. She didn't need public pressure in the face of a private medical decision.

I couldn't be there for her when she had the abortion, but keeping it out of the public sphere gave her a chance to come back on another season of *Love on the Line* as the girl next door. Or to do whatever she wanted, without it being dredged up on the internet or spilling into her professional life.

The video Wendy posts, calling me her best friend and talking about spending a week together drinking and hanging out and bonding, goes viral.

Lea drives us back to LA and for the first time in days, I turn on my phone.

There are no messages or calls from Gabe. I didn't realize how much hope I was holding onto until it was crushed.

On the bright side, nothing from my parents.

I answer messages from Jessie and Lauren and scroll through my email. The director Nic introduced me to last week promised to email, but there's nothing there. I suppose I'm too toxic for the role of Clare. Silly to get those hopes up too.

"What the hell?" Lea's voice draws my attention from my phone and I look up as she stops as close as she can get to my house.

There's a gaggle of paparazzi—unsurprising since they haven't caught me since the scandal broke—but what draws my attention are the police cars. Two of them, parked outside my house.

My stomach sinks when another officer walks out of my front door. My visibly broken front door.

The assholes with cameras press closer as I get out of the car. "This is my house," I say, barely holding my shit together as I approach the nearest officer, Lea close behind me. "What happened?"

My house was broken into, they tell me. No shit.

They give me a good idea of what I'll see before I go inside, but I'm still not prepared.

The sofa in my office is slashed. Papers from my desk are shredded. Anything glass is broken. The kitchen and living room on the first floor are just as bad. Everything breakable is smashed or slashed.

My bedroom is the worst. Every drawer is emptied onto the floor and the smell is bad enough I gag.

"What is that?" I ask from behind my hand.

"Bad milk?" Lea guesses, pinching her nose shut.

One of the officers nods. "We think so."

I don't have milk in my fridge. Someone deliberately brought milk here to do this.

And they wrote all over my walls with what looks like every lipstick I own. *Whore. Bitch. Slut.* The trifecta of the worst things a woman can be, according to far too many assholes in this world.

An officer clears his throat to get my attention. "Does anything of value appear to be missing?"

My jewelry box appears to be gone, and while I had a lot of nice, expensive stuff, none of it's sentimental. Only trinkets, given to me by wealthy partners that I set aside in case I needed to pawn one day.

We go back down to the office so I can check on my passport. It's there. In pieces.

My life is in pieces. I'm not sure how this can get any worse.

"Do you have any enemies, Miss Foley?" the officer asks politely.

I laugh. For a moment, I'm afraid I won't stop.

The other officer, who has been quietly judging me the whole time, nudges his partner. "She's from one of those trashy reality TV shows. Might as well add the entire cast and crew to the suspect list, along with half the internet."

The derision in his voice dries up my laughter. "I am a person," I say, keeping my tone level when I'd love nothing more than to strangle this bastard. "And my house has been broken into and my privacy violated. Have some fucking respect."

Lea clears her throat. "Maybe one of Kate Van Sandt's more disturbed fans is responsible. A bunch of them were camped outside last week. I believe a call was made to the police and nothing was done about it."

Our words do nothing to improve the situation. If anything, the officers get shittier and they make me jump through about ten million hoops before I can leave. And I have to leave. My house is uninhabitable.

"You can stay with me," Lea says when we walk back to her car. I've managed to fill a box with things that miraculously survived the carnage, and I cling to it.

Lea's apartment is too small and I don't want to burden her. "I can stay with my cousin." I hope. Lauren's staying at Timothy's house and the security is better. Not that I'm going to feel safe anywhere anytime soon.

Chapter Thirty

Gabe

THE PRESS TOUR FOR *The Last Best Man* is an unmitigated slow-rolling disaster. When all these professionals talk about their worst junket experiences, this one is going to top the list. Every interview is awkward and stilted, from New York to London to Tokyo. Even Kate's smiles can't save this cursed tour.

I'm jetlagged. I can't get comfortable, can't focus, can't make sense of what happened. Every time a minute ticks by, everything shifts.

Ashley betrayed me and hired that asshole to get photos of us so I'd have no choice but to make our relationship public.

Ashley had nothing to do with it.

Ashley forced me to choose, and I chose wrong.

I chose right.

Back and forth, every minute of every hour of every goddamn day.

I miss her. That's the constant. I don't know if her open vulnerability with me was real or an act, I don't know if she really loved me, but fuck, my life is empty without her.

Rose makes me tell her everything I told Ashley, so she can be prepared. She's warned me every day that goes by without Ashley spilling everything to the press and raining vengeance upon me is a day I should be thankful.

I desperately want to believe she wouldn't do that to me, but I don't know.

Any relief I feel arriving home disappears under the crushing weight of

Michael's expectations when I walk through the door.

He's been dead for ten years, but I still feel like that fourteen-year-old boy, caught stealing his watch.

Ash's ghost is here, too, tempting me with memories of her body, warm and ready in my bed. The fear and determination in her eyes while I taught her to float in my pool. Her laugh as she sat on my kitchen counter in my shirt.

Immediately I escape outside, down the wide paved path to a pair of sun loungers. With the ocean in front of me and the house behind me, out of sight, I can breathe again. I call David and ask him to find me a short-term lease for an apartment closer to the studio.

Filming starts soon after and my world shrinks to scripts, quick workouts, and long, grueling days on set. I put everything I have into the role like it will help me forget about the hurt in Ashley's voice.

Days pass, but I have no idea how many.

I'm exhausted after a particularly physical sequence, walking off set for lunch when David falls into step alongside me.

"It happened," he says in a hushed voice.

My heart stutters as I take in his pallor, the shaky breath he sucks in. He hands me his phone like he's about to tell me someone's dead, and I know.

Gabriel Sinclair is dead.

GABRIEL SINCLAIR'S SECRET IDENTITY REVEALED.

It's all there, in the article. Everything I told Ashley and more.

The name my parents gave me. Axel Gabriel Leddy.

They got comments from old classmates calling me short-tempered and dangerous. The kid I put in the hospital too—though he's not the victim they were looking for, as he's currently in prison for assault. He remembers me, but claims he beat my ass the following week. He didn't. Comments from teachers calling me troubled. A few shoplifting incidents. A lot of time in detention. Rumors about a stolen car.

I scroll, but it doesn't get better.

It goes into detail about who my dad was. And my mom. She'd died of a drug overdose years ago. Cora had only told me she'd passed away, and seeing it like this...

I click away. Other sites have already picked the story up.

GABRIEL SINCLAIR'S DARK SECRET.

HOLLYWOOD IDOL GABRIEL SINCLAIR'S TROUBLED PAST.

GABRIEL SINCLAIR'S SHOCKING FALL FROM GRACE.

After weeks of waiting for the sky to fall, there's something like relief when it finally starts to collapse. But mostly, there's anger.

"This is Ashley's work," I say, shoving David's phone back at him. My stomach is churning. She really did this.

Of course she did.

David clears his throat. "Maybe we should talk about this somewhere more private."

"She sold me out. She told me I'd regret leaving her, and she followed through."

"Gabe," he hisses, eyes darting around the room.

I glance around. We're still on set as the crew breaks it up and people are watching us. "Who cares? Everyone already knows everything about me—they might as well know what I'm thinking." My voice rises, my arms lifting as I turn slowly. "Hell hath no fury like a woman scorned, am I right?"

David pushes me through the crowd, but I'm laughing. The brittle sound silences everyone we come across and they all pause, staring at me.

"Hey," I say to one of the extras, stopping abruptly. "Never trust someone who tries to seduce their—"

"You need to stop before you make this worse," David says, grabbing me by the shoulders. He's tall, but he hasn't been enduring months of training and bulking up. He shouldn't be able to move me, but he does.

"How can it get any worse?" I demand, laughing again.

The moment my trailer door slams behind him, David rounds on me. "Stop acting like a dick."

"You didn't have your dirty laundry laid out for the whole world to see," I snap.

"Your childhood trauma isn't your fault, for one. It's also not an excuse for you to act like an asshole. You don't even know if Ashley is behind this—"

"She's behind this." The only other living person who knows anything about it is Cora. No one from my old life has ever recognized me. Cora and Michael gave me a new name when they adopted me, and as far as I was aware, those records were sealed. "Ashley—"

"I don't like Ashley and I'm a little pissed off you're making me defend her, but you just publicly called her out and you have no proof. How do you think this makes you look? You are losing it."

I find a bottle of water in the mini-fridge and tear off the cap. "No shit."

David's phone chimes and he glances at it before looking back up to me. "Meeting at your apartment, eight o'clock tonight, to strategize our way forward. You're locked out of social media and your official response is 'no comment.'"

"Was there any mention of Michael?" I ask, dropping onto a chair.

"Not yet. I talked to Lilah. She's going to take the boy to visit a cousin out of state for a while. She'll call me if anyone approaches her."

"Good." Hopefully, Ashley will keep this secret to herself. Although what good is a piece of information if it can't be used?

I'm going to see her, I realize. Tonight, tomorrow, soon. She'll come by to let me know she can make me regret her by hurting Michael's legacy too.

The rest of the day passes in a series of fight sequences and I'm glad to have someplace to put my anger and resentment.

"You're channeling the darker aspects of the character perfectly," the director tells me at the end of the day. "You've embraced this role. Well done."

It doesn't feel good.

I walk into the luxury apartment David rented for me after eight to David, Emma, and Rose all sitting around my table, tablets, phones, and laptops up and running. Damage control is underway. Korean takeout covers the table, but David pushes a salad toward me.

"Is there anything we can do?" I ask, dropping into a seat.

Rose takes a sip of water. "You show the world you grew into a man who can handle his own mistakes and do better. People love a redemption story."

"They also love a downfall," I grumble.

"You're a good actor, you're hardworking, and the people who matter aren't going to change their minds because you had a traumatic childhood," Emma says. "And let's face it—however much of your career is down to your talent and drive, your uncle was Michael Sinclair and that helped you get where you are."

That makes me laugh. My scandal might bring Michael's into the light. He helped me up, I might help him fall.

Emma gives me a pointed look. "The tabloids will give you hell for a while, but everything will settle down. This is simply another embarrassing breach of your privacy. It deserves our attention. But your career is going to be fine. This is not the end of the world."

It feels like the end of the world.

Rose nods. "Get used to being the butt of a few jokes on the late-night talk show circuit for the next month—or until someone else eclipses you with a real scandal."

A month. A whole ass month of this is the best I can hope for. I groan again.

"So the plan is to lie low during the frenzy," David says, summarizing his notes. This whole meeting, I realize, was finished before I walked through the door. My life decided, without my input. "The official response is 'no comment' while the lawyers look into this, then we'll shift into talking about this as a breach of privacy, about your childhood as something traumatic that you've moved past. Some charity work for a youth organization or two and a solid donation."

"Would you be willing to do an interview with Julia Spencer to take the narrative back?" Rose asks. "It would build sympathy with the public to hear more about the hardships you faced growing up."

I scrub my hands over my face. I don't like the idea of showing off my scars on TV.

"The temperature right now is more upset that you hid these things," Rose says, "and still upset about how things with Kate panned out. So building sympathy and incorporating your past into your brand is the way forward."

"I'll do it," I say with a sigh. "But what about Ashley?"

"What about Ashley?" Rose asks sharply.

Seriously? "She sold me out, and she's getting away with it."

"You will say nothing about her to the public," Rose says sternly. "If she did this, the lawyers will handle it. If she didn't, our asses are covered."

"What do you mean 'if she didn't'?"

Rose steeples her fingers and sighs. "Look, Gabe. You're a big name in this industry, but Celia Foley knows people—why the hell do you think we agreed to her plan for this fake dating business? There were other ways to give you an edge."

"She's a TV chef—what could she possibly do to me?"

Rose laughs. "She might live in one corner of the pool, but you'd better believe a shark can swim wherever the fuck she wants. I don't know if she can effectively kill your career, but she knows enough people to make it challenging for you to get the roles you want if she decides she wants to get involved."

I cross my arms. "If her aunt could do that to me, why can't she get Ashley on a movie or TV show?"

Rose shrugs. "Family can be complicated, and it's easier to torpedo a career than build one. But if you go pointing fingers at Ashley, Celia might come for you and that's a battle I can't win."

"Who would win in a fight?" David asks suddenly. "Michael Sinclair or Celia Foley?"

The question barely earns a moment of consideration. "Celia," Rose and Emma say in unison.

David crosses something out in his notebook and stands. "We done?"

"Gabe?" Emma glances at me.

I nod, staring into space as everyone packs up their stuff. I manage to rouse myself enough to walk them to the door. Rose, last out, turns to me.

"This thing with Ashley is complicated, but you've handled it badly since the beginning. Let me handle it, okay? Don't reach out to her. If she tries to reach out to you, call me. This might feel like rock bottom, but trust me, if she wants to nuke you, she can make things a lot worse."

Things get worse the next day.

SPURNED EX ASHLEY FOLEY'S REVENGE?

"Sources close to Gabriel Sinclair say the actor believes Ashley Foley, his ex-girlfriend, is behind the salacious rumors about his past."

"Did you do this?" Rose demands when I finally call her back after my worst day on set ever. She gives me no time to deny it. "Are you fucking kidding me? You were supposed to stick to the plan. If you can't follow my instructions, Gabe, I'm out. I'm not going to war with Celia Foley for you."

I pinch the bridge of my nose and lean against the kitchen counter. I've had a hell of a headache all day and now that I'm in my apartment, I want to be left alone. "David and I talked about it on set. Someone must have overheard and fed it to the press." I don't tell her I said it loudly so people would hear. Why stop lying now?

There's a long pause. When she speaks, her voice is flat. "You two talked about this on set?"

I grit my teeth. "In hindsight, that was a mistake."

"No shit."

I promise to follow her instructions from now until the end of time and make a note to have David send her some expensive wine.

I'm about to take tomorrow's script to the office when there's a knock at the door. I'm not expecting anyone, David has a key, and it's late. A photographer could have slipped past the concierge. I should ignore it.

I don't, because I'm itching for something. A fight, I don't know. Something.

The first thing I notice is Ashley's light brown eyes, red-rimmed but dry. Her face is bare of everything except emotion. No lipstick, no smoky eye. The foot she sticks in the door, preventing me from closing it, is wearing a flip-flop and she's in a slouchy shirt that leaves one shoulder exposed. She's holding a large fruit basket, probably her ticket past the concierge.

"You can't be here." My voice sounds too tight and I hate how badly it betrays that she's wrecked me. I have to remind myself I owe her nothing.

"We can do this in the hall, where your neighbors can hear," she says softly. "Or inside. Your choice."

I let her in. She takes a few steps before stopping. A little of her composure crumbles and her chest rises as she takes a deep breath.

My hands clench at my sides. I want to throw that fucking fruit basket across the room and pull her close so I can breathe her in. I want her to tell me this is all a mistake as she wraps her arms around me.

Or maybe I want her to scream at me so I can scream back.

"The second day we were on the road, I texted my assistant, Lea," Ash finally says, "asking her to dig up anything she could find on you. I needed to know you weren't the perfect man you show the world. I forgot I asked her. She turned up at my place weeks ago with an entire dossier on you. She's really good at research."

I knew it was Ashley, but the confirmation of her betrayal is still a punch to the chest.

She barely pauses. "She promised she would keep everything she found confidential, and she has—this wasn't her fault. I tossed the file into a drawer and forgot about it, and when my house was broken into, it was stolen. I should've destroyed it—I meant to destroy it—but I didn't. I'm so sorry, Gabe."

My heart slams against my chest, pushing me to take a step toward her. "Your house was broken into?"

Her eyes narrow. "You didn't know?"

"No." I rub my aching forehead. If David knew and didn't tell me...

She takes a deep breath and her shoulders relax. "Well. Now you know. I didn't do it."

The unconcerned tone of her voice gets under my skin. "You threatened me. Told me I'd regret leaving you. How am I supposed to know you didn't do this?"

Ashley stares at me for a long moment, her eyes finally registering that she understands. I don't believe her.

"It wasn't a threat." She shifts her grip on the fruit basket, her voice dropping to a whisper. "I thought I meant something to you, that you would regret your choice. That you saw me for who I am and liked me. But you didn't, did you?" Her voice breaks, tears beading her eyelashes and even though I shouldn't, I want to wipe them away. Ashley's a brilliant actress and I'm not going to fall for it, but goddammit my skin itches for her.

I liked her too damn much. She became my weakness, and I had to let her go while I still could. While I still had something worth protecting. And she took it all away. "Why did you do it, Ash?"

"No," she says with a sad little laugh, her eyelashes fluttering as she blinks away tears. "I didn't do anything, but you...you told them it was me. Some spurned lover bullshit."

"Wasn't it?"

Her eyes shimmer, but she doesn't look away from me. Not for a second. "I've lost the only job opportunity to come my way since *Love on the Line*. Your lawyers are threatening me, saying I breached the NDA. I can't afford to fight them, let alone settle. They're combing through my phone records and my bank accounts and every aspect of my personal life. Another violation of my privacy. And that break-in? That was one of Kate's fans. You did this. To me. I loved you, for whatever it's worth." She finally looks down at the fruit basket she's still holding, sniffles, and hands it to me. "Welcome to the dark side, Gabe. You'll do just fine here."

With that, she walks out the door.

Chapter Thirty-One

Ashley

THE ANGER I FEEL deserts me the moment Gabe's door closes. I'm empty as I take the elevator down, leaving him behind in his new lofty tower. I thank the concierge, but the effort it takes to smile at the older gentleman drains me.

Gabe doesn't believe me. He will never believe in me. He'll turn himself into what he fears most, trying to measure up to his uncle, and nothing I can do will change a goddamn thing. I can't fix this or save him. I've never felt so powerless in my life.

It's late when I get back to Lauren's. Staying with her has been good. She's really stood beside me, helping me find Gabe's new apartment or providing a shoulder to cry on. I was worried her boyfriend Jax would be on Gabe's side since they work together, but he appears uninterested and entirely neutral. He's curt, but not in a way that feels unkind.

Odds are good both Lauren and Jax are asleep, so I lock the front door behind me, kick off my flip-flops, and walk out to the pool.

I sit on the edge of the shallow end to slip my feet into the water. A silent tear slides down my cheek and I brush it aside.

I love Gabriel Sinclair, whatever he's turning into, and I don't know how to stop. This is too much like breathing.

He's hurting. The gossip sites are still frothing over his secrets and the horrors of his childhood. It's sickening. It was hard for him to open up to me on the road. He must hate reliving all this again.

And he believes I did this to him. It might destroy me.

I should've destroyed the dossier. Or at least remembered it after the break-in. I suppose the SuperVan that broke in sold it. Although I wouldn't put it past those cops either.

Gabe's past is going to continue to bleed out into the public, and nothing short of a major scandal is going to knock him off the top.

I freeze and a laugh bubbles up from deep inside.

Well, fuck.

I'm a walking scandal. I could steal the spotlight from him with one phone call.

Except I'd never work again. Not in entertainment. There'd be no chance for me to claw my way back. Worse, I'd destroy my relationship with Jessie and the parts of my family I'd like to be closer to.

It's a big risk. It wouldn't fix anything, but it would ease his suffering a bit. It's what the hero or heroine would do, right? Sacrifice themselves for something bigger? That's what the movies say, and what's bigger than love? I'd be honoring what we had and who he helped me become.

It would also show that asshole how wrong he is about me.

Okay, so my motives aren't pure and spite is one of them, but I'm only me. Just a little better than I used to be.

I think I'm going to like this Ashley Foley.

I book a flight to New York before heading to bed, but I don't sleep. After a few hours of tossing and turning, it's time to get up. I pack an overnight bag and walk downstairs.

Celia is standing in the kitchen, her back to me as she makes a coffee.

She must be here to see Lauren. Or maybe to check on the property for Timothy. Or—

She glances over her shoulder. "Oh, good, you're up," she says brightly. "We need to talk." Her brows knit together when she sees my carry-on bag. "Are you going somewhere?"

"New York." I leave the bag by the door and join her in the kitchen. "What do you want to talk to me about?"

She sighs and hands me a cup of coffee, turning to make another. "I'm sorry this whole fake dating thing turned into such a mess. That was never my intention when I suggested it."

I perch on a bar stool and take a sip of coffee. "It's not your fault things got messy."

"Well, I'm here to help clean up, whatever my role in this. My lawyers are ready to represent you and they're already looking into our legal options."

"That's not necessary."

She gives me an unimpressed look as she tucks a loose strand of auburn hair behind her ear. "It really is. You shouldn't have given his lawyers access to your personal records—they don't prove anything, as you could've received a cash payment and used a burner phone. But I hired an investigator. I met with him yesterday."

My eyes burn with tears. The aunt I sold out when I was a kid believes in me and the man I love doesn't. It twists my heart a little harder. "You didn't have to."

Celia waves it off and pushes a box of doughnuts toward me.

"Aunt Celia, I'm sorry I told your secret to my father—"

She hisses. "Don't mention that man." With a heavy sigh, she leans over the island and grabs a doughnut for herself. "You were a child. You didn't know."

"I knew." This was where it all started. My villain origin story. She can say I was a child, and a part of me wants to believe her, but the day I went home with her secret in my head, wrapped up with Jessie's warning about why I couldn't tell anyone, I made my first real choice to use something that wasn't mine to get what I wanted, even though I knew people would get hurt.

"I didn't blame you then, and I don't blame you now." She takes a bite of her chocolate doughnut. "Which one of the kids told you, anyway?"

"Jessie. She saw you and your...friend." It feels weird to say *lover* with my aunt.

"Olivia was my friend. And for a time, she was something more." Celia sighs, but it's wistful. "You didn't know the whole story. Neither did Jessie. William and I opened our marriage for a while. We were so young when we got together. We didn't have time to explore all the facets of our sexuality. But at the end of the day, William is my person, and I'm his. We chose to close our marriage again to ensure our personal lives stayed private. We should've been upfront with the kids. Jessie and Timothy were teenagers, and Amanda was an adult—they probably would've understood. We told ourselves it wasn't their business. Until it was."

"I'm sorry."

Celia smiles. "We had a few months to live out some fantasies. Besides, my friend and I had some wild, dirty times together, and William enjoyed his time with another married couple. We learned a lot about ourselves and our relationship. This one time, Olivia and I—"

"I have to get to the airport," I say quickly. Celia isn't my mother, but an aunt is close enough and this is way more than I need to know about her sex life.

Celia laughs, completely unembarrassed. "At least we didn't defile a gas station bathroom."

"Oh my god." I lower my head to the smooth surface of the island to hide the tears. I can't hide the little sob that bursts out. I'd give anything to have Gabe want me enough to defile a gas station restroom again.

"It'll be okay," Celia says softly, coming around the island to gently rub my back. "It might not seem like it now, but things will work out."

In a way, she's right. Things can work out, though not in the way I want them to. Gabe is lost to me, but that doesn't mean I can't do something meaningful with my life.

On the flight, I pull Wendy's script out of my bag. It's about a reality TV dating show gone horribly wrong—research for it was a big reason why she wanted the chance to go back on the show. It immediately pulls me in with its sharp humor and heartwarming relationships, and I can see the places where my notes and experience added depth. I loved the earlier draft and I love this one even more.

When the plane lands, I message Wendy and ask her to email me a copy and can I pass it along to a few people. I doubt sending it to Celia will do anything, but the woman has money and connections.

If things go well with Jessie and Nic, I'll pass it on to him. But I don't expect this to go well.

I used to imagine myself in control, moving the pieces around the chessboard because that put me above it. It kept me safe. It didn't hurt to be unloved when love was never the goal. When I used people first.

This is something new, and it's incredibly uncomfortable.

The shame of what I tried to do weighs down on me, but I walk up to the stoop of the beautiful Upper West Side brownstone—Nic and Jessie's new house, according to Lauren—and ring the bell.

Nic opens the door, clearly surprised to see me. And uncomfortable. "Ashley. I didn't know you were in New York."

"Just got in," I say, trying to sound bright. "Can I talk to you and Jessie for a few minutes?"

He ushers me in and calls out to Jessie after shutting the door. "Want a drink?" he asks me, leading me to the kitchen. Their house is stunning. Fully renovated sometime in the last decade, white walls hung with beautiful artwork that looks like Jessie's, it's warm and welcoming. I sit at the dining room table, trying to get my nerves under control. I have no idea how Jessie is going to take this, and I desperately hope this doesn't devolve into a hair-pulling brawl.

Nic pours me a glass of wine and goes back to cooking dinner. It smells divine.

"So," he says carefully, then swears and vigorously stirs a pot on the stove. I glance at him and he's rigid. He hasn't made eye contact with me once since he let me in.

He knows. Timothy must have told him after he met with me in LA.

Fuck.

Jessie comes into the room, her auburn hair in a ponytail, and a streak of green paint on her cheek. She smiles widely and I know Timothy didn't tell her. "Ashley! How are you doing?"

"I tried to seduce your husband on your wedding day," I blurt out. "But my assistant sent Gabe to the room instead of Nic. I'm taking this to the press, and I want you both to be prepared."

Jessie's eyes go absurdly wide, then stormy. She takes a few steps toward me and pauses as her brow furrows. For a long moment, she stares at me. Without a word, she grabs the bottle of wine from the island and sinks into a chair a safe distance from me at the table.

She takes a swig from the bottle, wipes her mouth with the back of her hand, and abruptly bursts into laughter. "Are you fucking kidding me?"

Nic brings her a glass, kissing her on the top of the head and glaring at me.

"I'm sorry," I say to her, then turn to Nic as he retreats into the kitchen. "I'm sorry, Nic. I thought I was in love. I wasn't."

"It wouldn't have worked," Nic says, lifting a steaming pot from the stove and bringing it to the sink. "I love Jessie."

"I know. I was messed up and I...I thought we had some kind of understanding. That we got each other."

"We barely know each other," Nic points out, draining pasta.

He's angry.

I glance at Jessie. She's looking at me like she's puzzling it all out.

I'd rather deal with Nic's anger.

"I know," I say to him. "I'm sorry. I don't have any feelings for you, I promise I'll never try to interfere—"

"Then what are you doing here?" he snaps.

"You love Gabriel Sinclair," Jessie says quietly. "That's why you want to take this to the press, isn't it? Because they're shredding him to pieces."

My throat closes, so I nod.

"They'll shred you to pieces."

Again, I nod.

Jessie stands. "How long until dinner?"

"Twenty minutes," Nic says after the slightest hesitation.

She turns to me. "Come on."

"I really am sorry," I say as I follow Jessie upstairs. I don't know if she believes me. Sincerity never sounds authentic from my mouth.

She walks into a room that she's turned into an art studio. "I love Nic. He loves me. You couldn't have changed that. Maybe you could have ruined our day, but you couldn't have driven us apart. See that board with the green tape? Bring it here."

I glance where she's pointed, and against the wall spot the board and the piece of paper taped to it. When I hand it to her, she sets it on the easel and hands me a brush. "Are you familiar with watercolors?"

"Why aren't you mad at me?"

"I'm not happy, but your plan failed so spectacularly you fell in love with another man and to be honest, you look like shit. It's hard to be angry with someone whose heart is broken. So slap some paint on that canvas and tell me the truth about you and Gabriel Sinclair. The whole story."

I stare as she pours water from a pitcher into a glass and sets it on the tray below the easel, alongside a row of colors in a rectangular box. A few little squares are empty of color.

"Mix colors here," Jessie says, tapping her brush on one. "More water will dilute the color, and paint whatever. It doesn't have to be anything."

She goes back to her easel, and after a moment, I dip a brush and wet the pink paint. Then I tell her everything, from the moment Gabe walked through that door to the moment I handed him the fruit basket and left.

I paint a pink sky while I talk. Reddish-brown mountains. A black ribbon of a highway. A six-year-old could paint better, but for a few minutes, I can feel the wind in my hair and Gabe's hand on my leg.

Reality sucks.

Nic calls upstairs that dinner is done, and Jessie drags me to the washroom, helping clean me up. I have paint on my face from wiping at tears, but she goes one step beyond, pulling out a makeup kit and doing what she can because I do look ghastly. I can't remember when I last had a good night's sleep.

Jessie insists I stay for dinner and makes the three of us squeeze together for a selfie.

"I should've been a better cousin when we were kids," she says, putting her phone away. "It might not help a lot, but we can stand together as a family now. After you tell your story to the vultures, I'll post this and let the world know there are no hard feelings."

"Are there hard feelings?" I ask, terrified of the answer.

"No," she says, pulling me into a hug. "But if you ever come for my man, I will end you."

I can't tell if she's joking, but I promise her I have no interest in Nic.

Nic, for his part, remains leaning against the stairs. Distant and aloof, as always.

"I'll talk to my parents," Jessie promises. "Timothy and Amanda, too, so they know we're good."

"Thank you," I manage, tears springing to my eyes again. Christ, I've never cried so much in my life.

When I return to LA, I light the match and torch my life.

ASHLEY FOLEY'S ATTEMPT AT SEDUCING NIC FONTANA—AT HIS WEDDING!

It's like watching dominoes fall as every outlet picks up the story. As it grows and gains speed, Gabriel Sinclair all but disappears.

Chapter Thirty-Two

Gabe

"You'll do just fine here."

I can't escape Ashley's voice or the dejection in her eyes or the crushing sensation that's been locked around my heart since I broke up with her.

"Did you know about this?" I ask David when he turns up at my apartment on Sunday. His day off. When he takes one glance at my phone and the images of Ashley's trashed house and gives a curt nod, I nearly lose it. "You should've told me."

The things people have said about it...

Pity she wasn't home.

She's trash, who cares?

OMG, did you see the pictures <horror emoji>

She probably did it to herself.

My stomach twists again. I can't look at the photos. The crude words written all over her bedroom wall.

Her bedroom.

Some creep was in there, touching her things.

The violation of her privacy shakes me to the core, but the fear of what might have happened had she been home...

David shrugs. "You said you didn't want to hear about her unless it was an emergency."

"This is an emergency!"

He shrugs. "For her, yes. Not for you."

"I want to know, okay?" Even now, even after everything she's done.

"Well, I'm here on my day off because you need to see this." He hands me his phone with a grim look on his face and I am so sick of this I swear to god I'm going to throw the phone on the floor and break it.

ASHLEY FOLEY'S ATTEMPT AT SEDUCING NIC FONTANA—AT HIS WEDDING!

I am a dead man if Rose thinks I leaked this. I drop onto the nearest chair and force myself to read the article for any clue how this got out.

I read it three times and I still don't understand. The language is unclear, but it reads like the source is Ashley.

"It wasn't you, right?" David asks hesitantly.

I shake my head.

He sighs, relieved. "Then it has to be Ashley or someone very close to her."

"Why would she do this to herself?"

David takes a seat in the chair across from me. "I don't know, but she's knocked you out as a trending topic. I spoke to Rose—I had to swear on my mother's life you weren't behind this, by the way—and she agreed we should be cautiously optimistic. Ashley's dumpster fire is drawing attention away from you at the moment."

I frown at the photo in the article. It's the one of us from the wedding, Ashley leaving the room. Someone has Photoshopped Nic over me and it makes me bristle. "Do you think she did this on purpose?"

I loved you, for whatever it's worth, she'd said.

Is it possible she meant it? That she did love me? If that's true, then I'm wrong and everything I've said and done is unforgivable.

"I doubt she'd make this kind of mistake on accident," David says after a moment. "But her motivations might have nothing to do with you."

Right. Ashley could be up to anything. She wouldn't blow up her life to protect mine—it doesn't gain her anything.

"You'll do just fine here."

Those words keep haunting me. But I can't be the bad guy. She's wrong.

Ashley is up to something.

Since I can't trust anyone on my team to tell me anything about her, I devote what little free time I have to monitoring her social media. For three days, there's nothing. Her last post is a photo of her in that jumpsuit, with the comment *New opportunities.* What opportunity was that? She said she'd lost it thanks to me.

Four days after her story dropped, Ash comes out of hiding with a vengeance, filling her social media with photos. She's all dressed up, out with people she calls friends, but I've never heard her speak about.

When I see pictures of her in a club, her arms around some douche—musician, apparently—I have to get up and do one of Jax's stupid workouts so I don't explode.

Even then, it's not enough.

I can't bring myself to put down my phone. I set an alert for anything she's tagged in. Next thing I know, it's 2 a.m. and she's shitfaced, flashing the paps when she gets out of a car.

I'm halfway to the door—I don't care if it's the middle of the night and I have to be in my trailer in three hours—before I realize I cannot do this. I'm trying to rehabilitate my image. Chasing after my drunk ex and getting into a public altercation over what I'm doing there is the exact opposite of what I need to be doing.

I call David. Bodyguard duty—if he trails Ash and keeps her safe, I'll give him a twenty thousand dollar bonus and a holiday.

I don't sleep. Ashley doesn't stop.

Every break I get on set, I'm watching her. She's getting tagged at some rich asshole's mansion, where the party's still going. David was able to sneak in, at least.

The director yells at me to get my head out of my ass—how can I forget the one fucking line I have in this scene?

I want to tear my hair, but the moment I touch it someone will descend upon me to fix it and I'd rather keep every human at arm's length right now.

If Ash is celebrating the end of her career after telling the world she tried to seduce Nic, she's not going out quietly. She stops for a wardrobe change, then she's back at it, surrounded by the usual types of hangers-on.

She's killing me.

David too.

> I haven't slept in days. When is she going to stop?

DAVID

I don't know if she stops. One day she's dancing on a bar, the next, she's gone. No new posts, and no one tagging her. Nothing from the paps. The only thing anyone is talking about is a cheating scandal where both partners of a celebrity power couple discovered they were sleeping with the same nanny.

I send David to Ashley's house. It was trashed so bad it's boarded up. No one is living there. She has a cousin in LA, so I send David on a goose chase to track her down. He does, and it turns out her cousin is dating my personal trainer.

Jax refuses to tell David if he's seen Ashley. When I call him, he tells me that if I even ask him once, he'll make my life hell and I still won't be any closer to Ashley. Which has to mean she's not there.

Next, I send David to find Wendy. It doesn't go well. Wendy chews him out, throws a shoe at him, and sends him on his way without giving up Ashley's location.

"She's not at Wendy's, I'm positive," David swears. I nearly send him back because I'm not so sure and I'm worried, but he tells me he'd rather face Jax again before he hangs up on me.

It's the weekend. I can't throw myself into work and my apartment is suddenly too small. I've been pacing like a caged animal all morning. I hop on my motorcycle and head to Malibu.

I don't need reminders of Michael's goddamn legacy—I need the beach. A paved path winds down the hill the house is perched on and I leave my shoes at the end of it, walking out into the soft sand.

The fresh air helps, but standing in front of the ocean drives home how small and helpless I am in the face of my problems. I drop down into the sand and stare at the waves rolling in.

Everything I've ever done in my whole life is out there. Someone can dredge up my secrets, or they could float up, and I can't stop it. I can't protect my reputation, Michael's legacy. Not from the whole goddamn world.

I can't even find Ash. She's blocked my number.

Everything she's done since handing me that fruit basket has been a giant "fuck you" because I hurt her. I didn't believe her when she came to tell me the truth.

"She didn't do it," I mumble to the setting sun.

I can't prove it, but I know it, deep in my soul. She loved me, and I destroyed that love.

I love her. I know that now too. All of me, every corner of my soul belongs to her and the realization settles over me in waves, each one a little bigger, a little stronger. Even when I thought she'd sold me out, I still loved her. Hated her, too, but loved her more.

Maybe it's better this way. We can't be together.

I miss her so damn much.

The sun sinks toward the horizon, but I don't feel like moving. So I don't. Maybe I never will. I'll stay on this beach until the wind and waves turn me to sand.

"Hey." David drops down next to me, handing me a beer.

"How'd you know I was here?" I ask, popping the top off and taking a long pull from the bottle. I'm too tired to be irritated.

"Heard the motorcycle." David takes a drink of his beer and shifts on the sand. He has something to tell me. The way my life is going, it's not going to be something good.

He clears his throat. "Ashley didn't sell you out."

"Yeah," I dig my toes deeper, relieved *this* is his news. "I know."

"We have proof. A sworn statement from that paparazzo saying she was staking out Ashley's place because a call came down to clear out and she was suspicious. She'd never spoken to Ashley or with anyone on Ashley's behalf. So it wasn't a setup. Just bad luck."

I close my eyes. My blood is rushing in my ears, drowning out the surf.

"And it turns out Ashley was right about a file on you being stolen from her house—it wasn't the intruder though. It was one of the cops. The dumbass leaked the photos of her bedroom to the press too. He's facing charges."

Good. The bastard.

David sighs. "Here's the bad news: we know all this because Celia Foley hired an investigator, who turned all this up. On the bright side, she hasn't sued you yet."

She can sue me. Ash can have everything. The house, the money, all of it. I'll pack some clothes and just drive. Wherever the road takes me. I need the wind rushing through the window and that long ribbon of highway fading off into the distance. The suffocating emptiness of it all.

My life, my soul, everything is empty without her anyway.

"And Ashley was the source behind the wedding story. It was very deliberate, according to the reporter." David pauses for a drink, then looks thoughtfully out at the ocean. After a moment, he shakes his head. "This might be nothing, but...that drunken party rampage? She wasn't drunk. I watched her. She was acting, playing it up anytime she saw a camera. From time to time, she'd step back, like she needed a break, and she appeared remarkably sober."

Ash is brilliant at playing the role of Ashley Foley. It's a relief to know she hasn't lost control. Makes her sudden disappearance a little less terrifying. She's chosen to hide.

"Rose was monitoring your media coverage," David continues, "so I checked with her. It's just a possibility, but I think Ashley was paying attention too. When you crept back up toward the spotlight, she put herself in the way. Because the moment that nanny scandal broke, she disappeared."

I acknowledge him with a slow nod. His words are sinking in, slowly rewriting everything I foolishly thought I knew about the situation. She did it to save me, to give me a break.

David falls silent, but he doesn't make a move to leave until he's finished the beer. "I told you on the press junket that you weren't Michael. I don't think you caught my meaning."

Fucking Michael. I loved and adored and idolized the man. He deserved less than I gave him. Ashley deserved more than I gave her. I can't get it right.

"Michael kept Lilah a secret, even when she might have been amenable to a public relationship because he wanted to preserve his legacy as this great, unimpeachable man who could rise above his philandering father and the worst of the industry that surrounded him. He felt the guilt, but he didn't struggle with it. He chose his image and never looked back. You look back. You struggle when you do something wrong. You can be better than Michael. It's not too late."

I snort. I'm so much worse than Michael. I've fucked this thing up so badly there's no coming back.

He stands. "I know I never gave Ashley a chance, but you did. You were happy for once." He seems to realize he's gone too far and clears his throat. "Anyway, you know where to find me. If you want to talk."

I don't deserve Ashley and I sure as shit don't deserve to be happy. The only thing I have now is my job—if I can pull my head out of my ass long enough to keep it.

"Thanks," I force myself to say, but his words are just another rock pulling me down.

"Welcome to the dark side, Gabe. You'll do just fine here."

CHAPTER THIRTY-THREE

Ashley

MY CAR WAS IN the garage when the intruder broke into my house, so of course they trashed it along with everything else. One call from my aunt's people and my insurance company made paying me out a priority. Plus, the money from Gabe breaking our fake dating contract came through. For half a heartbeat I consider sending the money back, but it's kind of like an asshole tax. Plus, he's rich and I'm not.

I bought a car. I chose this particular model strictly because I liked the look of it. Not because it reminded me of Gabe or the life we might have had.

Okay, maybe a little because of that.

It's a deep red, more rust than cherry, with sleek lines. A 1970 Plymouth GTX. I had to get Wendy to teach me how to drive a manual, but we had a blast. She screamed when I fucked up a gear change and panicked when I stalled out at intersections and laughed her ass off with me over the whole thing.

We take a bunch of selfies in the car too. She posts a few on her social media, but I'm not ready to post anything on mine yet.

I need to get out of LA for a while. Kate Van Sandt publicly condemned the actions of her fans and went so far as to personally call me with an apology, but everything here still feels toxic and intrusive. I need to clear my head. So I drive. I don't know where I'm going or what I want, but everything I own is in my car. I could go anywhere. Start over and be anyone.

It doesn't feel as good as it did with Gabe next to me, but there's something in the emptiness, once I leave the mountains behind, that soothes me. I have space to think and grieve and cry. By now, he'll know about the investigator. It won't change anything, but I'm glad he'll know it wasn't me.

I post one of the pictures Wendy took. My hand wrapped around the gear stick, in black and white. Very similar to the one I took with Gabe. I can't bring myself to comment and I have no idea if he'll even see it, but it's a new beginning for me, and this time, I'm driving. I'm not living my life trying to win the love or attention of anyone. I'm living it for me, loving myself for me. Taking the time to figure this newer, truer version of myself out.

I don't know if it will last, but I hope so. As terrifying as it is, for the first time in my life, I feel good.

Okay, maybe not good, but I feel like I'll survive this. Like I can find happiness in myself.

Hours and miles fly by and I drive as long as I can before stopping for the night. It's hardest in the dark, as loneliness bites while I toss and turn, but morning always comes.

The roadsides turn greener with trees and the roads get thicker with traffic. I stick to highways though. The interstates are boring.

I want the scenic route.

Chapter Thirty-Four

Gabe

I'M MISERABLE. IRRITABLE. I can't hide it or pretend everything's fine. The cast and crew of Warwick are giving me a wide berth, except for the director, who is almost giddy over what he mistakenly assumes is method acting.

I push through each day, but the relief I expect to feel when I get home—to my apartment, to the house in Malibu, it doesn't matter—never comes. Even David doesn't want to be around me.

He has a key to this goddamned apartment, and yet he's taken to knocking at the door.

Tonight, I debate ignoring the knock. Whatever this is can probably be an email.

"Gabe?" Her voice is muffled by the thick door, but that's not David.

I fling the door open and Aunt Cora sweeps me into a hug. Her arms hold me with the same firm but gentle embrace, and immediately I'm thirteen again, meeting her for the first time, terrified and angry and lonely. That scared little boy is still inside me, and he bursts into tears.

Cora makes a sympathetic noise and lets me cry it out. I haven't cried since Michael's funeral and it feels like I'll never be done. It passes through me like a storm, while my aunt holds me, and eventually, my eyes dry and I feel empty.

She sends me off to shower, insisting it will make me feel better. It doesn't. When I come out, she's in the kitchen, chopping vegetables. I help her while she catches me up on the latest news from her life in New Mexico.

I needed the reprieve of half an hour of lightness in my life. It's been so dark lately.

We sit with a warm roast vegetable salad topped with almonds and a pesto dressing. Cora watches me like a hawk and pushes a second slice of crusty bread my way when I finish mine.

"I can't eat this," I tell her, but the look on her face tells me exactly what she thinks of that, so I eat the second slice. And a third.

It's coming. The talk. The reason she's here. I put it off by doing the dishes when we're done eating, but Cora doesn't let me escape. She makes me a cup of tea and pushes me back to the table.

"What happened?" she asks in a soft voice.

I don't deserve the sympathy in her eyes. I turn my gaze to the table. "It was supposed to be fake."

"However it started, it was real by the time you arrived at my house," she says.

I don't want to remember the night Ash and I spent together there. The way she looked up at me from her knees. Her hands on my thighs. Every night we had together after. Just...*her*. I want to forget her. I need to.

"Things got out of hand," I explain everything as briefly as I can. I don't try to hide how wrong I was, or how mean I was, but I don't want to relive it.

"She's special," Cora says when I've finished. "You don't open up to others easily, but you did with her. And she cared deeply for you. I don't think she's the type of person who easily gives that away. Have you talked to her?"

My heart squeezes. "I can't."

Cora gives me a stern look over the rim of her mug. "Why not?"

"There's no point. I can't be with her. I forget who I am. What I'm supposed to be."

She gets it immediately. "This is about Michael."

"He wanted me to carry on his legacy—"

"Oh, fuck his *legacy*," she bursts out. "Do you think his legacy made him happy?"

I stare at her in surprise.

"Michael was a good man in many ways, and he should be applauded for his work and how he went about his work. But his idea of good and bad was very black and white, formed entirely by his desire to be better than his crappy father. He was never happy. And he was far from perfect."

Fear creeps across me, and guilt. Does she know his secret? If she doesn't, should I tell her? I really don't want to.

Cora stands and rummages around the fully stocked liquor cabinet until she finds a bottle of brandy, then tops up both of our cups of tea with it.

"I told him he was too hard on you, but I thought I could temper it." She takes a long drink and leans forward, arms crossed on the table. "I need to tell you something about Michael, and it's going to upset you."

I run my hand over my jaw, but I nod.

"I wasn't happy living in LA, so Michael and I agreed we'd rather have a long-distance relationship than separate. Well...after I left, he fell in love with another woman. They had a child together, a boy."

I exhale slowly. There's no heartbreak in her voice, no bitterness. Only concern for me. Sympathy.

"I know," I whisper.

"You do?" Cora picks her cup up again and drains the rest. "Thank god, I didn't want to be the one to drag him off that pedestal you both put him on."

"He told you?"

"He told me about Lilah and his son before he passed away," she says. "He was ashamed of his behavior, but never of them."

"He told you." He never told me. No, I had to find out by accident, ten years after his death, when our financial adviser retired and the new one started asking me questions about a trust fund I knew nothing about.

"He had to make sure they'd be comfortable after he was gone, and he knew I'd find out. He was afraid to tell you."

Bullshit. "He was a hypocrite."

Cora shrugs. "He was complicated. Most people are."

"He cheated on you."

"And I forgave him."

"How?" I can't find a way.

A sad little smile crosses her face. "Who does it serve, holding on to the hurt?" she asks. "I could carry the pain of his decisions around every day, but I'd rather not. Honestly, I pity him."

"You pity him."

Cora nods. "He suffered under the weight of his own expectations and standards. He could've been happy, had he divorced me and married Lilah. He could've been a real role model for his son as well as you. But he chose to stay on his pedestal."

"You're a saint," I mutter.

Cora laughs. "No, but I know who I am and I'm happy with my life. And that's what I want for you, my dear. I want you to be happy. You don't need Michael's brand of perfectionism to be a good person, and I want you to see that and trust in yourself."

"What about what I want?"

"What do you want, Gabe? To spurn a woman who loves you because she isn't good enough for your dead uncle?"

I wince, but she's right. I chose myself over Ashley's love and I publicly humiliated her, calling her a spurned ex. How could anyone do that to the woman they loved?

Welcome to the club.

"You and Michael were wrong about me," I say, crossing my arms and dropping my head onto them. "There's no good in me."

Cora pats my back. "That's not true. You decide who you are. Only you. And you can change and grow, rise or fall. Every day you start again. And as long as I'm on this earth, I'll be here for you. No matter what you do, or don't do, I believe in you and you'll never be alone."

Her belief means so damn much, even if I can't bring myself to believe the same. I get to my feet to wrap my arms around her. "Thank you."

She hugs me back. "You are worthy of love, just as you are," she says firmly. "Promise me you'll think about what you want, and when you figure it out, you'll go for it."

"I will," I promise, squeezing her tight.

"That personal trainer of yours needs to ease up a bit," Cora grumbles. "It's like hugging a redwood."

"Maybe you could write me a note. Get me out of leg day." I know Jax though. He'd take the note, fold it into a bite-size chunk, and eat it while maintaining intense levels of eye contact.

Might be worth it.

An alert goes off on my phone—it has to be Ashley—and I glance around. Rose is talking with Julia Spencer about the interview we're about to tape and Cora's trying to persuade a stoic David to accompany her to an animal shelter tomorrow. He won't meet the nice young surf instructor she wants to introduce him to, so he might as well get a pet. A rabbit, she thinks. David is horrified and trying to very politely find a way out of it.

Everyone else is quietly doing their job.

I slip my phone out of my pocket and relief nearly takes me out at the knees. I grab onto the chair in front of me. The voices around me all fade into the background.

Ash is alive. She's okay.

She posted a photo on her social media. Just one, in black and white. Her hand wrapped around a gear stick. There's a glimpse of the empty passenger seat and a sliver of Ashley's leg.

This isn't the car she drove over to my place. That one was a sleek Mercedes convertible, five years old—a gift, she'd said, from her father, after she'd stolen a lover from her mother.

The car in her post is a classic car.

She doesn't leave a comment—only the photo. No indication of where she is or where she's going.

It doesn't escape me that her photo is the same as the one we posted on our road trip, but with one hand instead of two.

She's driving to New York, retracing our journey. I feel it, like a siren song calling out to me. I belong in that car with her, not trying to reinvent myself with a TV interview.

"Are you ready?" Rose asks.

"Yeah," I say, quickly turning my phone off and slipping it into my pocket.

"Nice to meet you, Gabriel," Julia says in a warm voice, shaking my hand. Her white blazer sets off her flawless dark brown skin and her eyes crinkle as she smiles. We take our seats and I thank her for taking the time to talk to me on such short notice and so late in the day.

Julia has been interviewing celebrities for decades, gently prizing out juicy little details of personal lives. She's not the softball interviewer working hand in hand with PR, but she's not a shark scenting blood in the water either. With her dazzling smile and kind eyes, she's someone people want to open up to. Viewers trust her, celebrities adore her. She's my last hope.

Finally, everyone is in place and we're ready to shoot.

Julia begins with some simple questions.

I've been playing the role of Gabriel Sinclair for so long, it should be easy, but it doesn't fit right anymore. There are little moments when I have no idea what Gabriel Sinclair would say, or who he is. Julia tries to keep me on track, but the problem is me.

My ass might be firmly in this surprisingly comfortable chair, but I'm not fully present. I'm with Ash, on an endless highway somewhere under the stars.

If I'm going to get my life back on track, I have to do this. This is what I've worked for. This is what I want. All I have to do is stick to the script. Show vulnerability. Be contrite and humble. Talk about my struggles so I gain sympathy from my audience, but make it clear I'm what I've always pretended to be—the good guy. The last few months were a blip brought on by the stress of taking on a grittier role given my childhood. I've strived to live up to the ideals of my uncle, who I miss. There was no relationship with Kate Van Sandt, I was still with Ashley and it was miscommunication from my team and the assumptions of reporters.

It's painful, talking about my childhood, but Julia smiles encouragingly. She asks me about going from foster care to Michael's care, and I answer honestly that it was hard, there was a steep learning curve, but he taught me about integrity and responsibility and a million other things.

Julia lets the silence hang for a beat too long, and for some reason, I fill it, even though it takes me off script and into deeper water. "It's hard to live up to his standards, to be the man he wanted me to be."

Julia leans forward. "And who did he want you to be?"

"He wanted me to be better than him."

"How do you 'be better than Michael Sinclair'?" she asks, and I know she's making a point, not asking a question. It's in the sympathetic lift of her lips and the slightest hint of a laugh.

I shrug, shaking my head. If I had the answer to that...

Or maybe I do.

"I can't."

Her brows furrow. "Why would you say that?"

"Michael Sinclair was an amazing director who treated people with kindness and compassion, who held himself to such impossible standards. But I'm not sure it was enough. I don't know that his legacy made him truly happy."

Julia smiles and lets that sink in a beat before pivoting away from Michael. "And what makes you happy?"

Ashley.

A little smile steals across my face before I can stop it. Ashley made me happy. I think I made her happy too.

"Ah," Julia says knowingly. "Your whirlwind romance with Ashley Foley was...unexpected. So you go into this hotel room, and Ashley is there, waiting for another man. Tell me what was going through your head."

There's a scripted version of our relationship history I'm supposed to follow, one Ashley changed when she revealed her attempt at seducing Nic, but she didn't out our fake relationship. Merely pivoted and said we sparked immediately. That's the one I'm supposed to stick to.

For a second, I debate telling the truth, disclosing our relationship was a publicity stunt. But that might backfire on Ashley and I've hurt her enough, so I don't.

"You know," Julia says after I answer, "a lot of people say she was a bad influence on you. Do you think there's some truth in that?"

I bristle. "No."

Julia waits, and I realize I'm supposed to elaborate, not glare. It's hard to shake my anger at the world—impossible to budge the anger I still feel at myself. "She challenged me every step of the way, but she encouraged me to be myself. For that, I'll always be grateful."

Julia tilts her head and says in a soft, conspiratorial voice. "It sounds like you still care about her."

So much it hurts. "I know the real Ashley Foley, the one the rest of the world doesn't see. She's painted as someone she played on a competitive TV show, but that isn't her. We all know reality TV feeds on drama and thrives off of shock and outrage, so they push the people on the shows to be their worst and edit the footage to fit a pre-determined story. Ashley knew what she was doing, and she played to win, but the side of her the world saw isn't all she is."

"And who is the real Ashley Foley?"

"She's kind. She has a great sense of humor and she's fun to be around, but she's also been incredibly supportive and nonjudgmental. She's smart and brutally honest, and she knows who she is. She's made mistakes, but so have I."

"You believed she was behind your childhood being leaked to the press. Do you still believe that to be true?"

"I was in a state of shock, and while talking with a close friend, someone overheard us and passed on the conversation without context." The lie doesn't sit right on my tongue and I reach for my water. At the very least I owe Ashley a public apology, but that's not in the script and I have to get back on the script.

"What would you say to her, if she was here now?"

I take a deep breath. The answer I'm supposed to give? I like it even less than the last one. I take a long drink of water, my eyes seeking Cora. My eyes land on Rose first. She's watching me with rapt attention and a tinge of concern because I've already gone off script, talking about Ashley like this. Next to her, David has a tablet out, probably checking my schedule for the week.

Cora's sitting a little further back. She smiles at me encouragingly, and I think back on our conversation last night. All she wants is for me to be happy, but my happiness has never been my priority.

Ashley would never take me back. All I have left is this. My career. Fixing my reputation.

Or maybe I'm telling myself that so I can pretend I don't have a choice. So I don't have to give up on the person I've needed to become. So I don't have to face who I am.

Shit.

I'm doing it again, putting my reputation first, my job first, Michael's hopes first. It will never make me happy. It never made him happy.

What if I made a different choice? Maybe if I just let myself be myself, if I leave Michael's version of Gabriel Sinclair behind, I'd stop feeling like a fraud and a failure. I could choose happiness.

I could choose Ashley. Even if she'd no longer choose me.

My thoughts are a jumbled mess so I speak slowly, "I would tell her she was right about me. When she needed me, instead of standing by her, I chose to protect myself. I told myself my image was more important than how I felt about her, or how she felt about me, so I ended things. She trusted me, believed in me, and I refused to do the same for her. I was deliberately cruel when she deserved kindness and compassion." I can see Rose's frown as she takes a half step toward us before David stops her with a tap on her arm.

Cora's eyes are wide and hopeful. I manage a small smile for her, and then I throw out the script. "I would tell Ashley I'm sorry I put her second. I'm sorry I didn't stand by her. And I'm sorry I blamed her and refused to see what was right in front of me." I take a deep breath, letting it out in a carefully controlled exhale. "The truth is, Julia, I felt I had to be this perfect person to earn the love of people who already loved me. I owed it to my aunt and uncle for taking me in, for giving me a home and an opportunity at a life I could never have dreamed of. And I let that need get in the way of what I want in life. I hurt someone special. I became someone I didn't like. I see that now and I want to change. I'm going to change. And maybe I can't live up to Michael Sinclair's standards, but I like to think, if he'd lived, he'd understand. That he could be proud of the man I'm still becoming."

Julia smiles at me. "Tell me about *him*. Who is the real Gabriel Sinclair?"

"He's complicated," I admit. "But he's trying."

"Would he rescue a kitten from a tree?"

"Of course."

"And help little old ladies with their groceries?"

I laugh, rubbing the back of my neck. "If any of them will trust me again, yes."

Julia's eyes sparkle as she leans forward again. "But he also rides a motorcycle, vandalizes public restrooms, and loves a reality TV villain?"

My jaw clenches. Off set, Rose silently slaps a hand against her forehead.

"She's not a villain," I say firmly.

"But you love her?"

"That's not something you tell someone for the first time on TV," I say pointedly.

Julia takes the hint and moves on, after a smile that says she knows the answer. "You've been America's golden boy in rom-coms, dramas, and comedies for years. You're currently filming Warwick, where you're playing the titular hero and I understand the director is taking the franchise into some darker waters. Are you interested in dipping your toes into some darker roles? What's next for Gabriel Sinclair?"

"I don't know," I say with a shrug. "But there will be something next for me because this industry doesn't care what I've done or who I am inside. It will reward me with sympathy and second chances because that's what it's set up to do. Because I'm a white man who inherited wealth and a name that means something. Because society can find something redeemable in me but condemnable in Ashley. The double standards in this industry, in our society, are wrong."

My publicist is waving her arms at me to stop talking, but I have nothing left to say that hasn't been said before by smarter people than me. I don't have any answers or solutions. Nothing new to contribute.

Julia thanks me for talking to her and reminds everyone they can see me in *The Last Best Man*, which is out in cinemas everywhere next week, and the interview is over.

I thank Julia and head straight for David.

"I'm getting a philodendron," he announces before I can say anything. "Can you tell your aunt I don't need to go to the shelter tomorrow? I have allergies. To everything with fur."

Cora's biting back a smile. "Reptiles don't have fur."

David pales.

"Sorry," I say to my aunt, "but I need David, and trust me, he's going to wish he was sneezing over dogs and cats with you."

Cora's smile lights up her face. "You're going after her?"

"Yeah." I take a deep breath and shakily blow it out, turning to David. "I need a flight to New York. Tonight, early morning, whatever you can get."

"You're due on set tomorrow," he points out. "And the next day."

Two days until I have a few days off for the premiere of *The Last Best Man*. We've already filmed the big expensive action sequences and the next two days are in studio, not somewhere on location. At best I'll be fined and my actual reputation as a reliable, dedicated actor will suffer. It'll cause problems for the crew and put us behind schedule. At worst, I'll be fired.

I care, but this is more important.

Christ, she might not even be in New York. She could still be in LA and merely went for a short drive up the coast. She could be on the road as long as she'd like, heading in any direction she'd like toward whatever destination she wants.

It might be my T-shirt she's leaving at some highway rest stop.

I don't care. She can have another one. She can have them all.

"I probably won't make it to the premiere either." Which will land me in more hot water and send the press into a frenzy of speculation that I'm hiding from Kate.

"I'll take care of it. I'm calling Emma now," David says. "Go home and pack, I'll send you your flight info as soon as I've booked you."

"Thanks," I say, gripping his arm briefly.

He manages a smile and a shake of his head. "Go get her."

Even if Ashley can't forgive me, at least I'll have put her first and offered her everything. I'll have shown her and myself, and probably the world at this point, how I intend to live my life going forward.

"You'll destroy your career," Rose says, joining us. She's overheard enough to be appraised of the situation. She doesn't look like she cares one way or another, and I remember every time she's said it's nothing personal against Ashley. I think I believe her. She was just doing the job I asked her to do, giving me just enough space to make all the wrong decisions.

"Nothing personal," I say, "but I don't give a fuck."

Rose doesn't even blink. "Dashcombe and Teale will no longer be able to represent you," she says. "It's a bad look to keep you on as a client when your PR problems keep getting worse rather than better."

"I understand," I say, because I don't want their representation and I'm anxious to get out the door. I turn my back on Rose and scoop Cora into a tight hug. "I'll call you when I get to New York."

"Good luck," she says, squeezing me back.

I'll take whatever luck I can get, but by the time I get to the airport, I have a plan. The perfect plan, because I've learned from the best.

CHAPTER THIRTY-FIVE

Ashley

I STOP FOR THE night in West Virginia, and as I check into my hotel, I notice I've missed a few calls from Jessie. As soon as I'm in my room, I call her back.

"Hey," she says, barreling over my greeting in her excitement. "How soon can you be in New York?"

"Tomorrow," I say, hesitantly. I suppose New York was my destination, but I don't know what I'm going to do when I get there. "Is something wrong?"

"No! We all loved the script your friend wrote. There's financial backing if you're serious about producing and your friend is in. We can meet tomorrow in the city if you can make it."

I'm too stunned to say anything, so I sit on the foot of the bed, staring at the black screen of the TV, my mouth ajar.

"Ashley?"

"I'll have to talk to Wendy."

Jessie promises to arrange for Wendy to attend remotely and gives me a time and location. She hesitates a moment, then asks in a soft voice, "Are you going to watch the interview tonight?"

She has to mean Gabe, and if he's doing interviews, it's likely about his upcoming release. "Probably not," I lie. Now that I know about it, I'll have to watch it.

"I think you should," she says. Then adds, "For closure, or whatever."

Right. Closure. Like that's something I'll get any time soon from that man.

But if Gabe discovered I didn't sell him out before he taped the interview, there's a chance he'll apologize and it might be the only one I get from him.

"One last little thing," Jessie says, and from the tone of her voice, I'm not going to like this. "I'm helping Mina with her underwear business, and our model pulled out. We've already booked this gorgeous penthouse suite for the set—would you step in? We can have this meeting in the hotel, and do the shoot after. It'll only take thirty minutes and you can have the room for the night if you need someplace to stay."

A free penthouse suite for the night sounds good, but I'm not feeling up to modeling. "I'm sorry, but I don't think I should."

There's a moment of silence, then Jessie's voice drops. "You tried to steal my husband on my wedding day. I need you to do this."

So much for no hard feelings. Although, I guess I can't blame her. If she'd tried that with Gabe, I think I'd always carry a little grudge. "Fine, I'll do it."

I haven't modeled in years, but I like Mina's brand. Wild Things is more about comfort and saving fabric from going to landfills than luxury, but maybe she's working on something new if her set is a penthouse. If she wants to attach her brand to me, that's her mistake.

I eat dinner and pull Gabe's shirt over my head before I climb into bed. The shirt smells more like me, but I'm glad I had it with me and it didn't fall victim to that SuperVan's sour milk.

I feel closer to him wearing it.

Which is pathetic and I should know better by now. But this thing with Gabe—it's real. It's going to take time, even after the things he said to me and the way he treated me. So I'll let myself be pathetic tonight.

I watch the interview on my phone in my dark room. I cry the moment I see him. He's haggard and haunted, his face sharper, the hollows deeper. He's hurting. He talks about his childhood and his uncle and aunt, and his eyes are swimming with emotion. Laying himself bare like this for the world must be hard, but I'm proud of him for doing this. Taking control of how his life is being told.

I knew it had to be coming, but I'm still startled when Julia Spencer brings me up.

"It sounds like you still care about her."

I hold my breath. He doesn't answer it directly, but the things he says about me are kind. I search his face on the screen for any sign that he means what he's saying, that this isn't him whitewashing our relationship with words he doesn't believe.

"But he also rides a motorcycle and vandalizes public restrooms and loves a reality TV villain?"

I gasp—not because she called me a villain but because she asked him if he loves me. I can see the muscle in his jaw twitch.

"She's not a villain."

"But you love her?"

"That's not something you tell someone for the first time on TV," he says.

Christ, what does that mean? I watch the rest of the interview and I still can't tell what's real, but my heart feels like it ran a marathon and jumped into a blender.

It takes a while to pull myself together again. That interview could mean everything or nothing. Odds are he's doing this for his image, and making it seem like I meant something to him goes a long way toward explaining some of his choices.

He apologized though, for not believing me, for blaming me for spilling his secrets to the press, and if that's all I'll ever get from him, I'll take it.

The meeting with my family and a couple of my aunt's lawyers is chaotic and somehow I walk out with a newly formed production company. Well, the start of one. I'll have to recruit a few more people because Wendy and I can't do this on our own. Timothy has a list of names, all people he thinks would be interested and might be a good match. Kate Van Sandt's on there, but when I laugh, he merely shrugs and tells me I should meet her.

Maybe I will.

"Hey, Ashley, can I have a minute?" Timothy asks as everyone else files out of the hotel's conference room.

I slip my newly purchased notebook and pen into my bag along with Wendy's script and wait. Considering his change in attitude toward me, I can guess where this is going and I'll take this apology.

"I'm sorry for the way I've treated you," he says, once we're alone. "My parents' scandal was hard on all of us. I blamed you for it, and even though you were a kid, I thought you were just like your parents. I didn't want you messing with Nic's head, so I kept you away."

I hold his gaze for a long moment. "Nic was my emotional support crush for years," I find myself saying. "When I was a kid, I felt like no one understood me or accepted me, and the fact that he'd been kind to me gave me hope that someday, he could love me. That *someone* could. I leaned on it so hard I thought I loved him. I think, if I'd managed to get past you years ago, I would've woken up pretty quickly to the fact that he's not right for me."

Timothy nods. "I should've minded my own business. I've been told I have a tendency to meddle in other people's lives, and in this case, I may have gone overboard."

I shrug. "You're a Foley. Of course, you went overboard. And I'm not paying back the money you gave me to stay away."

"Fair enough." He laughs and pulls me into a quick hug. "Here's the key. Mina's up there already, getting set up. Thanks for helping her out, by the way."

"Thanks for the luxury penthouse suite."

"Enjoy it," he says, walking down the hall with a laugh.

I will, as much as I can. But first, the photo shoot.

It's half an hour of posing in underwear. So why does my stomach drop as the elevator carries me up?

I shake it off. The elevator I'm in is a private one, the doors opening onto a small marble foyer. The double doors into the room are shut, and my one sad piece of luggage waiting against the wall. Leaving it there so it won't be in the way, I open the door and step through.

The air inside is sweet with the scent of flowers—that's what I notice first. I breathe it in, my eyes scanning the beautifully decorated room. There are roses everywhere, plump and red. The massive windows have a perfect Manhattan view.

And then I see him.

Gabe.

He's sitting on one of the elegant sofas, wearing the hell out of a suit, holding a glass of amber liquid as he stares at me. Not in shock or anger or disappointment. The look on his face is tormented, and I realize what this is.

Fuck.

I've been set up.

He did this. Got my family on his side to get me here. It's a trap and I can't move because I want it to be a trap, but I also want to throw the nearest vase of flowers at his head.

Gabe stands, closes the distance between us in three large strides, and stumbles to his knees.

Chapter Thirty-Six

Gabe

One minute I'm standing, the next, I'm on my knees, staring up at Ashley like she contains my whole world, because she does, or at least the parts of it most worth holding onto. My days and nights are empty without her, one long nightmare I'm waking up from. I hope.

Her expression is closed off, and she crosses her arms. Protecting herself. From me.

The pain is so sharp it steals my breath. I did this to her, and I'd give anything to take it all back and do things differently.

"What are you doing here?" she finally asks, her voice shaking.

I shouldn't touch her. She's not mine to touch and I don't have permission, but my hands move to grip her hips, stopping inches from her. "Can I touch you?" My voice breaks.

Her expression doesn't soften, but she uncrosses her arms and her fingers thread through my hair. I melt into her touch. God, I've missed her. I grab handfuls of her soft summer dress and hold on tight.

"What I did was inexcusable. I'm not going to ask your forgiveness because I don't deserve it." I rest my forehead against her stomach and breathe her in while her fingers slowly comb through my hair. The relief I feel from the simple touch brings tears to my eyes. "I'm sorry I asked you to be my secret. I'm sorry I chose my reputation and image over you, and more than anything, I'm sorry

I let my fears get in the way of my trust in you. When you needed me, I tossed you aside. I'll never forgive myself for that."

Her fingers still. "How are you here? Shouldn't you be on set?"

My stomach dives at the reminder of what I've done to my career, but she's worth it. God, is she worth it. "This is more important."

"You walked off set," she says in faint shock.

I clutch her dress tighter, hold her closer. When I speak, my voice is raw. "I'll burn it all down for you."

Ashley's fingers leave my hair and she sinks onto her knees in front of me. Her fingers brush my cheeks for a few heartbeats before dropping away. "You're really here."

"I love you," I tell her. "I'm here for you now and I swear I will always be here for you. Give me another chance, Ash. Please."

Her soft eyes dim and she takes my hands, pulling them from her hips and holding them tight. "Nothing's changed. It might never change, and I can't try to be anything other than myself."

"I don't want you to be anything else. I've changed. You showed me how unhappy I was trying to be something I'm not. I'm done with that." I bring her hands to my chest, placing them over my heart, and to my surprise, she doesn't pull them back. "I love you. You are perfect. I promise, wherever we go, whatever we do, I will be on your side. The only legacy I want is one where I make you happy."

She sniffles and sits back on her heels, her hands sliding from my chest to rest on her lap. "What if I say no?"

My heart sinks. "Give me another chance. I'll do my best to earn back your trust and be the kind of man you deserve."

"Gabe," Ashley says. Tears shimmer in her eyes, but her expression is tight, her voice wavering on a watery edge. "You hurt me. I understand why, because I understand you, but you can't put me on the pedestal now that it's empty. I'm not replacing Michael as some ideal you have to live up to. The only kind of man I deserve is one who loves me."

"I love you. No more pedestals or impossible ideals, I promise. Just you and me. We can go anywhere, start over. Whatever you want, it's yours."

She sniffles. "I'll drag you down. You'll never have the life your uncle wanted."

"I don't want that life." I want to reach for her again, pull her into my arms. "And you could never drag me down. Not when you've helped me find my way up. I was drowning before you, in guilt and fear. You saved me."

Ashley rises to her feet, taking my hands and tugging. I rise more slowly, afraid that when she opens her mouth again, all hope will be lost. When her lips touch mine, it feels like my heart, time, everything, stops.

Her hands are in my hair, her body pressed to mine, and this right here is where I belong. This is happiness and joy and peace. Acceptance. Of our pasts and flaws and love.

"I love you," I tell her when she finally pulls back. I'm going to tell her every day. I'm going to show her.

"I love you too," she says, a big smile breaking across her face, forcing the tears from her eyes. "You've got a lot of work to do to make it up to me."

"I'll do it. Anything. Whatever it takes." I pull her close again and kiss away the tears before finding her lips and I'm so happy I could cry too. This, right here, is better than any award, better than all the things Michael told me were important.

"Here's what's going to happen," she says, breaking the kiss and holding tight to the lapels of my suit. "Tomorrow, you go back to LA and fix the mess you created when you walked off set."

I nod, but frown when she stops. "Not without you."

"Yes, without me. I'll have to drive back, and that will take days."

"No," I say, shaking my head. "I'll go with you. I don't want you driving alone, and I want to be with you right now."

"I want to be with you too," she says, soft but firm. "But you need to get back on set before they sue you for breach of contract if they haven't already."

"I don't care. I'll quit." It's not just words. I'll do it if it means Ashley's in my arms.

"No."

"You don't get to decide that."

Her eyes narrow. "This time, I think I do. You love acting—"

I pull her tight against me. "I love you."

"—and I don't want you to walk away from it."

"I'm not walking away from you. Not again."

Ashley's arms slide around my neck. "A week, Gabe. That's all I'm asking."

I don't want to give in, but maybe she's right. "Is Wendy doing anything? I'll fly her out and she can drive back with you. Or David can—"

She laughs. "I'll ask Lea if it will make you feel better."

"It'll help." I bend my head until our foreheads touch. "But I won't feel better until you're back with me." I brush the end of my nose against hers. "I want to keep teaching you to swim. I want you in my bed. I want dinners where we talk about our days and evenings snuggling on the couch. I want you with me for the rest of our days."

"I want that too," she says in a soft voice, reaching up to bring our lips together.

Little shocks of electricity zip through my veins, warming me, and it's a relief to finally kiss her. Ashley's hands slide down my shoulders to my waist, untucking my shirt, and just like that, a kiss isn't enough. It's nowhere close, but it's a start. We have all night.

We have forever.

Epilogue

Two Years Later: Ashley

This car drives like a dream. It's a 1960 Mercedes 190 SL—not the muscle cars Gabe usually prefers, but I fell in love with it. Cruising along this California highway with the top down and Gabe in the passenger seat makes for a perfect day.

He leans his tan, muscled arm on the door, his sunglasses reflecting the road ahead. His other hand comes to rest on mine on the gear stick.

The road winds along the cliffs overlooking the ocean, and he only grimaces a little when I ride the clutch.

The movie that just wrapped is going to win him his first Oscar—I can feel it. I think he can, too, even if he doesn't want to talk about it yet. That's okay, that's what these road trips are for. Gabe needs to unwind, get out of whatever role he was in, and drive.

I love these times, when it's just the two of us, no outside world. The break from the spotlight is good, even for me. I don't spend a lot of time in front of the camera, although I did play the role of Clare in what turned out to be a summer blockbuster. I hadn't lost that opportunity after all, but it's behind the camera where I've found my purpose.

My little production company is finally flying. *Trash For Love*, Wendy's part rom-com, part reality TV satire, wrapped last week. With Kate Van Sandt in the director's chair, we've generated a lot of buzz for our little independent film.

Our second starts pre-production soon and the third…it's nothing more than a screenplay and a few notes between me, Wendy, and Kate, but we've already whispered *award potential*.

Gabe and I stop late in the afternoon to fill up the tank. He goes in to pay, and I bend across the hood to wash the windscreen, timing it perfectly for when he walks out. Few sounds are as satisfying as a grown man running smack into a garbage can because he's too busy staring at my ass.

He presses up behind me, his hands slipping over the soft fabric that hugs my body.

"My wife is a menace," he complains in a growly voice that tells me there is no way we're making it to the beautiful secluded beach house we rented for tonight without stopping for sex.

I wiggle my ass against him. "My husband is a horndog," I say as I continue to wash the windscreen.

He takes the squeegee out of my hands, kissing my neck. "You do this to me. Want to vandalize the restroom, for old time's sake?"

It's tempting. I'm more than ready for him, but this gas station doesn't look promising as far as cleanliness goes, and I have a better option. I've been studying the maps, so twenty minutes later we're on a private road, tucked out of view of everyone and everything, but even if we weren't, I'm not sure it would stop me from hiking my skirt around my waist and climbing onto his lap.

Our lips meet in a hungry kiss, his hands sliding over my body as I free his dick from his pants. I sink onto him, reveling in the way he fills me, in the strangled sound he makes when I move. His fingers dig into my hips, and his mouth is hot on my neck, kissing down to my collarbone. Before he can rip my dress open—he's destroyed far too many, the man needs to be stopped—I pull it down, my tits spilling out. He's on them immediately, licking and sucking, dragging his teeth over each taut nipple in turn while I run my fingers through his thick hair.

There's always this thrill with him, even when we're somewhere our privacy is guaranteed. The chemistry between us is as strong as it's ever been. Maybe even stronger. The way he reacts to me, the way I react to him—we're perfect together.

He makes me come twice before he follows me.

When our hearts have slowed and we've both caught our breath, I kiss him long and deep before saying, "You're going to be dripping out of me for the next two hours because you couldn't wait. The brand new upholstery is going to be ruined, and it's on you this time." I was the one who couldn't wait, I pulled over on this secluded road, but whatever. He was just as impatient.

Gabe kisses me, then reclines his seat as far back as possible. "Get up here, baby. Sit on my face."

I don't need to be told twice. Sometimes it's good to be a little bad.

The End

Acknowledgements

This book would be an absolute disaster without the guidance and help of my amazing critique partners. Alexandra Kiley and Maggie North as always helped me work through what the book was actually about when all I wanted to do was write spice and chaos. If it weren't for them, Gabe would be in that woodchipper for good. So thank you both for all the chats that helped me figure out where I was going and how far was too far, for reading my messy draft and stepping in to read the cleaned up final draft. Not to mention all the moral support and guidance. Thank you and I love you both!

Speaking of moral support, having a shoulder to cry on/lean on is incredibly important and I'm lucky to have Kathryn Ferrer in my life. I'm fortunate that she's not only willing to read and give feedback on my messy drafts, but she's also a good friend. Thank you for everything Kathryn!

And a big thanks to my other beta readers, Michelle Merritt, LE Foley, Kathryn Ferrer, Chrissy Hopewell. Your feedback was so thoughtful and valuable. Thank you so much for taking the time and helping me out.

Thank you to everyone in the FridayKiss community and the writing community at large. And to my RomDoms in particular—I love watching you all smash it out of the park with every new book. World domination, one romance book at a time.

Writing wouldn't be possible if not for the love and support of my family. Thank you for giving me the time and space to realize this dream. Love you all!

THE VILLAIN EDIT

And last but not least, thank you readers for picking up this book, this series. Thank you for the reviews and for taking a chance on me!

About the Author

Sarah Brenton (she/her) writes steamy, sex positive romance with strong characters getting dropkicked by love. She lives in New Zealand with her husband and kids and wishes she had enough time to write all the stories in her head.

Want to know more? Visit www.sarahbrenton.com, sign-up for my newsletter, and follow me on Instagram!

Also By Sarah Brenton

<u>Over the Top Love series</u>
Love and Other Risky Business (book one)
Holiday Vibes (book two)
The Villain Edit (book three)